Isla Gordon lives on the Jurassic Coast of England with her T. rex-sized Bernese mountain dog. Isla has been writing professionally since 2013 (and unprofessionally since she can remember). She also has five romantic comedies published under the name Lisa Dickenson.

Isla can't go a day without finding dog hair in her mouth.

# A New York Winter

## ISLA GORDON

SPHERE

SPHERE

First published in Great Britain in 2023 by Sphere

1 3 5 7 9 10 8 6 4 2

Copyright © Lisa Dickenson 2023

The moral right of the author has been asserted.

A CIP catalogue record for this book is available from the British Library.

ISBN 978-1-4087-2893-2

Typeset in Caslon by M Rules
Printed and bound in Great Britain by Clays Ltd, Elcograf S.p.A.

Papers used by Sphere are from well-managed forests
and other responsible sources.

MIX
Supporting
responsible forestry
FSC® C104740

Sphere
An imprint of
Little, Brown Book Group
Carmelite House
50 Victoria Embankment
London
EC4Y 0DZ

An Hachette UK Company
www.hachette.co.uk

www.littlebrown.co.uk

*Dedicated to those who dream big . . .*

# Prologue

Sixty seconds. That's all that's left of this year, the year I felt like I lost so much. Then I took myself to New York City.

Below the famous Times Square Ball is a big screen counting down the seconds, one by one, moment by moment. And the crowd, who were singing and dancing only minutes ago are now all focused on calling out the descending numbers.

Just like that, the hours of waiting feel like nothing, the ache in my feet has disappeared, the numbness from the frosty air thaws, and I'm caught up in the moment. This is it.

And I'm in the wrong place.

'Stay. With me.' His eyes are pleading, lonely. I hate that he's lonely.

'I have to go,' I shout over the noise. 'Happy New Year.'

I squeeze under arms and through packed torsos. My vision is blurred by the people dancing before me. The crowd in Times Square is pulsing, whooping, a sea of smiles and laughter, and I have to jostle and push through

1

them since none of them can hear my polite requests to pleeeeeease move.

As I duck under a couple who haven't been able to save their kissing for the stroke of midnight, I'm struck by an almost heart-stopping awe that I'm *here*. Despite everything I made it to New York, I'm living, I'm breathing, I'm in the moment.

I have thirty seconds to find the one I'm meant to be beside.

I stand on tiptoes to try to spot how far he is from me, and I can't see him. I can't see anyone I'd been standing near. I don't get it – did he leave?

I call his name into the air, my voice a little fish swimming among the tide of numbers being hollered up into the night sky.

*Come on, come on, come on, where are you?*

Twenty seconds.

I whirl around, searching, calling, my heart choking my words as it rises to my throat.

New York City. They say you never sleep, but I wholly believe I'm about to make some new dreams here with you.

Starting at midnight.

# Chapter 1

'Ashling, you've got your head in the clouds again.'

'Leave her be – she takes after me.'

This gentle exchange between my mum and my gran floats into my head every day I do my job, probably because I heard it so often growing up that it could have been one of those family mantras, perhaps written in curvy calligraphy and framed above a household toilet.

I was that kid who was always bumping into things while I was staring up at the sky. Always falling off swings as I tried to loop right up above the threshold. Always lying on my back on summer grass lost in daydreams and creating cloud animals, leaving friends and games and the rest of the world to happen around me.

I always had focus. It's just that my focus landed, well, not on land.

Right now, my focus, and my head, is far, far above the clouds. In fact, through the cockpit window, as I reach cruising altitude, I'm looking down onto a panoramic vista of peach, sun-coated white duvet.

As first officer of this aircraft, I can confidently say, conditions are perfect.

'Ready to spot a UFO today?' I ask my captain, Rebecca, who sits beside me.

'Today's the day!' She laughs, and the cockpit door opens, revealing our flight's purser, Alex, carrying two cups of steaming coffee for us.

'You two say the same thing every day,' he comments.

'One day it's going to happen,' I sing out, swigging my drink, already enjoying today's easy flight of four hours to sunny Athens. It's early June and the happy holidaymakers are en route to try out their new swimsuits for the start of the summer season.

This is the best part of my job. Of my life. Sitting above the clouds, eyes on the horizons I'm chasing, a panorama of colours. I'm keeping a plane-full of passengers safe, I'm monitoring and checking and tweaking to keep them comfortable during my operating sector, and I'm doing it all with views that are, literally, out of this world.

Some pilots love take-off, some love landing, some love layovers, some love witnessing a dazzling Northern Lights show, some just love sleeping back in their own beds. I love *this*. This is where I'm completely in control, completely calm.

I roll my neck from side to side. Oof. 'Do you want to know something really ridiculous?' I ask Rebecca.

'Always,' she answers.

'I was playing baseball the other day—'

'You play baseball?'

'No.' I shake my head. 'But it's so hot out this summer already that my friend, Flo, and I decided to *A League of their Own*-it and try a bit of pitching and batting in the park. Turns out, I'm great at batting, not so great at pitching, and I somehow absolutely yanked my shoulder out.'

'Ugh! Are you okay?'

'I thought I was: the next day it seemed totally fine. But actually, I can feel it again right now.' I roll my shoulder a little and wince.

'Those UFOs only want fine specimens so I guess they'll just take me,' Rebecca quips.

I laugh and my eyes trail the skies, reaching up to adjust a couple of the dials in the overhead panel, and that's when a pain shoots through me, from my shoulder all the way down my arm.

A few swears spill out while Rebecca takes over my duties and alerts Alex to come back into the cockpit.

'What happened?' she asks. 'Are you all right to keep flying?'

My eyes meet hers. 'Yes. But something's wrong.'

# Chapter 2

*Nearly five months later . . .*

'I'll take a treat, please,' I croak out and laugh at my own joke, since nobody else does. 'Because it's . . . you know . . .' I point down at myself. 'And this all has to be a trick?'

Betty, from HR, scans me from head to toe and I find the pity in her eyes, and the confusion as she tries to figure out my costume.

'I'm the bridge from the TV show *The Bridge*,' I tell her. 'One half of it, anyway. Rebecca is the other half. I'm Sweden, she's Denmark, that's why I have a torso and she has the legs.'

'I haven't seen it . . .' says Betty.

'You should, it's really good.'

I'm feeling a little self-conscious in my Halloween costume now, to be honest, especially with a papier-mâché face looking up at me. Every year my airline puts on an informal costume contest on this day, for those not on shift. With me being off work, I went full steam with my costume, and it's only now occurring to me how awkward I am to have worn *this* to *this* meeting.

In front of a rain-drenched window, Betty shuffles her papers and I know it's not good news. Nobody shuffles papers before saying, 'Congratulations, all is well!' So when she says, 'We had the medical assessment back, Ashling,' I think I know what's coming next.

It's been almost five months since I buggered my shoulder playing baseball, five months since my last flight and my licence having to be suspended, and three months since I had surgery to try and fix things.

'And?' I gulp.

'I'm sorry,' she whispers, her eyes on mine, and I know she means it. She clears her throat and says it more clearly. 'I'm sorry, but, even after your surgery, even after all the work you've been putting in with your physio, we can't clear you to fly.'

I knew, of course I knew. When I was up in the air that day, my seemingly mild injury magnified into a large rotator cuff tear. It was agony, and I was recommended for surgery but even with all their amazing help, they couldn't fix the permanent damage I'd caused. Now I don't have the full range of motion I once had, and that I need for my job. But day to day my shoulder doesn't cause me many problems any more, now the pain is finally, slowly, slightly, beginning to subside. So a part of me prayed it could all still be okay. 'For how long?' A hot sweat floods my body. *Do NOT cry, Ashling.*

Betty and my management team are the most supportive airline leaders Living In The Air could ever ask for. I know in my soul they'd be doing everything they could to get me back up in the skies, which is why I don't need her to say out loud what I already know to be true.

'Is it really over?' I say, a tear escaping.

'At this point in time, under the advice of the medical experts, we can't clear you to fly. The flight simulation you took part in showed you wouldn't be able to perform your duties in an emergency. And it's not looking likely that anything will change.'

'But it's just a little shoulder injury, it's going to get better. It's so much better than it was – it doesn't even hurt now unless I reach upwards.'

Betty shakes her head. 'You know it's more serious than that. But I hope you know how gutted we are for you.'

I hear what she says for the rest of the meeting, a lot of words about reassessing in three months and finding me a new position if there's no improvement, but Betty is stressing that, honestly, realistically, it's the end of the line for me flying commercial planes. At the same time, I've checked out, my eyes unseeing, my brain thumping, my stomach hollow. My world just faded to grey and, even at the end when I stand and accept a hug, as she bends around my ridiculous costume, I am numb.

## Chapter 3

The first thing I do when I get back to my home in Sunbury-on-Thames is punch my stupid pumpkin right in the face. With my good arm.

Well, that showed him.

With an ice pack for my hand, I walk through my kitchen, the whole house silent except for my footsteps, like I'm not welcome here at this time of the day. Like it's busy sleeping and I'm supposed to be out, living life. My house likes to come alive at night, creaking and groaning and clanging pipes as if it's auditioning for the role of a haunted house.

But now, it's quiet, and I'm alone. I sigh into the silence.

Sliding open the back door that leads to my tiny garden, I sit down on the step and wince as the ice touches the skin of my hand. Stupid pumpkin. I thought it would be softer since he was all hollowed out, but nooooo. Hard as a rock. I guess I'll have to add busted-up knuckles to my failed medical record now.

The weight of reality pushes against my back, hunching me over, curving my spine until I'm a ball, my face between my knees, my eyes on the bronzed leaves that paper over my grass.

Shit shit shit shit shit. This can't be real. It can't be true. I can't not be a pilot any more, it's *me*, it's everything I've worked for, everything I've dreamed of. My mind races as though I'm seeing an Instagram Reel of my own life, one-second clips that montage the years of training, the expense, the hours and the flights and the joy and the pain and the fear and the fun. Being a pilot was my dream, it's part of me. I am a pilot.

Oh my god, but I'm not any more. I am not a pilot.

So, who am I?

I sit on the step for a while, tears dropping onto the leaves below, the chilly October wind finding its way through the holes in my crochet jumper, my bridge costume a sorry heap on the mulchy ground.

'All right,' I whisper to the leaves before lifting my head and taking a big sniffle. 'So one dream has gone to shit. It's not the end of the world, and I'm bloody well going to be okay.'

I stand, all stiff legs and tense back, but as I reach my patio doors, a thought hits me, a thought that causes a lightning bolt of panic in my chest, a wave of sickness in my stomach, and I have to hold the doorframe.

No. No, that can't be right. I have to check something, right now.

Stumbling through the kitchen, I leave the back door open and allow any heat inside the house to dance free. I crash up my stairs, falling at one point with a thump, and into my bedroom, where I yank open my desk drawer, and dump onto the floor an absolute hoard of hairy hairbands, my birth certificate, an eyeliner cap, the half-read copy of *Dracula* I keep meaning to finish, a string of expired condoms, a phone-charging cable from the mobile I had seven years ago and, eventually, uncover the thing I'm looking for.

*My Dreams* I've written on the cover of the journal, in twirling marker above an illustration of a flamingo. Flamingo print seemed to be really big when I was nineteen.

It was ten years ago now that I bought this in a summer stationery sale at the airport bookshop. I was on my way to New York City for a long weekend, whisked away by my gran who saw I was in serious need of a bit of inspiring, as I had zero clue what I wanted to do with my life. All my friends were at uni or already had jobs, and I was milling about like an undecided, unanchored jellyfish.

You could say, my head was in the clouds. I knew I had big dreams inside me – my name even means 'dream', and was suggested by my gran who, too, was a big dreamer. But I needed to go somewhere big to unlock them, get out of my hometown, out from the shadows of life plans being made by those around me.

While in New York, I filled the pages of this journal with everything I wanted to do, to be, all those ideas and ambitions and wants and needs, and by the end of the trip I narrowed them down to five dreams. Five big life goals.

I remember the moment it all clicked into place. I spent days prioritising, re-prioritising, de-prioritising my list. In between sightseeing with my gran, who'd spent time in New York as a 'young un', I'd sat in cafés and diners, poring over my journal pages. I read them aloud to a bored but kind Swedish girl in our hostel lobby to see what she thought I should do. Then on our last day, my gran sent me out to be on my own. Finally, up there it felt so clear, as clear as the dawn's cloudless sky. I knew what I wanted for my life.

And just like that, I was no longer the lost nomad of a friend, the head-in-the-clouds girlfriend, the drifting daughter. I had a structure, a purpose, a plan.

Now, as I flick the thin pages of the journal to the last entry, scanning past-me observations about life and bullet-pointed lists of all the languages I intended to learn and hairstyles I wanted to try out, sketches and doodles of the things my eyes viewed a decade ago, my heart thuds loudly. It sounds particularly ominous to my ears inside my silent bedroom.

My list. My finalised list – there in black and white. Well, blue biro and off-white paper. I know this list by heart. It is *in* my heart. I just haven't thought to look at it for years. At least not as a full collection, as this anthology of dreams. But it was my compass, my life summed up into those five goals. My ultimate to-do list. I might as well have laminated it.

Grabbing a red Sharpie from a pot on my desk, I sink down beside the foot of my bed, and read.

1. Get accepted on the Young Artists' Residency.
2. Marry Hugh.
3. Take Gran on her own trip of a lifetime.
4. Move to New York City.
5. Be a pilot.

That last one – that was my biggest dream of all. Nothing has felt more right than when I accepted that was what I was meant to do.

I first felt the pull to be a pilot when I was seven and my mum and gran took me to a fairground and I rode a big wheel. I don't think I blinked the whole ride, and my heart soared as we rose into the air. But I kept pushing the idea aside: it felt unrealistic, too hard, too expensive, too out-there, and it wasn't until New York, at nineteen, that morning on the top of the world, that I stopped fighting myself.

For the next few years my whole world became about the sky. I earned and then trained alongside earning, and built up my flying hours, and took tests, and got licences, and eventually, a long time and a lot of money later, I qualified. Then I just wanted to fly *all* the time, and thankfully I was taken under the wing, as it were, by the beloved commercial airline, Living In The Air. I've been there for nearly five years now, flying short-haul all over Europe, and it's everything I ever wanted, even before I quite knew it.

Until today, and now it's over.

Taking the lid from my Sharpie, I draw neat red lines through my dreams, one at a time, the reality of my situation settling over me.

I cross out my dream of getting a place on the Young Artists' Residency. I cross out marrying Hugh. I cross out taking Gran on her own trip of a lifetime. I cross out being a pilot, a tear dripping onto the page and smudging the decade-old lettering.

Every single one of my goals has collapsed, apart from the one about New York, I suppose. But I'd always figured that would happen far, far down the line. I thought that perhaps I'd change airlines one day, work for a US carrier, or even a private airline based out of America, and then with their help I could get the necessary work visas and sponsorship and make my transatlantic move. I was enamoured with New York from the moment I stepped out of the airport shuttle bus into Manhattan. And when the city inspired me to map out my life in just a long weekend, I knew it was the place to go if you wanted to think big and be something. But there was no rush. I had a whole lifetime.

Only now, with my thirtieth birthday barely three months away, it doesn't feel that way. This list was a promise I made to a younger me, and I haven't been able to give her a single win in ten years. How quickly will another decade slip by?

My mind zooms about, clutching at fading images of my future that disappear like cloud mist. What the hell am I going to do with myself now? And how can I grip hold of this final goal before it, too, slips from my grasp?

# Chapter 4

'I don't have any dreams left. They've all gone.' Three hours later, I'm sat on my floor in front of my mirrored wardrobe, my phone on loudspeaker. I've been in crisis mode since getting home and have called my best friend Flo for help.

'What are you talking about?' her voice crackles out. 'You don't dream any more at night?'

'No, I don't have any *life* dreams left. They've all . . . crumbled. My goals. My aspirations. Gone!' I pile my hair on top of my head and tie it with a scrunchie.

'Oh no. What happened at your meeting today? Did it go badly?' she asks.

'It went supremely badly,' I answer, and my voice hitches, but I can't cry any more today. I've turned off the waterworks, I've had my pity party and I've moved on to mild panic. I don't have it in me to reverse. 'In short, I can't fly any more.'

'*What?*' she yelps. 'For a while?'

'Most likely, ever.'

'I'm coming over.'

'You're at work!'

'Who cares?' Flo cries.

'No, no, don't leave work and trek all the way out to Sunbury, I'm fine. Well, not fine . . .' I examine my reflection and raise a pair of scissors towards my hair. 'I've just got a lot of shit to figure out.' I let the scissors hover. 'Oh my god, there's just so much shit.'

'As in, you need to figure out what to do next?'

'What to do at all!' My voice is high and shrieky. I drop the scissors and grab my journal from the floor beside me and read the four failed dreams out to Flo, one by one. When I've finished, I sigh. 'All my twenties I've been living around these goals. Now, thanks to me either leaving things too late, or breaking up with someone, or getting into a stupid accident, I've let them all slide away.'

'Didn't you say you had five goals? What was the fifth?'

'Moving to New York City.' I pause, cloudy ideations taking form somewhere in my mind.

'You could still do that,' Flo says, breaking into my thoughts.

She's right, except, 'What if I don't have time? What if something, somewhere, sometime stops me? What if I get some new skills, and find some new international company to join and eventually work my way through the ranks, only by then the laws have changed or something and then that falls through too?'

Flo hesitates on the end of the line, then dodges the

16

question with another of her own. 'Do you have any idea what you're going to do now?'

'No, not one.' I swallow down hysteria. 'I have spent the last three hours sitting here on my floor, completing online career tests and taking personality quizzes, and I just don't know. I don't know who I am or what I want. I don't know, Flo!'

'All right, chill,' she says. 'What did the career tests and things say?'

'The career test said I should be a ... wait for it ... *pilot*, a personality test said I was best suited to work in a job where I can travel and keep people safe, and a Buzzfeed quiz told me my next big career move should be acting.'

'So ... maybe you could play the role of a pilot in a TV show?'

'I'm sure the Duffer Brothers are just gagging to hire me.' I tighten my scrunchie again, holding the ends of my ponytail down over my forehead and angling the scissors. I snip at a few straggly split ends and a tiny wave of satisfaction ripples through me as they flitter onto my open journal. 'So then,' I say, moving the scissors an inch higher up my pony. 'Then I started reading back through my old journal, at all my lists of all the other things I wanted to do with my life. All the littler things that didn't make the cut for the Big Five, but I still imagined I'd get round to doing, sometime. And you know what? I've barely done any of them. So now ... I'm doing them.' *Snip.*

'Everybody ignores to-do lists, especially ones written ten years ago in some old diary. Wait, what do you mean you're doing them now? What kind of things are listed on there?'

17

'Remember once I told you I used to have a huge crush on Chris Evans? One of my aims was to write him a love letter. So I started by sliding into his DMs.' I guess my crush is still there, somewhat.

Flo laughs. 'That's fine, I'm sure he has hundreds, maybe thousands, of those a day. I thought you were going to say you'd been taking more drastic actions.'

I slide the scissors another inch higher. *Snip*.

'What I'm hearing is,' Flo interprets as I hold my ponytail aloft above my head and study its now shorter length. I think I should take a little more off, just to make it spot-on. 'You're worried you don't have a lot of frameworks for your life any more, and you need some new goals to work towards, and in the meantime, you're ploughing through a few things that have been hanging around your to-do list?'

'Yes, exactly!' I say. 'Well, not exactly. I don't just need new goals, it's like I need a whole new *me*. It feels so much bigger than me just sitting down with a notepad and picking a couple of new bucket-list items.'

She's quiet for a moment, and I take another snip. A message from my mum, the fourth in the last hour, slides onto the screen from the top, checking in on me, and how the meeting went. Oof. A knot of apprehension in my stomach prods at me at the thought of telling her all of this once I've finished chatting to Flo. Mum will be lovely, sympathetic, caring, but I know underneath all that she'll worry about me.

'You know something I've always wanted to do?' I say, swiping away the message.

18

'Tell me,' Flo says.

'Get a "Rachel cut".'

'As in, a "Rachel from the first couple of seasons of *Friends*" cut?' she clarifies. Flo is a hairdresser; she knows what I mean.

'Yes.'

'Okay. It's actually a lot of maintenance you know—'

'I want a *peach* Rachel cut.'

'Peach.'

'Peach. I've always wanted to dye my hair a lovely light peach.'

'Well, make sure you come into the salon and I'll do it for you properly—' At that point I snip again and her words halt, changing into a gasp. 'I know that sound – that was scissors on hair. What are you doing?'

I yank out the scrunchie and shake out my brand-new mane. 'Oh, bollocks.'

'What have you done?'

It is not the reflection of Jennifer Aniston in the early years of *Friends* looking out at me. Instead, it's a girl with pink, mascara-smudged eyes and dirty blonde hair I've now hacked into a tufty, jagged bob that in places still straggles beyond my shoulders and in other places hits level with my jawline.

'Listen. I'll be thirty in less than three months. I can't be thirty and have no direction at all for the rest of my life.'

'You actually *can*,' Flo counters, sounding off-balance with my frequent changes of conversational direction.

'I need to do something drastic.' The clouds in my mind part, my view clearing.

19

'You need to give yourself a minute to let it all sink in.'

'I need to go to New York before it's too late. Before that dream gets scuppered too.'

'Well, one thing at a time, okay? You only just got the bad news today. Let me find you a bit of space and I'll bring you into the salon in the next few days and I'll give you the peach Rachel cut of your dreams.'

'You will?'

With an affectionate tut, Flo says, 'Of course I will. Please always come to me first before you start chopping at your own hair.'

'Thanks, Flowy.'

'Just promise me you won't do anything wild until then, okay? Don't fly off to New York, or something.'

'I won't,' I reply, dragging my laptop close to me.

'And don't cut any more of your hair off.'

'I *won't*.' I laugh, tucking some locks behind my ear, which then fall out, just as the search page on Google brings up the list of flights to New York City.

## Chapter 5

Three days later, on one of those November mornings that are so gloomy and grey it's like you've stepped right into a film noir, I sit cosy and warm inside Flo's salon, which has already strung up its white and gold decorations ready for Christmas. The rain is splattering down on the window beside me, as if it's angry at the bright interior lights that reflect onto the glass.

Flo gives, in my opinion, an exaggerated sigh from behind my spinny chair.

'It's not that bad,' I say, watching as she fluffs my hair about, wincing at its lopsided layers and blunt hacks.

'Dude, the Rachel cut is iconic. This ...' She slides her fingers down two strands framing either side of my face, one side reaching the end a good few seconds before the other. 'This, would never become iconic. Why didn't you just come to me first?'

I shrug. 'It was all very sudden and I wasn't thinking

clearly,' I reply in my most clarity-soaked voice. 'I just wanted to get back on track, do something I'd wanted to do for a long time. But I didn't try and dye it, so . . .'

She meets my eyes in the mirror. 'Well, that's something.'

'Thanks for fitting me in.'

'You're lucky I had a cancellation. My next actual available appointment is January. Everybody wants their hair done before Christmas.'

'I am lucky. You're the best – thank you.'

'I am the best,' she agrees. 'Now, let's fix up this style, and then you still want to go peach?'

'Yes, please.'

'And you understand we have to lighten your hair first so the peach colour shows up?'

'Yes, please.'

Flo works around me, first weaving foils through my hair and painting a bleachy gloop over my head, while we chat away about everyday life. I smile and laugh and we both avoid the topic of me losing my dream job, and I know it's because she's waiting to see if I want to bring it up. But actually, there's something else I want to tell her. Just hanging in there for the right moment.

'All right, I'm going to give that about fifty minutes to start with and then we'll see how much the blonde's lifted,' Flo says a while later, wiping her hands on a towel. 'We're after a perfect, pale banana shade to develop before I wash it off then apply peach gloss to your damp hair. Do you have a book or anything with you?'

'I do, yes.' Ah-ha! I keep my head as still as possible as

I reach for my handbag, which is sitting on the counter in front of me.

'Want a cuppa?'

'A coffee would be brill.'

Flo saunters off to wash her bowls and make me a coffee and I pull out my New York City guidebook, finding a good page to have open for when she comes back. This one looks perfect – a big ol' image of the Empire State Building standing before a bright pink sky on the left-hand page, and a list of 'Six of the Best Sights When New York is Snowing' on the right.

I hold the book open until I see her in the mirror coming back, at which point I pretend to be ensconced, words jumping out like *ice rink*, *skyline*, *Rockefeller Christmas Tree*.

'Here you go,' she says, putting the coffee down and giving one of my foils a quick tweak. I peep up and watch her eyes move down onto my book. 'Nice photo. NYC. Wait. Are you still thinking of taking a trip?'

'I am,' I say, trying not to move my head too much but tilting my chin up in small defiance. 'Actually . . . I've booked.'

'You already booked?' She's trying to stop her voice from sounding scoldy, I can tell. 'When are you going?'

I take a large, relaxing inhale. 'Next week.'

'*Next week?* How long for?'

'All winter. Well, ninety days. Well, actually, less than ninety days. I come back late January, ready for another review meeting with the airline. Not that anything relating to me being a pilot will change.'

She blinks at me a few times. 'You're leaving for, just, the whole of winter. When were you going to tell me?'

23

'This was my way of telling you.' I pat the book.

'Do you not think this is a bit sudden? A bit ... you *just* lost your job. You need time to process all of this. I'm not sure jetting off to a foreign country for three months at the drop of a hat is the best thing to do.'

'It's hardly a "foreign country" to me – I mean, not really. I've been to New York before.'

'A long weekend when you were a teenager isn't the same as spending a whole season somewhere.'

'This is a good thing, Flo, trust me. Like I said on the phone the other day, I'm not letting my last dream slip through my fingers too. And what better place to come up with a whole new set of dreams – a whole new me – than the Big Apple? It worked before; I can make it work again.'

'Where better? I don't know, your own home? Your familiar living room with your familiar friends who can help you?'

'Don't be sad for me, Flowy,' I plead.

'I'm not, I'm just ... pissed off that you didn't take my advice.'

'When do I ever take your advice?'

She laughs, shrugging. 'Do you know where you're going to stay out there?'

'No.'

'Do you know how you're going to spend Christmas?'

'Nope.'

'Do you know what you'll do for money?'

'No. No! Yes, I mean, yes! That I do know. I can't work out there – I'll be a tourist on a visa waiver – so I'm going to use my savings.'

Flo picks the book up from my hands and flicks the pages, images of skyscrapers and taxis and Tiffany's whizzing by. 'Isn't New York expensive? You have a lot of savings?'

I nod. 'I still have the savings I was putting away for my trip with Gran.'

The Orient Express was going to be our next big trip together, as soon as I saved enough money to be able to fully treat her, like how she did for me when she took me abroad at nineteen.

My gran – Grooms, as I called her – was my *everything*. She raised me with my mum. She was my confidante, she was my comedy, she was my inspiration. When she used to say I took after her, she was right – we were both dreamers. The number of hours I used to sit and listen to her tales of her early life, where she followed her heart as a young dancer, travelling the world, meeting men, experimenting with lotions and potions, never stopping to give up on her dreams. She even began it all by following her heart and talent out to our favourite place, New York City, back in the fifties.

Then, ever since Grooms read *Murder on the Orient Express*, she talked about wanting to experience it for herself (the train, not the murder). I wanted to do that for her, repay and recreate the excitement we felt on our Big Apple trip, and along the journey ask her every remaining question I had, and listen to all of her life stories again. But it was expensive, and I wanted it to be perfect. I made promises, saved as hard as I could, trying to make sure we could do it all properly.

My gran was so full of life that it's like I forgot how little she had left. So when illness came and whisked her away to another world a couple of years back, with very little notice, I simply ran out of time. We never made that train together. The dream died alongside her.

'I think she'd approve of me using the money this way,' I say to Flo, nodding to myself, picturing Grooms dancing around New York City. 'I know she would.'

Flo hands me back my guidebook and does another of her exaggerated sighs. 'I know she would too.'

Fast forward to a long while later, while I munch on donuts and Flo chops my damp but peachened locks into what I know she'll make the perfect, bouncy Rachel hairdo, she brings up the subject of a going-away party.

'I haven't even thought about it,' I say, spraying a little sugar down the front of my black nylon robe. 'Where would we hold it?'

'My house? Your house?'

I make one of those non-committal huffing sounds that means no, while being careful not to shake my head. 'I don't want that. I don't know who I'd invite – I need a little space from the airline gang at the moment.' I meet her eyes in the mirror and she gives a small smile. I think she gets it.

Flo holds the scissors away from my head for a moment. 'What's happening with your house, while you're away?'

'I'm giving it up. I've already sent in my notice to my landlady. I'll have to pay for a couple of weeks when I'm not there, but ...' A couple of weeks' rent wasn't exactly nothing, but my flight was booked by the time I thought about my living arrangements, so that was that.

'Will she keep it open for you though, for when you come back?'

I hold her gaze in the reflection. 'Why would I live there again? I don't need to be so near the airport any more.'

'Oh, honey.'

'I am a little lost lamb,' I declare.

'I know. Do you know anybody in New York? Is there anybody I can count on to have your back out there, to make sure you're eating vitamins and refreshing your dye job at a salon and not over your bathtub?'

'I'm not going to be able to afford a place with a bathtub.' I laugh and try to change the subject, but Flo refuses to cut another hair until I spill. 'All right, there is one person I know out there, but he is *not* the reason I'm going, so don't start with me.'

'Who?'

'Hugh lives out there now.'

'HUGH? As in, the Hugh who always said he'd never move to New York with you because he hated big cities, and was so begrudging about living even this close to London?'

'Yep.'

'What's he doing out there?'

'I have no idea, and I don't intend to. I'm not planning to bump into him, anyway, I think there's over a million and a half people in Manhattan.'

Flo goes back to cutting, suspicion painted all over her face. 'You swear you aren't going there to try to rekindle anything so you can get that "dream" back again? Because he was no dream.'

'He wasn't so bad,' I argue. 'I loved him for a long time, and it was me who split up with him, remember, so, no, I'm not trying to get back together. Besides, he probably hates me. We never talk any more.'

It was sad, really. Hugh was significant, to me, to my life. We grew up together but drifted apart in our twenties, eventually splitting up around a year ago.

I should never have based a dream around a boy, in retrospect. Hadn't my gran, and my mum, two women who lived their lives fully and followed their hearts without a man at their side, taught me anything? We met when he joined my school in Year Eleven and I made my list a couple of years after getting together. It was teenage love at first sight and we connected in a way that felt new and familiar all at once. Because of that, he always felt like an anchor home.

I have this photo of him, one of my favourites, that's still tucked inside that flamingo journal. In the picture, he's leaning against the front door of the flat we rented when we first moved up to London, back when I was in those early days of pilot training and he was super-supportive. Before he got irked by my work schedule, and our reasons for being together felt like they were distancing, and, nearly a decade after that first kiss outside the science block, our futures separated at a crossroads that took him to live out in the countryside and took me back up in the air.

It's fine. It's a good thing we split up – I'm the one that called it off, and, after some time wallowing, I now think of Hugh with a fondness, a sadness, a guilt and a relief. He was my high-school sweetheart, and I loved him hard, for half of my life.

Maybe I would look him up when I hit the city, just to say hey—

'Stop that.' Flo holds a hairdryer aloft like she might clunk me on the head with it. 'Stop thinking about contacting him.'

'I'm not,' I insist, and go back to my donut while Flo dries the rest of my hair.

She's spun my chair away from the mirror while she works and as she sweeps a big round brush through the ends, I can tell just from the way they tickle my neck above the robe that they're shorter and silkier than the mess I made previously.

With a few final flourishes of a butterscotch-scented serum and a brief foray with a pair of straighteners, she smiles down at me. 'When you first told me you wanted a peach-coloured Rachel, I thought, well, it didn't seem very you. But actually . . .'

She turns my chair around, giving me a big reveal moment, like I'm on *Queer Eye* with JVN or something wonderful like that. I gasp. Literally.

Leaning forwards, I reach up to touch my tresses, angling my head from side to side. It's bouncy, it's flicky, it's cool and it's new. The colour is a pale, creamy peach that looks like apricot ice cream.

'Rachel from *Friends* would be very proud,' Flo says.

'I love it,' I whisper, flicking the whole lot over into an exaggerated side-part. 'It's exactly what I've always wanted. I think you did a better job than me.'

Flo chuckles. 'I'm glad you like it. It looks lovely on you.'

'Wow! Gorgeous,' comments one of Flo's colleagues, who shoots past with a pair of trimmers.

'Thank you!' I grin. 'I really, really love it. Thank you, Flo.'

'You can thank me by treating it well and finding a good colourist to maintain this shade when you get to New York.'

'I will, I promise. This is definitely the hair of someone with a whole new set of dreams just waiting to be uncovered, don't you think?'

'Absolutely.'

# Chapter 6

'You have your passport?' Mum asks.

I tap my rucksack. 'Yep.'

'And you've sorted your ESTA visa waiver thing?'

'I have.'

'Are you meeting any of your friends at the airport for a cup of tea or anything before you go?'

When I take holidays, my mum likes to talk to me like I've just finished Sixth Form and am embarking on my first trip abroad without her. Rather than like someone who has been travelling internationally as a pilot for the past five years. But I don't mind. Where Grooms and I were always more your lobbing caution to the wind kinda gals, she's been the one reining us in and keeping us careful.

'I'm not meeting any friends, but I'm sure I'll see some there, organically.' Preferably not, of course. I'd like to start my new quest for self-discovery without reminders from my recent and pain-soaked past. At least I'm flying to New York with a different airline than my own.

Since I moved the last of my things out of my Sunbury-on-Thames home and into my mum's house only yesterday, she's insisted on driving me to the airport, saying that my shoulder must be aching from all the lifting and that she doesn't want me having to haul my suitcase up and down train steps. I will miss my mum.

I shake the thought away – I'm going for less than three months. Sometimes life gets in the way and we don't see each other for nearly that long anyway. I'm just feeling lonesome, and I need to get past it, pronto.

Mum swings the car into the drop-off area outside the terminal and after a little weeping and a lot of hugging, I say, 'Grooms would be excited for me, wouldn't she?'

'Of course she would,' Mum answers, her face lighting up at the mention of her mother. 'She loved New York. And she loved you, so if this is what will put a smile on your face again, she'd be all for it.'

I nod. It's what I know, really, but it doesn't hurt to hear it again. 'And you're excited for me? Even though I won't be around for Christmas this year?'

'Oh, don't worry about that – there's always plenty of fabulous festive movies on Netflix. I can probably even find some set in New York.'

'And you could have Eric over, if he's free,' I suggest, knowing that Eric, my mum's lifelong friend and my biological father, will probably be round at hers with them talking each other's ears off, as usual, before my flight's even left the

UK. 'Which reminds me, tell him he can borrow any of my books while I'm away.'

'Absolutely. You'll call us on your birthday, won't you?' Mum says, her eyes on mine.

'Of course.' Thirty years ago, Eric donated to my single mum so she could have me, and he's always keen to be a part of my birthdays. Occasionally I feel a stab of sadness at the thought of my homebody mum being lonely, though I know I shouldn't. As well as Eric, she has a strong circle of friends, and a new potential love interest in the wings. So, though I'll be away, and though Mum hasn't had a girlfriend for a while, I know I don't really need to worry.

'I'm very excited for you. And proud.'

Hello, watery eyes. 'Okay, Mum, I have to go so don't make me cry any more. You have my flight details, and the hostel info, and I'll be back in January.'

'Call me when you get there; it doesn't matter what time it is.' Mum gives me a giant final squeeze and pushes a clump of my peach hair out of my face. 'This new do has a life of its own, doesn't it?'

I sniffle a yes.

'Go,' she says. 'Make the most of this dream, make us all proud. Maybe start with a stiff drink.'

I've managed to get myself so lost in thought on the plane it takes a couple of tries for the air steward to get my attention. I've been thinking about my gran coming to New York in the fifties. How did she get there? Did she fly? Did she take a boat? Where did she stay when she first arrived, or did she go right to the dance company and they put her up there? I'm struggling to remember – did she have a job already lined up or land one when she arrived? I should know this. I should have asked her all this when we came here together, but I was too distracted by the present to think about the past.

I'm searching my mind in case the answers are locked inside the stories she's told me over the years, but I can't quite recall, and suddenly someone is saying my name.

'Ashling? Ashling?'

I turn from the frost-peppered oval window and blink up at a familiar face. Hannah, from Manchester, who used to work for my airline. 'Oh, hi!'

'Living In The Air couldn't comp you a flight?' she asks, handing me a tray of breakfast food with a friendly smile.

'This one just worked out better, with my timings.' *And my insecurities.*

'Well, if the plane flies into any trouble, we know who to call.' She winks. Beside me, the lady passenger turns her head and scrutinises me. 'Do you want anything?'

I mean, a fancy first-class brekkie wouldn't go amiss, if I'm honest. But I'd also like to remain a little elusive. Like a celebrity, but with less money and a hostel room booked at the end of my journey. 'I'm fine, thanks so much, though.'

Hannah's attention is drawn elsewhere, further down the cabin. 'I'll be right back.'

Am I a number one super-bitch for wishing she wouldn't be? I loved my colleagues (most of them), past and present, but right now I just want to push that part of my life away.

Which is hard enough when you're an ex-pilot sitting on an eight-hour flight.

What will my new life look like? What am I going to do with my time, my energy, my love? What am I going to save my money for or spend it on? By the time I fly home, will I be unrecognisable? And is that what I want?

'Hey.' Hannah's returned. She has a glass of mimosa for me, and one for the woman next to me – I'm not sure if it's out of kindness or if she thinks we're travelling together. She also gives me a hot towel and three packets of mini pretzels, so my seat-back tray table is positively brimming. 'My inflight manager house-shares with several Living ground crew. She'd heard of you and told me what happened,' Hannah says, handing me yet another hot towel, her eyes fixed on mine. For a moment, I feel myself flood with a shameful blush. I don't want to talk about this now. I don't want to talk about this. But then Hannah surprises me by simply saying, 'I'm sorry. If you need anything, you know what to do.'

# Chapter 7

This is lovely. Relaxing, even. Exactly where I want to be right now. I am absolutely not thinking about the fact my ambitions got lopped short before I ever got to cross the Atlantic in the pilot seat.

We begin the descent over New York, and I want to glimpse the view that never gets old, the one often reserved for sweeping drones in the establishing shots of TV shows, or those that are still pilots.

I shuffle my hand in the pouch in front of me and dig out my phone, switching on the camera so I'm armed and ready should a *National Geographic*-worthy photo suddenly display itself to me. I also find the bread roll I stored away from the lunch serving. I'm pretty full, and a little gassy to be honest, but I rip into the plastic and chew away at it anyway, eyes on the window, ears bubbling.

'Noooo!' I say out loud through a gummy gob-full of

dough as the plane takes a sudden dip to the left, sliding my view from approaching city to blue skies above.

It's been a good flight, very little turbulence, and, actually, it's nice to experience a trip here in the main cabin instead of looking through those gigantic panoramic windows of the cockpit. I totally believe myself.

Seriously though, the flight has been great. Very steady, and word clearly got around the cabin crew that I was recently-but-no-longer a pilot, and they lavished me with mini bags of pretzels. One even gave me a sleep kit from business class, which was nice. I'll save it for a day in New York where I just can't sleep because I'm having too wild a time figuring out the new me.

The plane curves again, and my window fills with the islands and coastline alongside Long Island, while my ears pop in my head. Far in the distance, if I lean forwards, I can see the hazy glitter of the Manhattan skyline.

The little sadness in me that has kept me company on this leg of the journey backs away, making space for excitement, and . . . relief? Yes, relief. I'm nearly there, and there are two things I know:

1. This is the last goal left on my list I can plausibly tick off, and now it's happening.
2. New York City is going to sort out all my problems. It is a city where big dreams can be made and it will show me the way to my perfect future, one more time.

Usually when I exit an airport, I'm met by a Living In The Air shuttle bus that takes me to our partner layover hotel. Now, after getting some cash out of an ATM and then breaking some notes inside a shop on a massive bag of peanut butter M&M's, I'm standing in the middle of JFK's arrivals hall. Passengers rush past me, ruffling my hair in their breeze. The clack of high heels, judder of suitcase wheels and muffled announcements fill my ears.

All right, let's just follow the signs to public transport. I'm sure it'll be obvious how to make it into Manhattan.

I pause to figure out whether to take a right or left, standing like a rock in a river of people inside the terminal. A conversation filters closer to me: two people arguing.

'Would you hurry up?' she's saying, her eyes focused on the screens above the array of check-in desks while he drags a giant suitcase behind him. 'What's wrong with you today?'

'I'm just nervous, you know—'

*Thunk.* Plastic meets canvas, wheels slide out from underneath, cases crash to the ground by my feet.

'Watch where you're going, all right?' the man says, an easy American accent tinged with chargrilled words.

The guy and I lock eyes – his dark, like his hair, mine light, like mine. His stressed, overhung with a frown, mine bright with new beginnings.

'Whoops!' I say, lifting my case, which his monstrously large burgundy suitcase has taken a flying wallop into. 'I was stationary though ... maybe you should watch where *you're* going?'

'Sorry,' he mutters, reaching down to do the same, his

holdall swinging and nearly clipping me on my bad shoulder. I jolt sideways only to catch my hair in its zip.

I yelp as a few strands are pulled out, and rub the side of my head.

The man looks confused, until he glances down at his bag to see three bright peach hairs dangling against the black of his holdall. He runs a hand through his own hair and sighs. 'I'm so sorry, I don't know what's wrong with me. Are you okay?'

'I'm fine,' I say, and then add, 'Are ... you?'

Beside him, the woman sighs. 'Come on, get your bag, let's get going.'

'Wait, just one moment,' he tells her, and then starts to reach towards my head but I must have flinched back. Touching a stranger's head is a bit weird, right? Unless he's a doctor? He seems to catch himself at the last moment though, stuffing his paws into his pockets and saying, 'You're sure you aren't hurt?'

'I'm sure.' I smile. Then I give the woman a smile, too, but her return is a little tight. I stoop to pick up the handle of my case again. 'Go, catch your flight. Enjoy your trip.'

The man nods at me, distraction painted all over his features, and goes to follow the woman. He half turns a heartbeat later and adds, 'Welcome to New York.'

Welcome, indeed. There's a chill in the air as I step outside, not dissimilar to back in the UK. It's mid-afternoon now and the sun is lowering in the sky. In front of me are a string of yellow cabs, and the sounds of New Yorkers talking quickly into their phones, planes taking off overhead, and suitcase wheels rattling along the tarmac flood my ears.

I love it all.

A woman in shades and a cool, casual flight outfit walks past my vision. Is that Alicia Keys?

'Miss? Are you getting on the bus?'

'Yes!' I focus, clutching my massive suitcase and hoisting my rucksack further onto my other shoulder. I scrabble in my pocket for my ticket, which I hand to the driver. 'It's a one way, please.'

'Dropping off where?' the driver asks.

'It's a hostel, right by Columbia University, let me just grab the name ...'

'I can drop you at Columbia, no problem.'

'That sounds perfect.'

'Are you attending Columbia this semester?' asks a woman sitting behind the driver, after I heave my case into the bus's underbelly and climb aboard.

I take the empty seat behind her, and wonder if she thinks I'm a sprightly freshman rather than a practically thirty-year-old. 'No, I'm just hostelling nearby for a few days, while I find somewhere to stay over the winter. Do you live here?'

'I'm just visiting from Ohio: my son is at Columbia.' The woman smiles. 'I'm not sure I could live in a city this big, but my son says it's amazing.'

'He's right,' I say, settling back in my seat as the bus pulls away from the airport.

I made it. Not just to New York, but through the journey. I didn't appreciate (maybe I did) just how on edge I've been ever since arriving at Heathrow that morning. Even the early morning whisky and coke hadn't taken the edge off, nor the mimosa on the plane. I felt like I was at a high school reunion but I was the kid who failed at life and then had to stand in front of all of her peers naked.

That was a bit of a mixed metaphor, but I think you know what I mean. I felt exposed, vulnerable, but now I'm driving away and I don't need to set foot inside an airport again for over two months. And by then, I will be new and improved and goal-oriented again, and I will have all my shit together and *I'll* be the one in the cool flight outfit, striding through the concourse.

I glance back at JFK retreating in the distance, at the criss-cross of contrails streaking the sky, the lowering sun making them the same peach as my hair. And then I face forwards again, my back to my past, facing my future.

A while later, after the bus has trundled through the busy streets of Manhattan, we pull into a shady spot beside a cream-stone building. The sun is well behind the skyline now, and a shiver of cold dusk breeze creeps under my coat as I step off the bus. I pull my suitcase out, minding not to hit any passing college students as they make their way from class or to a frat party or any other cool thing American uni kids get up to.

My hostel is one block away from the campus, and as I start walking I take a subtle sniff at my armpit. A dip in a pool often helps me beat jet-lag, but I don't think my hostel stretches to such facilities, so a cool shower will have to do instead.

The air feels magic. It probably isn't, it's just big city air,

I guess, but it's full of fall leaves and the promise of change and the smell of peanut butter or maybe that's just me and my M&M's.

'Hello,' I say to the girl behind the counter of the hostel. She is dressed in a fluro-orange shirt the colour of the autumn trees and she has a septum piercing, and I wonder if she's looking at me and thinking how my hair looks like Rachel from *Friends*. Will everyone in New York be admiring my haircut? Will they notice my subtle nod to NY life? My humble homage? My—

'Hey, what's up?' she replies with a lovely big smile.

I never know how to answer 'what's up' but I feel like it's the equivalent to a Brit's 'all right?', which doesn't warrant a detailed answer of whether or not life is currently kicking the crap out of you. Instead, I launch into, 'I have a room booked for a week – Ashling Avalyn.'

'Is it a dorm?' she asks, clacking on her computer.

'Yes,' I answer, looking around while she pulls up my reservation. It's been a while since I was in a hostel – in fact, aside from a long weekend in Newquay with some friends for a twenty-fifth birthday, my stay in New York a decade earlier was the last time. My lips twitch, a chuckle threatening to escape, as I remember Grooms insisting (despite Mum's protests) that the two of us stay in the dorm room so we could make friends with the backpackers sharing our bunks. I hope my roommates tonight are as nice as the ones back then. I hope they aren't quite such party animals, though.

Who knows, maybe 'party animal' is part of the new me?

I'm just about to ask what the price would be if I switched to a private room, when the receptionist says, 'Okay, you're all checked in. I just need to take a copy of your passport.'

She chatters away explaining hostel rules and how there'll be free breakfast bagels each morning but you have to slice and toast them yourself. She points out a notice board covered in printouts about cars for sale, trips, tours, adverts for odd jobs and one for a request for a nude model.

'Does anyone advertise apartments on there?' I ask her.

'To live in? Yeah, sometimes. They go pretty quickly though. Whereabouts are you looking for?'

'Anywhere, really. I'm just here for three months – a little less than. I guess I'm playing at living here, rather than actually doing it, in a way . . .' I trail off.

'So, you need a couch, or a room? Or a sublet?'

'Erm, any of those, I guess,' I reply. Wow, I sound totally prepared.

'Well, keep an eye out, but you might have better luck finding a place online.'

She shows me up the stairs to my room on the second floor, a four-bed (two-bunk) dorm with signs of two other people already occupying it. I slide my case into the corner, put my rucksack on one of the empty top bunks, and look out of the window towards a section of the Columbia campus opposite.

Maybe I should go to university, after all. I never went – it was one of the decisions I made back when I was nineteen and trying to figure everything out. Hugh left, and I jumped straight into earning money so I could start my pilot training

43

once I had enough in the bank. Perhaps that could be a new beginning for me?

I don't see my mystery roommates for the remainder of the evening, but, after grabbing a slice of pizza from down the street, calling Mum to let her know I'm still alive and kicking, and forcing myself to stay awake until nearly nine p.m., I drift off just as two laughing women enter my room.

They quickly hush each other and I would have stirred and said hi but before I can even wipe the drool away that's already pooling on my pillow, I've drifted off again.

# Chapter 8

Okay, living in New York really suits me. I mean, I'm not about to get a spot on *The Real Housewives of New York City*, and I don't actually have somewhere to stay yet, and I only arrived yesterday, but I just know. You know? And I knew it a decade ago, and I was *right*.

Yay me. See, all I needed was to get some space from the old me, start over, stop panicking, and I feel much more myself and far more positive about my situation.

I step from my hostel and into the morning sunshine. There's a bagel dangling from my mouth with a smear of peanut butter on, and I'm holding a coffee in a reusable cup that I bought from Reception, which bears the hostel's logo.

I cut through the grounds of Columbia University towards the top western corner of Central Park. With my coat flapping in the soft breeze, my boots crunching over the November leaves, and my New York Yankees baseball cap on my head, I feel right at home.

Even if I did spend fifteen minutes that morning

memorising the route on Google Maps so I could walk confidently and look like a local.

Strolling along pretty, tree-lined streets, I take in the neatly imposing architecture. Vast apartment blocks and campus structures overlook me, and one even has bright green foliage creeping over the lower brickwork, like the building is wearing a scarf.

My bagel is delicious and my coffee is full of half-and-half so it's creamy-dreamy.

Entering Central Park, I join one of many pathways and begin my nearly three-mile walk down towards Midtown Manhattan.

Around me, people on benches read books and newspapers. Joggers in bright tops with long sleeves puff and pant their way past, AirPods firmly in. Walkers watch their dogs of all shapes and sizes as they snuffle at the verges. Squirrels zoom between the trees. I hear the sounds of the city but it's muffled behind the closer music of friends chatting, wheels rolling over crunchy leaves, happy barks, trainers rhythmic on tarmac and birds singing.

Am I breathing slower? I feel like I'm breathing slower, like I would at a yoga class. Being out here in nature must be doing my soul some good.

A plane flies overhead, far, far above, and I watch the streak of white cross the sky, wondering where it's going to, until somebody snatches the remaining third of my bagel right out of my hand.

'Oi!' I shriek, looking down at what is now just a streak of peanut butter on my palm.

'*Roger!* I am so sorry,' comes a female voice and I look around for this arsehole Roger who's nicked my brekkie.

I spot a woman crouching in front of a wriggling, chunky yellow Labrador with a blue collar. She has her hand up to his mouth and I see they're wrestling with my bagel.

'I'm so sorry,' she calls again. 'He's a teenager and I looked down at my phone for one minute—'

'It's okay.' I smile, bending to stroke Roger on the head, just as the woman manages to tug the bagel third from his mouth.

'I guess you don't want this back?'

'I'm sure it's fine.'

She looks mildly disgusted for a moment before she realises I'm kidding, and drops the bagel into a nearby bin, putting Roger on leash. 'Can I pay you for that?'

I wave her away with a thanks – it was free anyway, and I had enough creamy goodness in my coffee to keep me full for a while. Besides, today I'm walking all the way down the length of Manhattan, so I'm sure I'll pass a million delicious-looking eateries and food carts en route if I get snackish.

It takes me about an hour just to walk from the top of Central Park to the bottom, maybe more, winding along paths and over bridges, past ponds and through tunnels of bright orange trees. By the time I exit the park at the south-east corner, I'm about ready to duck into the mammoth Plaza hotel for a sneaky wee. I do just that, clip-clopping through the revolving door and down the gleaming corridor, in awe of the marble walls and gold ceiling accents and glitz and glamour.

Once my business is finished, and I'm back out in the autumn sunshine, I check the map on my phone. There are lots of potential routes I could take to reach the bottom of the island, but which would be the most interesting?

Fifth Avenue. It has to be done. Is there a more all-encompassing street to get you fully immersed in New York life? I walk past the icons: Tiffany's, St Patrick's Cathedral, Rockefeller Plaza, the New York Public Library, the Empire State Building, the Flatiron . . .

There's so much to see, so much to look at, and my head is, as they always said, well and truly in the clouds as I try and look up at everything. Dog leads tangle at my ankles, traffic and bikes whoosh past my side, steamy subway grates threaten to blow up my skirt, Marilyn-style, if only I was wearing one. As I pass, sales assistants move about inside big window displays, hints of the upcoming holidays glittering on the tinsel they're draping.

Ouch, though. I pause by the Flatiron to wriggle my toes in my trainers, my feet throbbing a little. Since leaving the hostel I've been walking, almost solidly (bar a few photo stops), for over two hours. It's definitely lunchtime.

I find a café with lovely-looking giant 'hero' sandwiches, and take a seat by the window so I can keep watching city life rush by while I chew. Although . . . I swallow my mouthful. Really, I should be looking for a place to stay. I've only got a week before my hostel stay runs out.

But it's only day one, right? I can have one day before we get down to the business of figuring out my whole life. Maybe two days. I can get some tourist fun out of the way first.

The buffalo chicken is spicy on my tastebuds and I manage not to get all *When Harry Met Sally* but in my mind I'm making a lot of yummy noises. I let myself focus on the present moment, the sounds of the café, the fashions scuttling past the window, the cars crawling, the people talking, the city life living. It's so busy, like a giant airport terminal, and I am just one person, one little life, munching on one giant sandwich.

Enough philosophising. I've still got about an hour's walk to make it down to The Battery park at the bottom tip of Manhattan.

Onwards I go, this time veering away from Fifth Avenue and zigzagging down through Lower Manhattan, past impressive architecture, and parks filled with happy dogs, until I reach the tip with sore, possibly bleeding, feet and a sense of satisfaction.

I lean on the railings, the cool, autumn winds whipping off the New York Harbor waters. Liberty Island is in the distance, Lady Liberty herself standing with her torch raised, just visible in the afternoon mist.

I take a seat on one of the concrete steps and watch for a while, as people wander back and forth between me and my view, snapping selfies with the statue behind them, one woman making her partner do a full-on photo shoot while she wears what looks like a prom dress. Good for her.

But as much as I'm enjoying the leg-rest, after a while it gets just a little too cold. I flex and wriggle my stiff soles inside my trainers, three more hours of being on my feet causing tantalising thoughts of the subway to flash through my mind.

A breeze hits my face and I look up to the sky, basking in it. Mmm. No, I don't want to be underground for even a second today.

I buy myself a bright white I HEART NY sweater to layer under my jacket, and a matching red lipstick from the first Sephora I pass. Looking picture-postcard perfect to walk back up the length of Manhattan, if I do think so myself. I start with a stroll along the long and serene Hudson River Park on the west side, the Hudson River on my left and New Jersey across the water.

When it comes time to rest my soles again, I cut back into the bustle and enter a pop-up art gallery, and flop down on a bench.

Imagine if I never followed up being a pilot. If I never put the Young Artists' Residency on the backburner, never let it become something I'd do 'someday' and then let myself slip past the age limit. Would I have made a career out of it?

I squint at the painting before me, tilting my head.

Honestly ... probably not. Art, for me, is – was – definitely more of a hobby than a honed skill. I love it, mainly sketching and line drawing, and I'm okay at it. My work has been called 'very realistic' by a local paper and 'jolly nice' by my mum. And managing to get a place in my favourite, dreamy-sounding art foundation in London and Paris as a young artist would have been a monumental thing for me – for just four weeks taking me to new environments, new boundaries, new horizons. But I couldn't have even applied without spending time getting better first, and honing takes a looooooong time. Each year, I kept telling myself to get on and take an evening class or buy some proper materials, but, well . . . it never happened.

Onwards. This time I skirt the east side of Central Park and stop in the Metropolitan Museum of Art and finally the Guggenheim, where a really loud and pretty rude yawn escapes me. Perhaps I'll come back another day, when I'm not hobbling like a two-hundred-year-old hag with jet-lagged bags under my eyes so huge I should be paying excess baggage charges.

Finally, shattered, I climb onto my hostel bunkbed and peel off my smelly socks, throwing them straight into the bin thanks to the holes that have worn right through the toes.

I'm just about to flop backwards and open my phone to start a bit of house-hunting when one of my dormmates throws open the door, lobs her day bag across the room in the general direction of her bed, and shouts at me.

'You've got mail!'

'Where?'

'On the roof!'

'What's it doing up there?' I ask, bemused.

'The movie – the hostel's showing it on their rooftop cinema, and it starts now.'

What time is it? Midnight? Oh, six p.m. 'I don't know, it's cold out and I'm pretty tired—'

'There are heat lamps,' she says, looking at me like I'm being quite ridiculous wanting to be inside on this gorgeous autumn evening when there's a screening of a gorgeous, New York-set autumn film on. 'And free popcorn.'

Ignoring the screams of my feet, I find myself standing, my hip flexors shaking, and hobbling towards the door. How could I not end this perfect day with this perfect-sounding nightcap? 'Sold.'

## Chapter 9

I wake up early with a muffled groan when I see the time. I went to bed way later than I should have following rooftop movie night. But once I've cranked open both my eyelids, I remember: *today is the day I'm getting my life back*.

This morning, as soon as it opens its doors to visitors, I'm going to the one place in the world I know can give me the answers I need.

The Empire State Building!

My heart flutters and a smile spreads across my face as I stare up at the ceiling. By the time I'm taking that elevator back down from the observation deck, I'll be awash with inspiration and ideas and a future mapped out again. Or at least, roughly sketched out.

Okay, maybe *all* the answers won't fall on me from the sky, but being here, in this city, is already expanding my mind to possibility once more. I feel nineteen again.

The memory, so clear in my mind's eye, blossoms inside

me. Standing on the 86th floor observatory as a teenager only months from entering her twenties. It was September, and it was still warm. Back home, Hugh and my friends were heading off to university, some beginning their freshers' weeks, some starting their second years, or even embarking on careers, and Grooms picked that moment to plonk me on a plane with her. She knew I was feeling left out, and mildly terrified at having to make some decisions about what the heck I wanted to do with *my* life. That last day in New York, I went up the Empire State Building, clutching my journal, and stayed for two hours, absorbing everything I could see and everything I could feel until I knew in my soul what I wanted. From then on, I had it all mapped out.

Despite the ache in my feet, I can't wait any longer, and hop out of bed, dressing quickly. Grabbing another bagel for breakfast, I begin the long walk back down through Central Park all the way to 34th Street.

The gilded, Art Deco lobby of the Empire State Building welcomes me into its grandeur. *We've got this*, it would tell me, if it happened to remember who I was. But I have peach hair now, so it probably doesn't.

I show my ticket and follow the stream of visitors past information displays, exhibits, even a photo opportunity with King Kong, and my pace quickens, along with my heart, my eyes straining to see the first glimpse of the view as I reach the open-air 86th floor observatory.

God, at this time, all those years ago I left Grooms at the hostel and arrived here, alone. Now here I am again.

A rush of cold wind and bright daylight sweeps my features as I step through the door to the outside. The sun is peeping out from morning clouds, and my hair dances a quickstep around my face so I force it all into a hairband, stat.

It's busier than I thought it would be at this time of the morning, but then it is such a beautiful day. I move to the edge, facing down to the bottom of Manhattan, the sun in my hair in the same way I felt it ten years earlier, only now with the addition of a bitter November breeze.

The view is incredible in this light. It's like the whole world is stretched before me, for the taking.

Below me, the melody of sirens and horns – sounds common on these city streets – drift up, reaching my ears even from this high in the sky. The noise mixes with the chatter of other visitors, and the distant propellors of helicopters and planes far off in the sky.

Was it this noisy last time?

I close my eyes. I'm sure it was, it's just that back then I was more relaxed. I take a deep breath and allow the sounds to become a background soundscape.

*Come on then, dreams, out you come.*

Perhaps my eyes should be open. I need to absorb the inspiration of my surroundings, after all.

After another gaze into the distance, taking in the windows of shorter skyscrapers, the glittering waters of the Hudson and East rivers, I step up to look through one of the heavy iron viewfinders. My eyes trail over the rooftops and along the roads below me, in case I spot something that way. No, no flashes of inspiration yet . . .

I'll take a lap. I probably just need to get my bearings a little more, settle into the experience first.

Walking to the west side, I'm hit by the gustiest of winds, which seem to be lurking here, secretly. My layered hair is immediately pulled from my hairband in wild clumps and by the time I've scuttled to the north side of the observation deck, which is far less breezy, I know I'm a mess.

Fixing myself before views of the Chrysler Building, Central Park and the just-visible flashes of Times Square, I take my journal from my bag and hold it close, ready to fill in a few new dreams when they show themselves.

You know what, the south side was really a very lovely view. And the most meaningful to me. A break in the onlookers lets me squeeze to the front, and I put my fingers on the cold silver railings and inhale a big ol' gulpful of breath.

This is where I was standing, when I knew. It was much less busy up here that day, and I remember leaning here with my journal in front of me, clutching it tightly. I spent a while skimming my eyes over the pages, at all the notes and hopes and dreams I scribbled down over the past few days, and like a magic-eye image, they reformed into pictures of my life before me.

I wanted to fill any spare space I had in my time and my heart with art, and let it take me to London and Paris and maybe beyond.

I wanted to be with Hugh for ever. I loved him, and I wanted to marry him.

I wanted to take my wonderful Grooms on the adventure of her lifetime, on the Orient Express.

I remember gazing out at Manhattan and knowing I wanted to come back here, one day, to live.

And I looked up at the sky, above me, surrounding me, at the top of one of the world's tallest buildings, knowing I wanted to make my career up here in the clouds.

It all just came to me back then. So now I guess I . . . wait?

Several minutes later and I'm still waiting for the big revelation(s), and it's getting awkward as I think there are people behind me who would like to squeeze in and get a cute couple photo together. Just because they just got engaged or something.

Fine, I'll do another lap, give myself another 360-degree view of New York City. I'm in no rush.

Over the next hour or so I search and I search until the cold wind is stinging my eyes, down all the criss-cross streets below me, in every one of the millions of windows, on every rooftop garden and from every angle, but I just can't find the inspiration that I found back then.

Have I lost that, too?

*Come on, dreams. I need you to appear and tell me how to live the rest of my life. Come onnnn, work with me here.*

I lift my gaze to the sky, like I did back then, and it's as if the weight of the atmosphere is suddenly pressing down on me, heavy and sad.

I was so sure this was going to work. Am I broken?

Tears begin to stream from my eyes, changing direction on my cheeks as they're whipped by the wind. I'm barely breathing and let out an audible, choking sob.

Heat from my blush prickles my skin as several people turn to look at me.

'Are you okay?' asks one woman, her camera lowered, her face full of worry for me.

'Yeah,' I squeak, wiping at my face. 'Yep.' But my lips are doing that Wallace and Gromit thing where they stretch out to the sides and I'm blinking at the tears to try to stop them but I just know they're creating big mascara splotches under my eyes. What the hell? Where did this come from? Stop it, Ashling!

'Um,' the woman says, looking around. 'Are you here with anyone?'

'No, I'm alone.' I actually didn't mean it in a bad way but given my weeping face it comes out sounding pitiful, even to my own ears. 'I'm fine, just having a moment.'

'Can I get you anything?'

I shake my head. 'I'm just going to nip to the restroom.'

I walk quickly inside the doors, my head down, taking long, shaky inhales and exhales to control my breathing. I really need to get it together.

Breathe in, breathe out, blow nose, wipe eyes. *Lalala*, everything is fine. I give myself a shake and head back out onto the observation deck, but through the opposite doors, so I'm facing the direction of Central Park again.

However, the minute I'm back outside, the taps get turned on again, and I'm forcing myself to be silent but my breathing is jagged, my face is hot and soggy and I'm pretty sure there's snot trickling out of one of my nostrils.

I can't see it – I can't see my future. All the little ways I thought it would look: my hair grey under my captain's hat, the collage frame I bought in an Ikea sale that I planned to use for our Orient Express photos, all the small things that weren't even fully loaded images in my mind, so much as imprints and impressions of the things to come. Now I can't, I won't, ever see them. I don't know what to replace them with.

I can't leave yet, I've not got anywhere closer to figuring anything out, I need to ride this out.

Another vocal sob splutters out and I turn it into a cough, which is maybe worse now I see the nearby tourists scatter away from me.

*For God's sake, Ashling.*

All right, I know I have to go. And I guess that's about the only thing I do know.

## Chapter 10

Well, crap.

I sit in a diner, two thick slabs of cheesecake under my fork acting as my lunch, and process what just happened.

Wasn't the Empire State Building going to get me out of this mess? I thought I'd have a bit of direction right about now, but I'm no closer to figuring my life out than I was before I went up there. Less, even. At least I went up there with hope.

'I still love ya,' I whisper into the glass of the window, looking up at the building, poking up into the sky from behind nearby skyscrapers. It wasn't the Empire State's fault – maybe I just need to go back when I've had a little more sleep, when I'm a little more settled.

I fork in a huge scoop of creamy vanilla cheesecake and pull out my phone. I scroll about for a while through different property apps, looking for rooms or sublets going in Manhattan over the next three months. Hmm, pickings are

slimmer than I thought they would be. Don't get me wrong –
there are hundreds of adverts, but once I've narrowed down
the length of time, the price and the location, the fruit isn't
as plentiful as I assumed it would be. And I don't want to
get stuck paying for a six-month-plus contract, but I'll need
it to be furnished, even if it's absolutely tiny.

I huff and suppress a cheesecake burp that rises up in
protest, before stuffing more in and calling a couple of the
listings. After a handful of duds (already snapped up / it's an
old listing / 'actually the price in December is extra because
it's a popular time of year') one woman gives me a magical-
sounding 'Yes' on the end of the line.

'Can you get here in under thirty minutes?' the letting
agent asks me.

'Yes, sure,' I say quickly. I'm sure I can make it to the
Lower East Side in that time. She's telling me the address
and the directions as I throw down a handful of bills, wave
a thank you to the waiter, and scoop up the remainder of
the bigger of the two cheesecake slices in a napkin and run
out of the door, chomping it from my hand as I stride down
the street in the hopes of stumbling upon a subway station.

I hear them below me; I see the steam pouring out from
the grates. There must be one somewhere . . .

'Ha!' I cry out loud, happening upon one outside the
famous Macy's, and run down the steps, my cheesecake
gurgling in my stomach.

Once I'm ticketed and through the barriers, on a platform
and definitely facing the right direction, I step onto the train
and collapse into an empty seat in the corner. I check the

map. I'll need to transfer to a different line in a bit, but I'll just rest my weary eyes for just a few minutes . . .

'The next, and last, stop is Coney Island-Stillwell Avenue . . .'

The announcement infiltrates my dream and I wake with a dribbling jolt to find myself in a much emptier carriage, sunlight on my face in a way that shouldn't happen deep inside a subway.

'Coney Island!' some kid near me shrieks at her dad, teeth showing in a wide grin.

'We're not at Coney Island,' I say. Not really to her, more to myself. But myself is quickly shut up when the train rolls to a stop in front of a big sign reading 'Coney Island-Stillwell Av'.

What time is it? '*Ffff* . . .' I stifle a swear from popping out in front of that little girl. An hour has passed. I slept for an hour, which is a full thirty minutes longer than the apartment woman gave me to get over there. And now I'm in Coney Island and to be honest, I'm not sure where that even is, but it ain't the Lower East Side of Manhattan.

It's now mid-afternoon and I step off the train to call the woman back, apologising profusely in my most sorrowful and British voice. Perhaps she might take pity on me.

She doesn't sound like she has much pity, but she does say we can try again when she's done with a couple of errands.

I am not risking getting lost during a 'quick' walk around Coney Island, so back on the train I go. I rub the crick in my neck, my eyes and brain all post-nap blurry. I think I have warm, squished cheesecake in my coat pocket but I'm afraid to check. En route back to Manhattan, I force myself to stay wide awake, and jump off as soon as we reach my stop.

The dark is creeping in by the time the woman, in clacking heels and a no-time-for-nonsense look on her face, meets me outside a red-bricked apartment block.

'Are you Ashling?' she says, unlocking the front door and walking briskly in out of the cold.

'I am.' I follow her inside.

'And you just want short term, right?'

'Yep, just until January.'

She nods and we begin walking up the stairs when she asks, 'What do you do?'

'Uh . . .' I hesitate. You tell me, lady! 'I'm between jobs at the moment.'

The agent stops and turns to me, two steps higher than me, which, to be honest, makes me feel a little inadequate. I move up a step and end up eye-level with her boobs and closer than either of us would like me to be.

'You don't have a job?'

'I'm just looking for somewhere to stay for a couple of months, then I'm heading back to the UK. I have savings to cover all the rent,' I explain.

'Wait.' She holds her hands up. 'You don't have citizenship, tax returns, a social security number or anything like that?'

I gulp, and put my hands in my pockets so she doesn't see them shaking.

*Bollocks*, I do have cheesecake in there.

'Do I need them?'

She sighs, and proceeds to give me a bit of advice in the

form of: I might have trouble renting a home here – even short term – as a tourist. 'You could get like, a holiday let, or a hotel, or stay with friends or something. But you need the right paperwork to rent a place directly. Isn't that how it would work in the UK?'

I nod, dumbly, because of course it is. Of course I can't just rock up to some flat and ask to rent it without any of the legal necessities. I should have known this. I would have figured that out, quickly, if I'd stopped for five seconds and thought about what I was doing, rather than just rushing into all of this.

I am feeling like a prize dumbo today.

Everything is noisy. The subway home is noisy, the streets are noisy, the hostel is noisy, even my dorm room is noisy, with the other girls having drinks while they get ready for a night out in the city that never sleeps. But man, I need to sleep.

The communal kitchen bubbles over with people fixing snacks and dinners and by the time I get to blast some rice, the microwave stops working after twenty seconds.

I go up to the roof terrace, which is deserted, and munch my lukewarm, gritty rice with zombie eyes staring at the ground. Where'd all my excitement go? Where's that electric feeling that buzzed around my body all of yesterday? I made a good choice, coming here, right? Things are just very up in the air right now ...

As soon as the girls have left the dorm to go to a cool bar, I climb into bed, make-up on, cheesecake still in my coat pocket, teeth unbrushed, and am asleep before I even sense the small churning inside my stomach.

Four hours later, it wakes me up, and I leap out of bed without even giving my brain a chance to think of anything other than some quick-fire directions out of the dorm and into the women's bathroom.

I throw myself into a stall, crouching in front of the toilet, and, to cut a gross story short, that's where I essentially stay for the next two days, after having given myself food poisoning from not handling that bloody rice properly.

Sometimes I crawl back into bed and sleep some more. Sometimes I just sit on the floor of the toilet cubicle, sweating and heaving, and then crawl into the shower, and then back into the toilet stall again. Often, I slump my forehead against the dorm window, looking at New York City waking up, living, breathing, and putting out the nightlights, all without me. A truly glittering start to life in NYC.

Then, finally, I start to feel better.

# Chapter 11

I can't believe I've been here nearly a week. I feel like I have literally been flushing time down the toilet.

I'm feeling waaaaaay better now, and yesterday and today I poured everything into finding somewhere to live. Via holiday rental websites and short-term sublets, the internet and local newspapers, I saw a studio in Soho, a little room in Little Italy, a one-bed just off Broadway and an apartment in the Upper West Side that was way over budget but I couldn't resist viewing. But ... nothing. And the legalities of where I can rent and what's actually allowed are a minefield I didn't anticipate. A nervous feeling is settling into my stomach that maybe I'm not going to find a place to call home for the next couple of months, after all.

Arriving back at the hostel, I join the queue for Reception, where Septum-Ally (who I'll just call Ally from now on) is manning the desk. I've clearly hit check-in time, and by the time I'm at the front I've eaten my way through three of the six donuts I bought on the way home.

'Hi,' I say, wiping cinnamon frosting from my lip.

'Hey,' Ally replies, greeting me with a smile. 'Any luck with the house-hunt?'

I shake my head. 'To be honest, it's not going well. I was really hoping to live on Manhattan but everywhere is over budget, or a twelve-month lease, or only available for some of the time, and I'm limited by not being able to rent directly . . .' I trail off.

Ally thinks for a second. 'Do you know anybody at all in the city? An old relative? Some exchange student you went to school with? What you need is someone who already lives and works here and has a network. There's always somebody who knows somebody who has a room.' She meets my eye and adds quickly, 'Myself not included; I moved here from Wyoming six months ago, I live at the hostel and I only hang out with backpackers and tourists as yet.'

A thought flutters by. There is one person I know here . . .

No. Nope. I reply with, 'In the meantime, I'm due to check out tomorrow. Can I extend by another week?'

Ally turns to the computer and frowns. 'Umm . . . I can place you for three more nights, but then we're booked out.'

Crap. I can't see myself getting a house lined up in just three days, not the way I'm going. Maybe I could move to a hotel for a couple of nights, then come back. 'For how long?'

'Right through Thanksgiving,' she clicks, 'and then it gets pretty busy up until Christmas, and we're fully booked over Christmas and New Year's.'

'Can you recommend any other hostels?'

'I mean, yeah, there are a lot. But I don't know what their availability will be like, coming up to the holidays. I'm sure you'll find something, though,' she adds, seeing my frown-furrowed face.

'All right, um ... Can you book me in for the three extra nights, and I'll ... I might make a phone call to someone I know. Or at least, used to know.'

Ally nods and taps on the computer. 'Will do. And do it – make the call.'

I step out of the queue and head back up to my dorm, the autumnal spring in my step having fallen a bit flat. The room is empty of people, so I take out my phone and find the number I haven't called for a long time.

His name, and a circular smiling picture of him, stare out at me from above the options to call or message him. Hugh.

I cannot phone him, admit that I, too, am in New York, and ask if he can help me find somewhere to live. What if he offers me a spare room at his? If he even has a spare room. Maybe he has flatmates. Maybe he lives with a new girlfriend. I don't know anything about his life now, beyond a few nuggets he's posted online, and he's never been much of a social media-er.

What if he's still angry or upset about the break-up? What if he just hangs up on me? Or doesn't answer at all? Will that be worse ... or better?

I swipe away the Contacts app and re-open the billion browser tabs I've bookmarked. Perhaps some perfect new apartments will have been added since I checked last night?

No, nothing. I call three places I've already viewed to see if they're still available, and none of them are.

Perhaps I should just hostel-hop the whole time I'm here instead? It's a lovely sense of community, and sharing a dorm for nearly three months might not be *quite* what I had in mind but it is just like proper backpacking, I suppose.

Only ... I didn't come out here to backpack. I wanted to experience *living* in New York City. As close as I could get to that, anyway, as a tourist.

If the roles were reversed, and I was the one who moved here first, and Hugh came into town and needed somewhere to live, I'd want to help him. I wouldn't want him to not call me. But maybe that's because I'm the bad guy trying to make amends. If he broke my heart, maybe I wouldn't feel the same.

'Maybe, maybe, maybe,' I mutter, shaking my head and internally giving myself a quick telling off for trying to mind-read what the whole world was thinking. I reopen Hugh's contact page and hit the phone icon, before I can talk myself out of it.

The phone rings and I sit atop my bunk staring out the window towards the Columbia campus.

He probably won't know of anywhere, anyway.

I watch two students in university-emblem sweatshirts exit a building and turn left down the leafy street.

He probably won't even answer—

'Hello, Hugh's phone?'

That voice. So familiar, yet no more than a memory to me over the past year, until now. He still answers the phone in the same way, like his mum and dad always had, stating his name for the unknown caller. Ah, of course: he doesn't have my number stored any more.

'Hi,' I say, or more, croak. I wish I brought a glass of water up here with me from the kitchen. I only have a bag of sour jelly sweets so I briskly jam one of those in my mouth just to loosen a little saliva. 'It's Ashling.'

There is a pause as long as the Brooklyn Bridge, and then he says, 'Oh. Hi.'

'Hi. How are you?'

'Isn't it quite late at home? Is this a drunk dial?'

He thinks I'm in England, missing him. 'Actually … I'm in New York. Not for you. I mean, not in a following you kinda way. I know you're out here too – again, not in a stalker way, but you know, we still are friends, on Instagram and things.' Always good to state twice in one ramble that you definitely aren't stalking someone. I swallow my sweet. 'Anyway. Surprise!' Oh god, this was not how I wanted our first re-encounter to go.

'You're in New York?' he asks. He doesn't sound *completely* furious.

'Yes. And I have peach hair now. So if you think you see someone that looks like me but with a cool new hairstyle, it probably is me.' I laugh so I don't cry.

'What are you doing here? Since it's definitely not to see me.'

That was pointed. Maybe he is a little furious. I take a breath, and prod in another sweet. 'I'm really sorry to call out of nowhere, perhaps I should have just texted. I've been doing a few things without thinking much lately. But my job situation at home ... changed ... and I decided it was time for me to experience living in New York. Temporarily. Like you always knew I wanted to.' I wait to see what he says next.

'Okay ...'

I guess it's up to me to keep talking. That's fair. 'So here I am, until late January, and I'm just calling to say hi and to ask if, well, do you ... Am I allowed to ask a favour of you, Hugh, or is that really out of line?'

'You can ask.'

It cuts me how cold he is with me, but I don't blame him. Gone was my right to warm chit-chat and cosy catch-ups. 'This is a long shot, and I'm sorry if me asking this is super inappropriate – please tell me to bugger off if you need to – but I'm struggling to find somewhere to stay for the next couple of months. You're the only one I know here and I just wondered if you happened to be aware of anyone, at your work, or through your friends—' (I'm mega-tempted to add 'or girlfriend' but it would be as transparent as a pair of ten-denier tights) '—who might have a room to let for a bit. Or a sublet. Or even a sofa, haha.'

'Are you asking to stay on my sofa?'

'No,' I reply, quicker and louder than I probably should have, and at that moment my two dormmates fling open the door and walk in chatting loudly about which bar to hit that night. I cup my hand around the phone and angle away from them, saying, 'No, not at all, I'm just asking on the off-chance if you happen to know of anywhere. It's fine if you don't, and please don't spend any time on this. Sorry.' I cringe.

'Where are you?' he asks.

'I'm at a hostel. Near Columbia University.'

After a drawn-out sigh, Hugh says coldly, 'I'm fine by the way, thanks for asking.'

'Oh—' I thought I asked?

'Let me have a think and I'll come back to you if anything springs to mind.'

'Really? Thanks, Hugh, I so appreciate it.' I can't keep the gush out of my mouth and I think he hears it too. My roommates certainly do. They've stopped talking and are helping themselves to my sweets that I left on the side and watching me with interest.

'I guess I've got your number again now, so I'll call you.' With that, he does the thing they often do on TV shows and hangs up without a goodbye.

'Who's Hugh?' asks one of my dormmates.

'And what did he do?' asks the other.

'He's just a guy I know that lives over here. He's going to help me find a place to stay.' Sort of. I wonder if I'll ever hear from him again? 'He's my ex,' I blurt.

They both raise their eyebrows and chew slowly on my sweets, waiting for more info.

'We broke up about a year ago,' I begin. 'We'd been together a long time ...' As I explain our history to them, I remember the day I called it quits with the guy I thought I'd marry. I say day, but – at least to me – the break-up had been dragged out over a matter of weeks, a desperate clutch onto what could have been. After a number of years living in London, Hugh was prodding more and more about when we could finally move out to the countryside. But like I said to him, many times, it just didn't seem feasible with my job. My job that he was starting to show a big dollop of resentment towards. But I loved my job. And actually, if I had to give up one . . . I realised I loved it more than him, and that made up my mind for me, as sticky as it made me feel.

'Did he have a job out in the country?' asks one of the girls through a mouthful of jelly sweets.

I shake my head. 'That was part of what annoyed me. Maybe if he'd had something he loved like I loved being a pilot—'

'I can't believe you're a pilot, man,' the other interrupted, shaking her head and reaching over for a sugary high five. 'You seem so . . .'

'I know. Anyway, so Hugh had nothing lined up, he just wanted a change. I knew it was never really about being closer to nature.'

'So him coming to New York wasn't out of spite, just . . .?'

'I guess it was just all part of his own journey? Finding himself and what he wanted out of life.' Without my dreams clouding his.

The girls nod, like I'm wise but a bit boring to listen to, then one of them asks, 'You wanna come out with us tonight?'

I'm not really in the mood. With the looming reality of having to be out of here in a matter of days, it's put things in perspective a little that I'm not just here on a happy holiday and instead need to pull myself together. 'Not tonight, but thanks. You guys have fun. I'm going to have an early night.'

# Chapter 12

I spend a sleepless night on my top bunk, tossing and turning with guilt, and by sunrise I'm feeling like an absolute shitbag. That was so selfish of me to call up my ex, the guy whose heart I broke, out of the blue and ask him for a favour. How would I feel, if someone I used to love did that to me? If they came into my space and interrupted my life and wanted me to use my time and my friends and connections for their benefit? I'd feel pretty mad, I think.

I'm fairly certain I won't be hearing back from Hugh, and I don't blame him.

On the tiny roof terrace, I stand under an overcast Tuesday morning sky. I'm four storeys up and the chatter of university students walking past rises, along with the morning squeak of car tyres and distant horns. I wrap my coat around me and suck on the mini pencil I'm holding in my fingers as if it's a cigarette. It feels like the kind of morning to smoke a cigarette on a roof terrace and ponder the shit-bagginess of yourself, but I don't smoke, so . . .

Perhaps I should call Hugh again. I could apologise and tell him not to worry about doing anything for me. I could even tell him I found somewhere and it's all good. But I haven't. And maybe calling him again would make him even madder.

With another drag on my pencil, I groan and stub it out, which breaks the nib.

I won't call him again. I'll just let it be.

Lugging myself back to my dorm, I grab my rucksack and head back out onto the streets. Yesterday I thought about bunking off from my responsibilities and spending a large part of today exploring the American Museum of Natural History, but the exhibits might have to wait a little longer. I have more pressing needs at the moment.

I spend Tuesday and Wednesday extending my house-hunt away from Manhattan. I visit Brooklyn, Long Island, I even take the train as far up as Westchester County. It's certainly opened up some more options, and there are some nice places, some great places, some average places and some bad places, and I know I should just snap one of them up. But a tiny crystal of hope keeps glimmering, catching my attention, telling me that this is potentially a once-in-a-lifetime opportunity, and maybe I should hold out for Manhattan.

On Thursday, my last full day at the hostel, I take an early ferry out to Staten Island, to meet with a woman who has a room going spare, before she heads to work for the day.

The house is warm and inviting, and smells of bread and apple-cinnamon.

'This is my daughter's room,' she says, opening a door to a purple-painted bedroom with arty prints of London on the wall. 'She just loves London; she'd be tickled to know a Brit was living in her space.'

'Where is she now?' I ask.

'She's at college. I miss her a lot. She'll be coming back for the holidays but she can sleep on the pull-out couch in my bedroom with me while she's here.'

The woman shows me around, and the place has a nice vibe. Homely, warm, with rich colours on the walls and loads of cushions and stacks of books surrounded by cute knick-knacks. I ask if I can think about it for a couple of hours and she tells me, 'Sure!' and loads me up with cinnamon rolls for my boat journey back.

By lunchtime, I've made up my mind. Staten Island isn't where I thought I'd be setting up my temporary home, but it has a nice feel. I'm in.

With a slice from Joe's Pizza, I join the High Line – a rail line that was converted into a public park, which sits raised over the streets on the west side of Manhattan.

I swallow my final bite and lick my fingers, fuelled and excited, and take my phone out of my pocket to call my new landlady, but she calls me first.

'Honey, I'm sorry,' she says down the line, her voice as warm as those cinnamon rolls. 'My daughter just called and she's coming home.'

'For Thanksgiving?'

'No, from college. She didn't like it, she's transferring to somewhere closer by. I want to help you out, and if it were any other time, but . . . I can't rent her room out while she doesn't know what she's doing. Bad timing. I'm sorry.'

'Of course,' I say. 'I hope she's okay?'

'She will be when she gets here and has some good food in her.'

I consider asking if *I* can be the one to sleep on the couch in her bedroom, but she's not offering. Instead, I smile into the receiver. 'That's so true. It was good meeting you.'

We hang up and I hang my head for a moment. Dammit.

I walk the High Line lost in my own thoughts. I'm not really noticing the yellows and oranges of the leaves that scatter the wooden walkway, or the pattern the clouds make on the glass-fronted buildings I'm passing. I'm barely feeling the pitter-patter of rain on my face. How much would it actually cost to stay in a hostel or hotel long term? Can my savings even cover it?

Is this another dream that isn't quite working out how I hoped?

I wonder if I should hostel at least a little while longer, in case something opens up in Manhattan, or continue the search for a place to call mine out in one of the suburbs . . .

I sit on a bench, the wood cold through my leggings, and pull out my phone. I'm about to book a dorm room in a hostel across Manhattan when my phone rings in my hand, the second time in the space of an hour.

This time, it's Hugh.

It's been nearly seventy-two hours since we spoke, and I'd given up hope, basically. I press the button and answer. 'Hugh? Hi! How are you?' I *definitely* led with a 'how are you' that time.

There is the sound of traffic and street noise coming from his end of the line and he speaks to me in a loud voice as if to be heard. 'Ashling, do you still need somewhere to stay for a couple of months?'

'Yes,' I answer, my hope rising a centimetre.

'Well . . . I've found something. For you.'

'You have?' My voice is now loud, and I scramble up to standing upon the bench in delight.

'I have,' he says with a slight tone of martyrdom. 'I'm just on a late lunch break – can you meet me in Greenwich Village so I can hand over the keys?'

'Wait, the keys already? I don't need to see it first, or the landlord doesn't need to meet me?'

'No, he's a friend of mine and he's overseas. You can see it now and if you like it, you can have the keys.'

'Erm, what, *now* now?' I step down off the bench and twirl in a circle as if a giant sign saying 'Greenwich Village' with a down-pointing arrow might be sticking up from between the buildings. I know I'm in the right area . . . 'I mean, yes. I'm on the High Line at the moment.'

'Ah, you're not far then,' he says. 'Go to the Southern end and then you've got about a fifteen-minute walk.' It irks me – just a teeny tiny bit, which doesn't take anything away from my gratitude – how 'in the know' he is about Manhattan. It feels like it was my place and now it's his place, which is silly; it's neither of ours, really; he's only been here six months and I'm a tourist.

That doesn't matter, *this* is huge! I speed-walk my way back down the High Line, weaving between the trees and the plants and the other New Yorker walkers. I'm babbling my thanks to Hugh and arranging to meet him outside a coffeehouse in twenty minutes and when we hang up it occurs to me that I'm about to reunite with my ex-long-term-boyfriend. My would-have-been fiancé.

Yeesh.

But I don't slow down. He's pulled through for me when I don't really deserve it; the least I can do is try to be on time.

At the end (or the beginning) of the High Line, I scamper down the steps to the cross-junction, and check the map on my phone for walking directions to our meeting point. The way I'm racing over crossings and past pedestrians makes me feel like I'm in an opening montage for a TV show about a cool NYC gal who's got places to be and so very many things to do. I wish I was holding a coffee or wearing Louboutins, although actually my trainers are serving me well to be honest.

I've not visited the Greenwich Village area of Manhattan before and I do a déjà-vu double take when I round the corner of a block and see a building that I swear I've seen hundreds of times.

My hand raises to flip my hair back from my eyes before my brain has caught up with what I'm looking up at, and then it dawns on me – it's the *Friends* apartment building! The one used in the TV show! I dawdle for a moment beside some other tourists at the crossing, staring up at it, snapping a couple of pictures, and wondering if anyone has noticed my homage haircut.

The numbers are ticking by on the screen of my phone, and I drag myself away. Oh my god, though, imagine if the flat Hugh's found me is *in* the *Friends* building?

Anyway, my map tells me I'm now only a block away from the coffeehouse we're meeting in front of, so I slide my phone into my jacket pocket and slow to a confident stride.

There he is. It's jarring to see him here, leaning against the wall, looking down at his phone and wearing a suit and a smart wool jacket. His hair is shorter and neater, his face clean-shaven. He looks like my Hugh, only from a different part of the multiverse, as if there's a version of him still back in the UK wearing a hoodie, with a beard and in the house he moved to in the countryside with the fireplace.

'Hugh?' I don't know why it's come out as a question.

He turns to look at me as I approach, pushing his phone in his pocket, and I'm relieved that we both smile, almost involuntarily. It's not a beam, at least not from him, more soft, more reserved, but it's a smile. Then he takes in my hair.

'Wow. That's shorter.'

'And oranger,' I agree. 'You look different too.'

'It's been a while,' he says with a sigh.

I'm in front of him now, and I reach my arms out for a hug before I can decide if that's really something I should be doing, so I let my arms dangle in the air and say, 'I don't know why I'm trying to hug you, you probably don't want this, but, well, here you go. If you do.'

He accepts, with hesitation, and we have a lovely, brief,

awkward squeeze and I notice he still smells of the sandal-wood beard oil, even without the beard.

'Argh,' he says into my hair. 'I wanted to be so cool in front of you but it *is* good to see you.'

I could cry at the niceness of his familiarity. 'It's good to see you too.' I laugh, and squeeze him tighter.

Hugh pulls back, so I take a step backwards as well, giving him his space. He rearranges his features to look more stoic again, but we both know he's putting it on. We were with each other for a decade. We grew apart, we didn't grow oblivious to each other's expressions and mannerisms. 'All right, I'm on lunch so we're going to have to make this quick.' He begins to walk down the block with a fast stride and I fall into step beside him as best I can, leaning forwards to hear him while he continues talking. 'I put some feelers out for you to some people at work who've transferred overseas for a while. Just to see if any of them hadn't let their places, or had any tips for where they got their tenants, that I could pass on to you.'

He pauses and glances at me. I meet his eye and pop out a quick, 'Thank you.'

'One guy, River, came back yesterday evening to say the person he'd sublet to has just pulled out after only a week, or something. Something about moving back to California, nothing to do with the state of the apartment or anything. Apparently. I've never been over to his, but he's a nice guy, so I'm expecting it to be a decent place.'

'Good to know.'

'He didn't want to have to try to advertise and inter-view for a new tenant from all the way over in Europe, so I managed to convince him to give it to you for a really good rate since you'll only be there for a couple of months anyway, and I can vouch for you. Then when he pops back in the new year, he can readvertise for a longer sublet.'

He pauses again, and I thank him again.

'Not a problem,' he says. 'Hope you like it.'

'Seriously, I'm in a dorm at the moment and no idea where I'm spending tomorrow night. Unless this place is teeming with cockroaches or I'm sharing it with a family of serial killers, I'll take it. Thank you so much for finding this.'

He stops at a double doorway made of glass and black wrought iron, set at the bottom of a six-storey rectangular building of cream-coloured stone, with a classic movie-set of a fire escape zigzagging down the façade.

Unlocking the door with one of the two keys attached – 'I had to meet the building manager to pick up the keys on my way to work this morning,' he explains – Hugh leads me into a slim entrance hall with mail cubbies lining one wall and a noticeboard on the opposite. At the end of the corridor a staircase leads upwards, beside a lift with a metal gate pulled across it.

'It's on the sixth floor,' Hugh says. 'River mentioned the elevator but said it's tiny. Take it if you want, but I'll do the stairs.'

'I'm up for taking the stairs,' I reply.

We reach the sixth floor and Hugh reads the numbers on the doors aloud until we get to apartment 605, at which point he inserts key number two, swings open the door, and steps aside.

I enter the space and find my feet drifting straight to the window. This building, being a couple of storeys higher than the one opposite, gives me a view over the rooftops and above the sparse leaves of the treetops. A big, cloudy sky is above and a string of brownstones below.

I feel myself inhale in some calm. When I can see the sky, I feel . . . right.

'This is absolutely perfect,' I say. 'It's just perfect.'

I step backwards and return to the real world. The window itself is large and arched, placed at one end of the small living space the front door opens out into. Surrounded by exposed brickwork painted burgundy, the room feels both warm and cosy, but light at the same time. To my right I spy a bedroom, and behind that, back by the front door and opposite a tiny kitchenette, a bathroom.

Hugh is looking around too, assessing the space. I don't actually know where he calls home. 'Do you live in this area?' I ask. I tried to make it sound casual, but he gives me a wary look nonetheless.

'No,' he answers. 'I'm out in Brooklyn. You get bigger accommodation out there and it's more affordable, but you said you wanted something in Manhattan, so . . .'

'Yeah, no, that's right. I always thought that when I moved here, I probably wouldn't live right on Manhattan, but since I'm just here for such a short time, and living in New York is one of my big dreams, as you know . . .' He shuffles on the spot, hands in pockets. I'm really not meaning to make everything sound so pointed – I am *so* grateful to Hugh for finding this place for me – but I just have to know. 'To be honest, I'm kind of surprised you chose to move out here . . .?'

Now he's giving me that look again, the one that's guarded, perhaps? I can't tell if he's harbouring a lot of pain and anger at me still, is trying to impress me, or is genuinely just wading through the mud of talking to someone you've seen butt-naked like they're just an acquaintance. 'Yeah, well, like you said when we split up, people change and grow and this opportunity came up for work and I thought, *why not?*'

*Why not?* Where was that attitude when I suggested doing the same if the opportunity came up? Ah well, water under the Brooklyn Bridge now, I guess.

'So, do you want this place?' Hugh asks, dangling the keys.

'Yes, definitely, this is absolutely perfect. Seriously, thank you. I mean it.'

'It's okay. Take the keys, and I'll let River know. I'll email you his contact details so you can be in touch directly from here on.'

So, he hasn't wiped my email address from his life then.

I gush some thanks a little longer, until Hugh is edging out of the door. 'Should we . . . could I . . . can I buy you a pizza or something sometime? Just as a thanks for all this.'

He gives me that strange look again, then leans in for a final hug, which I accept, enjoying, for a moment, that old feeling of home. Then he leaves with a vague, 'Sure,' which could mean 'yes, that would be nice' and could mean 'I never want to see you again'. And then, the door closes, and I'm standing alone in an unfamiliar apartment in an unfamiliar neighbourhood, and outside the big arched window, the afternoon's sun must be dipping behind the thick clouds as lights are starting to blink on inside buildings.

I gaze around my new New York abode, and I couldn't be happier.

# Chapter 13

It's tempting to just climb straight into this stranger's bed, in this lovely little apartment, and have a nap. But all my clobber is uptown, and it's getting dark out.

I lock my new door, check the handle twice to make sure I've secured it properly, take a wrong turn down the corridor and end up at a dead end, reverse and find the staircase, and make my way back onto the streets of Greenwich Village.

The air smells different to me here than it does up near Columbia University. Up there it's all light, leafy scents of autumn, down here it's sugary baked-goods aromas spilling out of coffeehouses, the smell of steam rising from below the sidewalk and rain on tarmac.

An easy ride straight up Manhattan on the '1' subway train, and then it's only a short walk to my hostel. I stroll past Tom's Restaurant, as featured in *Seinfeld*, with a lightness that's mismatched with the heavy clouds above, and the light drizzle coming down on my baseball cap.

I'm smiling as I enter the hostel and spot Ally on the reception.

'I found somewhere!' I tell her with pride.

'Hey, that's awesome,' she replies. 'Is it cute?'

'Very cute – it's in Greenwich Village! It's a teeny one-bed apartment and I can move in straight away.'

'You're going tonight?'

I yawned. 'I think I'll go first thing tomorrow, when it's light again.'

'It's beginning to get dark early, huh? Feels like it might be getting festive. Anyway, I'm pleased for you. And glad you found somewhere over Thanksgiving.'

'When is that again?' I ask, checking the calendar on my phone. 'The twenty-something, right? The Thursday of that week?'

She nods. 'Thursday twenty-fourth – a week today.'

It's not late, so soon after I chat to Flo on the phone and make myself some pasta as I'm doing so.

'Are you getting ready for bed?' I ask into my headphone mic when it connects, leaning over a pan of bubbling water and stirring at the penne, lazily. It's ten over there, and Night Owl Flo will probably be up for another hour or two so I know I'm not disturbing her.

'No, I'm binge-watching *Stranger Things* for the second time. It's so good. I wish I could go back to the eighties.' I hear her shuffling on her sofa. 'What's new in New York? How's the house-hunt going?'

'Well . . .' I obviously called to tell her, even I can't lie to myself about that. But now she's on the other end of the line, I can't get the words out.

'What did you do? Did you cut your hair again?'

'No, I promise, my hair is looking great. But I did do something else.'

'What?'

I nibble on a bit of still-hard pasta, stalling for time. 'I met up with Hugh,' I say through a mouthful of hot food. 'But only briefly – he was really great, actually, and he's helped me find somewhere to live.'

'He helped you house-hunt?' Flo asks, and I just know her eyebrows are up in the air.

'He was a last resort, but he happened to know a guy looking to sublet. It's a great place, here in Manhattan, on a nice street and I can move in tomorrow morning.'

'So you actually saw him? How was that?'

'I did. It was nice, actually, kind of. We were both pleased to see each other, though he seemed to want to be a little pissed at me still, which is fair enough, so that makes it even more lovely that he came through for me.'

'Ashling . . .'

'What?'

'Just . . . You know Hugh has a bit of a habit of centring himself in any given situation?'

She's not wrong. The Hugh I dated for a decade was charming, funny, kind, but also very outwardly confident. He could brashly command a room and had a habit of pressing his ideas on other people. But I often saw his other sides.

89

The guy who was insecure about people liking him, the one who was unadventurous. He excelled in being a big fish in a small pond, as the saying goes, but tended to cock up and feel insecure when he was in the opposite situation. In fact, he seemed more like the small fish-big pond version of Hugh when I saw him in Greenwich Village. Maybe he's changed.

Flo continues. 'I'm just saying, it's kind of annoying that he's there in New York when that was always your dream, one that he didn't want anything to do with. I just don't want him to start making this about *him*, that's all.'

'He won't – I won't let that happen. We probably won't even see each other again. It really felt like he was just doing me this favour and then wanted us to go our separate ways again, for good.'

A friend in the city would be nice, but that's just the gratitude thinking, I'm sure.

'Okay,' Flo says. 'Now tell me about your new pad?'

I drain the pasta and babble on to my friend about my new place and my new neighbourhood. 'The owner is some guy called River, but I don't know anything about him, other than that he has good taste in interior design.'

'But you aren't going to meet him?'

'I think Hugh said something about him coming back over in January, so I guess I'll meet him then. But Hugh's going to send me all his contact details. I'll get in touch once I've settled in and "meet" him online.'

'I hope he has hair like Steve Harrington,' Flo says in a dreamy voice, referencing her favourite *Stranger Things* gent.

We get to chatting about her day, and end up talking all

the way through my pasta dinner, until I retire to my dorm for the final night. I fall asleep a while later to the sounds of my roommates – of their familiar chatter, book pages turning, a backpack being tipped inside out for a lost hair clip. In the middle of the night, one of them ducks out and comes back in snogging someone, then the other one takes a hushed phone call. Later, several snores drift around me in surround sound, interrupted by the latest Taylor Swift album suddenly bursting out at full volume when one of the girls dropped their phone from their bunk and their head-phones pulled out. I kind of like dorm life. But the thought of my new little apartment, all to myself, sends me to sleep with a smile.

At dawn, I'm awake, and silently tiptoeing around my snoozing and snoring dormmates while I zip my remaining clobber into my suitcase and rucksack. I don't need to be out of the hostel until mid-morning, but I've got a hankering to haul-ass downtown, dump my belongings, and then go for a massive pancake brekkie somewhere. With bacon. And maple-syrup. And those breakfast potato things.

I slide my case towards the door, whispering a panicked 'Shhh!' at it when it clonks the leg of the other bed, or some-one's leg sticking out of the bed, I'm not sure.

'Are you leaving us?' the girl croaks, sitting up in bed, rumpled hair and smudged lipstick.

I nod. 'Stay in touch, won't you?' I whisper, but her friend is now propped up too, pulling an eye mask off her face.

'We're going off on the Greyhound soon, but we're flying

out from New York in a couple of months, so maybe see you then?'

I lean in and give them both a quick hug, a mass of morning breath, tangled hair, warm skin and a yawn right in my ear.

Exiting the hostel with a sentimental sigh, I notice the air temperature has dropped a little. Or maybe it's because NYC is still waking up at this hour (I hear it never sleeps, though) and so the air hasn't been warmed by a million people's bodies pounding the streets.

Rattling my case down the pavement, I hoik it into the subway station and onto the train – the same one I took yesterday – and settle in for my ride back to Lower Manhattan, my shoulder twinging at the weight of dragging my crap around. I shake it off, plopping down in a seat, my body jiggling in excitement. I'm actually on my way to my own New York City apartment!

We reach Christopher St Station in the Village, so off I go with my suitcase, my rucksack and my rumbling stomach, to retrace my steps from last night.

The neighbourhood is waking up, a low, yellow sunlight creeping between the buildings and glinting against puddles on the pavements. The temperature is indeed a little colder today, and the sky is a frosty, pale blue with the clouds from the day before having drifted away.

Now where, of all of these coffeehouses and restaurants and delis I pass, looks like it would do the fluffiest of all the pancakes? I'm so distracted I nearly the miss that big double door that leads me into my new home.

Once inside, I hover at the bottom of the staircase, my

hand absentmindedly rubbing the ache in my shoulder. No way am I taking six storeys of stairs with this case – I press the button for the elevator.

Far above me, slow creaks and groans begin to sound, and cables and metal grumble as the lift inches its way down the shaft, and I wait a while in the still of the entrance hallway. I wonder if I'll like my neighbours. I wonder if I have any celebrity neighbours? I wonder what my landlord is like. Hugh's sent me his details now and asked me to get in touch to arrange rent payment and suchlike, so I'll do that later.

The lift arrives and it looks at me from behind a metal gate, while I stare back at it, before realising I have to slide the shutter open myself. I nudge my way inside and there's just enough space for me and my suitcase, thankfully, and we take off towards the sixth floor.

This feels very real, suddenly. Now I'm out of the hostel environment and moving into an actual home, with a mini kitchen and a bathroom and everything. I know it's not even for a full three months, and I know this isn't really an actual Big Apple Move like I always imagined, but right now it feels solid under my feet.

Opening the door to the apartment, I'm somehow surprised by the quiet. Not silence – I can hear the low soundscape of city life happening outside the window, and the noise of the lift closing up its doors and hinges again behind me – but I am alone.

I leave my suitcase in the middle of the living room area and walk straight to the window. I'm craving another look at the view, and for the first time I notice that if I crane right,

I can see the tip of the Empire State Building poking into the sky in the distance.

'Wow,' I whisper aloud, steaming up the windowpane with my breath.

I must have walked past the Empire State Building at least ten times now, since arriving in the city over a week ago, but even after what happened when I went back up, I feel like she's there, waiting to help me. I think I'm ready to start looking for that inspiration again.

I open my case, right there in the centre of the living room, and pull out my journal, its cover tattier than it used to be, the foil flamingo peeling off, the page edges rippled from sitting in the bottom of bags.

I've got my house, I'm about to get myself some breakfast. Perhaps afterwards it'll be time to knuckle down and get myself a new life.

# Chapter 14

... Or perhaps it's time to give my aching feet a rest, and put off finding a new life until another day. Moving into a new home, albeit temporary, is enough of a win today, right? I'll have a clearer head if I put off the whole 'figure out my entire life' thing until tomorrow, after I've had a day of chilling on the sofa, watching TV, and then finally having a good night's sleep.

I'm sure that's just what's holding me back – I'm a little sleep deprived, a little disoriented. Yes. Tomorrow, the journal comes back out, I'll retrace my steps, and we'll find who I'm meant to be again.

As day turns to dusk, I haul myself from the plush, burgundy sofa, take a long shower, lay my toiletries out on the little shelf in the bathroom, and pull my PJs out of my suitcase. I've left the case in the bedroom and I'll absolutely unpack the rest of it tomorrow. I found some local pizza delivery leaflets on a noticeboard down in the entranceway, and now I'm navigating the pizza place's app and tailoring my order.

'Extra pepperoni,' I mutter. I'm going for a large and am adding things left, right and centre as my stomach growls its order for a big, hot meal. 'Ooo, sweety drop peppers! Adding those . . .'

While I wait for my delivery, the world outside grows darker yet more illuminated, with lights painted across the city like stars coming out from behind the clouds. The Empire State Building is lit up tonight in warm red and green, which the website tells me is in celebration of the Radio City Rockettes' opening night. A festive feeling fills my heart and floats it up with excitement for the weeks to come.

Less than half an hour later, as I'm beginning to yawn and notice just how late in the evening it's gotten, the buzzer to the apartment rings, and I leap up, my stomach letting out a walrus-like growl as I do so. I put my hand on my belly. 'Soon, my love.'

'Hello?' I say into the intercom.

'Hey, ma'am, I've got a large pepperoni pizza for you?'

'Come on up!' Should I have gone to meet him? It's many flights of stairs for him to climb . . . I'm not sure what the etiquette is here so I pull a jumper over my head and jam my feet into my trainers. But pulling open the door I find a guy with a giant pizza box already there, and about to knock on my forehead.

'Oh! Hey, you got up here quick.' I dodge his rapping knuckles.

He looks at me in surprise and lowers his hand, laughing. 'All those leg-day workouts come in handy in my job.'

Pizza Guy has shaggy blond hair, not unlike my own fresh cut, actually, but more of a dirty blonde. He's wearing shorts despite the cold, and I notice that he does, indeed, have some very defined legs down there. He hands me the pizza box.

'Thank you,' I say, already smelling the rich tomato sauce wafting out from under the cardboard lid. Ohmygoddddd I'm going to eat this whole damn thing myself the second Pizza Guy leaves, and I'm going to watch American TV and drink American soda while I do it. I reach into my PJ trouser pocket and pull out a note to give him as a tip, and find myself saying, 'You must get hungry running up and down all those stairs – do you want a slice of my pizza?'

Could I sound any more desperate right now? I don't mean to. But with the way we're eye-contacting the shit out of this situation, and the fact I haven't flirted in a pretty little while . . .

'I'd better not.' He grins a handsome set of teeth. 'I've got a lot of hungry customers tonight. Thank you though, you're sweet.'

'No problem. I'm Ashling.' Like he cares.

'Danny,' he replies, and goes to shake my hand, which is holding the note, and we have a super-awkward version of when suave people pass a tip through a handshake. Far down on the ground floor, the front door of the building clangs open and the sound of something large being rapidly *clunk-clunk-clunked* up the stairs echoes up. 'Hey, doesn't Hawaiian guy live here any more?'

'Uh, maybe,' I reply. 'I'm subletting at the moment.'

'Are you from Australia?'

'The UK.'

'Nice. Well, if you need any more pizzas, or advice on where to get even better ones.' He whispers the last bit, leaning in a little, and I think he smells like I imagine Chris Hemsworth does, like chopped logs and sea salt. Mmm. 'Just give me a call.'

The clunking is getting louder. 'Do you think someone's dragging a dead body up the stairs?' I ask Danny, mildly nervous.

He looks down the corridor and I feel like he's puffed himself up a bit. 'I hear cursing – I live in a building like this and that sounds like me when I have to move a piece of furniture in that's too big for the elevator.'

I've opened the lid of the pizza box now, just to have a peek. Clearly my tummy is more concerned with getting fed than it is about impending furniture movers.

'Don't tell them about my pizza,' I say. 'I don't think I want to share after all.'

Danny glances back at me and laughs, just as a man reaches the top of the staircase. He's dragging an absolutely enormous suitcase, and the holdall on his shoulder has just bashed into one of the framed prints in the corridor. He has dark hair with a wave to it, though it's hard to see the exact style because it seems to be in a right mess. My eyes flick down to his face, which is full of thunder. His jaw is so clenched I don't think he could open it to put a slice of pizza in even if I offered. Which I wasn't about to.

Right then he looks up, directly at me, and drops the handle of his suitcase to the floor, which I think is a bit of an overreaction to the sight of my make-up-less face and platypus-print pyjamas.

The naughty suitcase starts bouncing back down the stairs, at which point Thunder Man shouts a curse word I won't repeat and I let out a giggle. Super rude of me, I know, but it was kind of funny.

Thunder Man catches the case with the help of Danny the Pizza Guy, who has sprinted on those athletic legs of his down the corridor to help.

'Hey, man!' Danny says when the two of them and the suitcase are upright. Why do I recognise that case?

Thunder Man moves his hair and looks at Danny, and I see a whisper of a smile form on his face as he breathes, 'Oh. Hey.' But then he faces me again and says, 'Who are you?'

'Who are *you*?' I counter.

But actually ... I know him. I *know* I know him. I'm just figuring it out when he shifts the holdall on his shoulder, a strand of longish light hair that dangles from the zip catching the overhead light. I see him taking in my distinctive peach locks with recognition. It hits me clearly at the same time it hits him.

'Wait – I've met you before. You're the stressy guy at the airport last week who almost scalped me with your bag!'

'I'm the guy whose apartment you're standing in. And I already said sorry for that. Your hair still looks ... fine.' He flusters, throwing his hands up in the air, and if a flash of thunder and lightning had appeared to punctuate his mood,

99

I wouldn't have been the least surprised. Despite his stormy mood, his voice betrays American smooth with a hint of New Yorker. He's—

'You're River?' I ask, the penny dropping.

'Hawaiian Guy.' Danny grins, pointing at River.

River gives Danny a tight smile and starts advancing towards the apartment. 'That's right. And you are . . .?'

I stand in front of the doorway, my giant pizza box acting as an extra barrier. 'How do I know you're who you say you are?'

He stops. 'Perhaps we could start by you saying who *you* are.'

'I'm Ashling,' I say, tilting my chin up, daring him to come any closer. I was a pilot, goddamn it. I moved to New York City on my own. I'm not a pushover. 'Prove to me you're the River that lives in this flat.'

A long, low groan comes out of River as he rubs his forehead. 'My photos!' he says, his head snapping up and looking me dead in the eye. Huh. I thought his eyes were dark before, but now I see they're a deep, forest green. They're nice eyes, I can't lie.

He gestures towards the inside of the apartment. 'I have photos on the bookshelves, and I'm in some of them.'

I narrow my gaze at him and then, still holding my pizza in front of me, I step back a touch and lean to the side to look at the framed pictures on the bookshelf. There are a few travel shots, one a canyon-backdrop selfie of a pretty brunette with her arm around . . . yep, pretty sure that's River. Also, pretty sure the brunette is the woman he was with at the airport. There's a family photo of what seems to be a set of parents and three grown-up kids, one of which is probably River. I squint back at the man in the door. Maybe if he had chin-length curls like this dude in the picture, then yes, yes it was him. Then I spot a picture of four friends dressed as various superheroes, I think, and I can pick out one of them staring seriously into the camera with clenched jaw, which tells me that yes, that River is one hundred per cent the same guy as *this* River.

Danny pokes his head into view and adds, 'It's really him.'

'So, Ashling? What are you doing in my apartment?' River growls as I stand aside to let him in.

'You got this?' Danny asks, checking the time on his phone.

'Yeah, it's fine,' I say. I'm bewildered, but not afraid. River is definitely who he says he is and he's a friend of Hugh's.

'All right, I gotta go,' Danny replies. 'Call me though, if you need anything.' He gives me one of those grins again before hopping down the stairs, two at a time.

'I will,' I coo after him, and close the door, smiling. River is there with a scowl melted all over his face, but before he can get a word in, I say, 'This is very uncool of you to come barging in, you know, don't landlords have to give twenty-four hours' notice over here? Hugh said you were in Europe or something, anyway.'

A moment of confusion is swallowed up by a groan escaping him again, and he slaps his face into his hands like he can't believe what a dummy he is. Or I am. I'm not sure at this point. Then he speaks through his fingers. 'You're the girl Hugh emailed me about.'

'Woman. But yes.'

He ignores me and pulls his phone out from his pocket, frantically tapping and scrolling like he's only got one per cent battery left or something. I perch on the edge of the sofa and open my pizza box. 'Are you from Hawaii?' I ask, through a mouthful of perfectly melted cheese.

'What?' He looks up. 'I'm from Saratoga. Upstate New York.' He glances at my pizza and then back at the door. 'I like to order a Hawaiian pizza from time to time.'

'Ohhhh.' I smile.

'I see you were making friends with my neighbourhood pizza guy. Already,' he says, his eyes back on the phone. It sounds pointed and accusatory, but I'm not sure why.

So I just say, 'Yep. He seems great.'

River puffs out another quiet curse. 'Dammit. I didn't see Hugh's email until now saying you were here already. I forgot all about him, and you, actually.'

'You okay?' I say, munching.

'It's been a real . . . shitty forty-eight hours.'

'Do you want a slice of pizza?'

He watches me as I pull myself out a second slice, and then glances towards the bedroom. I notice his eyes are gloomy and tired-looking, and he's rolling his shoulders. 'Can't you go and stay with Hugh or something?'

'No.' I laugh. 'You told him I could live here. I'm your tenant now; you can't just kick me out at ten o'clock at night.'

'Is it ten?' He yawns, then snaps himself out of it. 'Well, how about asking the pizza guy if you can stay with him, since the two of you seemed so cosy?'

'Excuse me?' I say, unable to stop a laugh escaping. What the hell is his problem with me flirting with Pizza Guy? Does River have a crush on him?

He ignores me and huffs through his nostrils. 'You aren't my tenant, we haven't signed anything yet, and I want my apartment back.'

Was he really kicking me out? Where would I go? 'How long are you back for? Why don't *you* go and stay with Hugh for a couple of nights?'

'Because ... this is my home!' His stomach lets out a giant growl, which somewhat takes the sails out of his impassioned plea for me to bugger off.

'Oh my god, have some pizza,' I say, shoving the box to him. I watch as he picks up a slice, folds it in half, and takes a bite, closing his eyes for a moment, and let him enjoy his minute of peace before saying, 'You wouldn't kick a woman out, in the middle of the night, in a city she barely knows after she shared her pizza with you ... would you?'

He opens his tired eyes. 'I just ... I've had the worst day. The longest journey. The shittiest break-up. And all I want to do is climb into my own bed.' He sighs onto his pizza slice then adds, 'But no, I guess I'll find somewhere else to stay tonight.'

Phew. 'Just tonight?'

River looks at me with daggers (just not very sharp ones).

'I basically just got a demotion, so I'm back in New York. For good.'

Hmm. He's kind of being a dick considering I have sub-letted from him, whether he saw the email or not. But ... 'A break-up and a demotion in one day?'

'One long, extended, crappy day.'

I hold the pizza box up for him to offer him another slice. He takes it and gives me a small nod, which I'm going to take as a thank you.

I really, *really* don't want to have to move all my stuff out to a hotel right now, not to mention start again with the whole house-hunting. But if he wants his place back, what choice do I have? He's not going to find somewhere *else* to sublet for three months while I'm in his house, is he?

A yawn stretches itself out of my mouth, and its conta-giousness causes River to yawn as well. 'Is this a sofa bed?' I point to the couch.

'Yes.' He exhales, as if he really can't be bothered with small talk right now.

'Then I have an idea. A suggestion.' I smile at him. I'm not sure why, since he doesn't deserve it, but despite the grumpiness and snide comments I do feel like we both have quite good reasons to want to just keep eating pizza and not have to leave the apartment again at this time of night.

River just chews and looks at me, no response, so I con-tinue. 'How about tonight – just for tonight – we both stay here. You can have your room; I haven't unpacked anyway. I'll take the sofa bed. Then in the morning we can figure it all out.'

'In the morning, you can figure out where you're going to go, you mean?'

I grit my teeth and deliberately reach for the slice of pizza closest to him, which is massive and has a really good spread of toppings, leaving him to pick the thin, shrivelled slice, which is basically half crust. But before I can say any more, he adds, quietly, 'You take the bedroom.'

'Wait, really?'

'Yes.'

'No, I mean, I don't want the bedroom, I'll take the sofa. That way I'm closer to the door if you try to murder me in the night. But you're okay with us both staying here tonight?'

'I don't love the idea, I'd like some peace and quiet,' he grumbles. 'But you're Hugh's girl so I'll do it for him, and I don't want to go back out into the cold and find a hotel for the night any more than you do.'

I'd hardly call myself 'Hugh's girl' but semantics could wait. 'And you're Hugh's friend so I think I can trust you.'

'Of course, you can trust me. I'm way too beat to murder anyone tonight.' He gives me that whisper of a smile that he gave Danny earlier, but it's gone almost instantly, and he stands up. 'Thanks for the pizza. I'm going to bed. You'll find extra bedding in the cupboard by the door.'

As a final act of chivalry, River wheels my suitcase out of his bedroom and stands it in the middle of the living room like an uninvited party guest who doesn't know anyone. He then disappears into the bathroom.

'Jeeeeeesus,' I say, flopping back onto the sofa and resting the pizza box on my horizontal stomach. I could have cried again at my dreamy new apartment being ripped out from under me. I could have cried at having to sleep on a sofa bed in a flatshare rather than in a proper bed on my lonesome. I could have cried, again, at being a big ambition-less nomad. But I'm not going to do any of that. I'm not planning on taking any of this lying down. Metaphorically.

River exits the bathroom looking even blearier than when he came in and with a vague wave in my direction, but without even looking at me, he goes into his bedroom and closes his door with a slam.

I wonder how he managed to lose his job and his partner on the same day? Poor guy. I expect I'll never know – he doesn't seem exactly open to forming a fast friendship.

Outside the window, off to the side, the Empire State Building is looking down at me as I shelter from the cold night air behind the glass.

'What are you looking at?' I mutter to it.

So, what now? Back to a hostel? Stay in a hotel for the remaining time here? Ouch, I'm not sure my savings will stretch that far.

This seems like a problem for Tomorrow Ashling.

I stand up, stretch out my bad shoulder, and head to the cupboard to grab some more bedding, pleasantly surprised to see it packed with plenty of sheets, pillows and blankets. An extra duvet wouldn't have gone amiss, but it's cosy and warm inside this apartment so the blankets will do just fine.

Transforming the sofa into a sofa bed is easy breezy, but I don't particularly try to keep quiet. A few clonks and bangs is just about the right amount of passive aggressive I feel

River deserves right now. I hunker down under my blanket pile with my head facing the window, leaving the curtain open so I can fall asleep to my view of Manhattan.

You'd think the traffic and noise and hubbub would keep me tossing about all night. But by the time I wake up at dawn, I'm not only deeply rested and in love with this super-comfy sofa bed, but I have an idea.

## Chapter 15

There's no sound coming from River's room, so by early daylight I set to work. Thanks to the small space and a spotlight bar on the ceiling, which seems to be more for decoration than use, judging by the lack of bulbs, I'm able to create a basic but functional sheet partition, behind which is my sofa bed, pushed up against the window. I only topple once, landing with an ungraceful slap on the wooden floor as I avoid falling on my bad shoulder, but no sound emits from the bedroom.

I stand back when I'm done. It looks quite charming, if I do say so myself. And with the bed in its sofa position and the 'drapes' pulled to the side, there's still complete access to the living space.

Pottering into the bathroom and feeling pleased with myself, I look in the mirror. My hair is a bit all over the place, but my eyes are less pink, less baggy, my skin a little dewier. I wonder what River will look like this morning. Better, for having a good night's sleep? Or will he have spent the whole night awake thinking about how his world feels like it's just crashed down? I might be projecting a little, but that's how I spent my first night after realising my dreams were all shot to shit.

He didn't have to be such a complete dick, though. What if I was his original subletter? He couldn't have just barged in then; I could have caused a right scene. He has no right to be here really.

Or is it me that has no right?

What a tangle.

'Play nice,' I whisper to my reflection, preparing myself for a battle ahead.

Changing into a warm jumper and a mismatched pair of leggings that I pulled out from the top of my suitcase, I brush my teeth and rub in some moisturiser. By the time I emerge, a low sound is coming from River's room, like he's talking to someone on the phone. His ex, perhaps? His office? The Landlord Association to help have me evicted?

A knock comes from behind his door and I stand still. What was that?

The knock sounds again, as if he's inside and knocking to see if he can enter the living room.

'Hello?' I call, for want of something more appropriate to say in this situation.

'Ashling, are you up, and, um, decent?' comes River's voice through the wood.

'I am, sire,' I reply in an overly British accent for literally no reason.

His door opens and River faces me. I'm expecting that grumpy scowl, arms crossed, a 'get out of my flat' look in his eyes. But what I see is, frankly, a different person.

Perhaps it's the forest-green tartan PJ bottoms and the ancient-looking summer-camp T-shirt that make him look softer. Perhaps it's that his bleary eyes are now awake and the green of them is coordinating appealingly with his outfit. Perhaps it's that his jawline has softened overnight and he's giving me a ghost of a smile as he leans against the door-frame, his phone in his hand.

'I'm so sorry.' It spills from his mouth before I can say a word. 'I'm really not that much of an asshole usually, and it was really awful of me to bust in here and try to kick you out.' I hear his New York accent more today, like the softer his voice the more pronounced it is. It's nice, deep; each word is a coffee drip.

My eyebrows are so far up my head they might hit the ceiling. 'T-that's okay,' I stutter. Perhaps a good night's sleep was all he needed to cause this change of heart.

'It's not.' He waves his phone in the air. 'I just got off of a call with Hugh.' River takes a breath and winces at me, as if embarrassed by his own actions. 'I was under the impression you and he were still together. That's why I didn't understand why you couldn't just go and stay at his place. I now realise you're not, so I'll go and stay with him instead.'

Why would he think Hugh and I were still together? I shake my head, shake away the battle defences I prepared instead of expecting any of this. 'Okay, we're going to circle back to that, but, for now, just hold on, I wanted to propose something.'

River then catches sight of my DIY bedcurtains. 'What did you do to my living room?'

'Hear me out,' I say. 'I get that if you're back for good you want to live in your own space again. And I appreciate you saying you'd stay with Hugh but nobody wants to do that.' I push down this trickle of annoyance at my ex that slinks into my voice. 'But you shouldn't have to leave either, after what it sounds like you've been through, and I *love* your apartment, so I was thinking, maybe, I could be your roommate. Even just for a few days.'

'Really, Ashling, the least I can do is just leave you to it.'

'No, hear me out. I made this sectioned-off bit so we can both have our privacy during the nighttime. And each morning I can fold the sofa bed back up so you won't lose your living room. I'm no trouble as a house guest. And if I can just stay for, like, a week—' I quickly check the calendar on my phone '—through Thanksgiving, then the hostels and hotels might be less crowded and I can be out of your hair.'

I pause, throwing my arms in the air like I'm a magician's assistant showing off my magic trick.

'But I was so horrible to you,' he said.

'I'm actually pretty tough,' I counter. 'And you don't scare me.'

He could go and stay with Hugh if he really wanted to, but there's something about his vulnerability this morning that makes me want to make this work for both of us.

111

'Look,' I say. 'Do you want to go and get some breakfast with me? And think about it?'

River nods. 'But I'm buying.'

'Fine,' I agree.

He turns back to his room to get dressed. 'There's a coffeehouse downstairs—'

'Can we go to a diner?' I interject. 'Like, a proper one? I want pancakes and coffee and the works!'

'Sure,' he says with a shrug, and through his glasses he meets my eyes. 'Whatever you want.'

This diner is perfect. We're seated in a booth by a window only a few blocks from River's (and my – fingers crossed) apartment block. In front of me is a giant stack of pancakes coated in maple-syrup and crispy streaky bacon, a steaming cup of coffee, and River, dressed in a knitted jumper, the sleeves hanging down over his fingers, a frown line of thought on his forehead.

'Hi,' I say to him, after I've swirled the deliciously creamy coffee around in my mouth for longer than is normal.

River glances at me and puts down his toast. 'Hey.'

Lower Manhattan is reflected in the glass he brings to his lips; I see busy New Yorkers walking past the window and a skyscraper in the distance. But beyond that I notice his face is kind, now it isn't pinched in a scowl.

'I'm Ashling.' I wipe my sticky hand on my jumper and reach it across the table to shake his.

He chuckles and clears his throat, accepting my hand in his own, toast-crumbed one. 'Hello. I'm River.'

'Nice to meet you, River.' I drop my hand and go back to my silky pancakes. 'Now, what the hell happened to you yesterday? If you don't mind me asking.'

River stares out of the window for a moment, as if pulling together his thoughts. 'Are you sure you want to hear about this? We're basically strangers.'

'No, we're not, we're roommates.' I flash him a grin. There's a shyness to him this morning, and so I start. 'Let's get to know each other a little more first, then. My name is Ashling Avalyn, I'm twenty-nine and I'll be thirty in January. I live, or lived, near London back in the UK and now I'm here, because I've always had a bit of a thing about New York. Your turn.' It isn't exactly an in-depth autobiography, but there's no need to info-dump on the guy.

'I've never been to London,' he says as a reply, before dropping his toast on his lap, and muttering quietly but audibly, 'Oh bugger,' in a faux-British accent.

I laugh. 'Are you trying to make me feel at home?'

'A little bit.' He smiles and then turns back to the window again, city life passing by his face once more. 'Okay, um ... I'm River. Thirty-five. Born in New York, but upstate. My parents still live there. And up until yesterday, or maybe it was technically the day before, I don't know, I was just beginning a year of living in Italy.'

'Oh! And that's the job you got fired from?'

'Not exactly fired, but ...' River pauses and we both slurp our coffees and accept refills from the server as he comes around. 'Okay, you're sure you're ready to hear the sorry tale of my life?'

'Hell yeah, I am,' I sit back in my seat, my paws around my freshly topped-up mug.

With a big sigh and a scratch of his hair, River starts. 'I work at a big IT company and about a year ago they started putting out feelers for workers to go overseas to help launch our new division. They wanted ten experienced people to go, get it launched, train local staff, et cetera. I put myself forward, met the nine others, one of whom became my girl-friend and for the past twelve months our lives have been all about preparing for Italy. Sometimes there were setbacks, and it looked like it wasn't going to happen. Once it even looked like some but not all of us were going to be allowed to go. But the closer it got the more everything was slotting into place.'

'Sounds like an amazing opportunity.' My nosy self is instantly wanting to jump forwards to what happened with the girlfriend. Chill, Ashling.

'So, during this time, the ten of us are forgoing any other opportunities for promotion or projects or raises because this, Italy, is what it's all about now. Everything, I mean everything, is now about this move. Late nights in the office making sure the launch details are perfect, late nights at home finalising travel arrangements and accommodation. Weekends at the office, all together. We've been in a bubble, really, the group of us. I'm pretty sure everyone else in the office was sick to death with hearing about *Italy, Italy, Italy* every time we went to grab a sandwich or whatever.'

River gives a smile that looks so sad I want to reach across the table and stroke his face, but that would be extremely awkward for both of us. Plus, who wants maple-syrup fingers smeared across their cheeks? I keep my hands in check and bestow upon him an 'Aw' instead.

'Thank you.' The smile widens, just a touch, and for a millisecond he meets my eyes.

'Then what happened?'

'Well, that brings us to last week, or was it the week before? Anyway, everything is great, and my sublet had moved in and me and Delilah – my girlfriend – are finally on our way to sunny Italy. But a few days in, something's not right.'

'With Delilah?'

'With the launch. I don't know what, but it's like this freight train of action, action, action has suddenly stalled and nobody wants us to do anything. Then I hear from my sublet that she's had a change of circumstance and is pulling out. I figure I'll think about this in a week or so, when everything's a bit more settled overseas, so tell her to just leave the keys with the building superintendent.'

I'm keeping up so far. Also, he has a nice voice and I like to hear him talk. Not that that's important to this very serious story.

River goes on. 'But as luck would have it, I guess, a day later I get an email from Hugh. We all do, just a shout-out asking if anyone still has a spare room going or whatever.'

'That was about me!' I smile.

'Yes, it was.'

'Do you know Hugh well?'

'Not as well as I thought,' he says, eyebrows raised. 'But

yeah, I've worked with him on a couple of bits of work. He wasn't coming to Italy because he only started in the New York branch, I don't know, early summer? But I like him. We hang out at work from time to time.'

I have a lot of questions about the Hugh situation, but I don't want to knock River off course while he's spilling his guts. 'All right, so Hugh gets in touch, you tell him your *very lovely* apartment has just become free, and then ...?'

'Then I forgot all about it. Because maybe an hour later the group of us get rounded up, all of a sudden, told we're taking a field trip to a vineyard, and while we're there, we get the bombshell that the funding for the new branch has been cut in half. Which means *we're* getting cut in half. As in, half of us are staying, half of us have to go home. The next morning. On the early flight.'

'Shit.'

'Right? And not just home – back to our old jobs. As if this opportunity, this stepping stone or promotion or whatever you want to call it, this whole year of planning, never happened.'

'Did you get any say in who stayed and who went?' I ask, guessing he wouldn't have voluntarily put himself in this position.

River shakes his head. 'They already knew. They'd already picked.'

His expression tells me the next bit so I don't make him say it. Delilah was asked to stay; he was asked to return to New York. 'Is that why she broke up with you? Because she didn't want to do long distance?'

116

The question must be making River uncomfortable. I see the frown lines reappearing on his forehead as he looks down at his hands again, now cupped around his coffee. 'I don't know. Maybe. Partially. We got into a huge fight because I couldn't – I can't – see why we can't give long distance a go. We'd been together through all of this, up until now. But she said she didn't want a boyfriend who lived in a different country, that so much of our relationship was based on the romance of us moving to Italy together and starting this exciting, exotic new life, that now she just wanted to move forwards rather than going back. Like I was.'

'Damn,' I say, accidently adopting an American accent for a second. 'That's kind of mean.'

River shrugs. 'It's true, though.'

'Really?' I wait to see if he's going to say more.

'I don't know what I'm doing with myself any more. I want to move forwards too but I'm not.'

We pause the conversation. Around me, diners are chatting, the coffee machine is puffing, forks are scraping, and low, indistinct music is playing. The air is perfumed with sugar and cinnamon, coffee beans and frying bacon, and my lips taste just how the atmosphere smells. I shuffle in my seat, causing the soft pleather to creak under my legs. 'So, you split up, and your company shipped you back here, only to find a rando Brit hogging the doorway of your home.'

'That about sums it up.'

'Sorry about that.'

'No, I'm sorry,' he says, and his hand reaches across briefly like he's going to pat my knuckles or something, but then he pulls it back. 'You had every right to be there, I just hadn't checked my emails in all the commotion. I'm sorry.'

'No more sorries, I totally get it.' I wave him away. 'I'm sorry for startling you.'

'I mean, you didn't startle me.' He says 'startle' in my accent again and it's almost endearing how he keeps letting it slip out. 'I was just surprised. Kinda shocked. A little confused.'

'Perhaps . . . startled?'

He chuckles. 'Okay, maybe a little startled.'

'Why were you so pissy with Danny the Pizza Guy?' I ask, remembering his weird attitude the night before. 'Don't you like pineapple on your pizza after all or something?'

'No, I love it,' he cries, as if I've spoken blasphemy. 'But at the time, when you said you were Ashling, I thought you were Hugh's girlfriend. And I was like, *this girl isn't using my place to hook up with other guys behind my co-worker's back.*'

I would snigger if I wasn't a bit affronted. But aside from River's commendable-if-misguided loyalty to my ex, I need to get something cleared up.

'I suppose that's fair enough. Now tell me all about why you thought Hugh and I were still together. We split up a year ago, you know.'

River drains the rest of his coffee and signals to the waiter. 'More coffee?' he asks me.

'Sure.'

He's silent as the waiter comes over and refills our cups, other than thanking him and asking how his day is going. Then he looks out of the window and takes the slowest sip I've ever, ever, ever seen.

118

'Are you biding your time?' I ask.

'No, I'm just ... enjoying the view. It's a nice morning. I don't do a lot of breakfasts out.'

'You're not supposed to be in work this morning, surely?'

'No,' he says, with a touch of resentment. 'I'm giving myself a day to mope. Next week is a short week because of Thanksgiving, so I'll go in on Monday.'

I nod. 'So ... Hugh?'

River cringes. 'I feel bad talking about him. Maybe you should just call him up and ask him what's going on.'

'I feel weird talking about him too, to you, his friend who I am only just getting to know, in the middle of a city I've never spent this long in before. But here we are.'

'When did you arrive?'

'Don't change the subject. Did Hugh actually tell you we were still together, or did you just assume that for whatever reason?'

River squirms, the seat creaking again. 'He ... look ... I don't know, maybe I misunderstood. But when he first started at the office, I remember him talking about his girl-friend in the UK a lot.'

Well then, he can't have been talking about me. He must have had a new girlfriend who he left behind. I find myself smiling. I'm glad he moved on – it alleviates my guilt a little. But then River says, 'He talked about you all the time. Ashling this, Ashling that. We all thought your name was Ashley for a while but then he set us right.'

Oh. 'Why would he say that?'

'I don't know. But that's why when he emailed and said,

"Hey, Ashling's coming out but needs somewhere to live for a little while until we find a place—"'

'Until we *find a place*?'

'He lives with roommates so it didn't seem weird to me.'

'It's weird to me,' I splutter. Hugh is such a bloody weirdo.

'I get that. Now. But that's why last night, when I came back, I thought you could have just gone to stay in his room or something.' He holds his hands up to stop me from combusting. 'But I get why that would be very weird and inappropriate now. And I also get why it was totally *not* inappropriate for you to be flirting with the pizza guy.'

'I wasn't flirting,' I mumble, which is a lie.

'All right,' he says, dropping it. 'But if you didn't come out here for Hugh, what brought you to my home state?'

Eesh, I'm not sure how deep to go with this. But then, he did tell me his sorry tale, so . . . 'I got let go as well, in a way. I'm a pilot.'

'Wow,' River says, his eyebrows popping up. I love that reaction. People are always surprised that I do what I do, and not even necessarily because I'm a woman, though that can happen and it can be SO tiring, or because I'm young. I think *they think* I'm just a bit 'charmingly chaotic', to quote myself. But I'm not when I'm up there.

The warm pride dissipates as I remember I can't seek that reaction any more. 'I *was* a pilot. Then I had an accident, and now my shoulder isn't as mobile as it needs to be for that job.'

'Shit,' he echoes me from earlier. 'They can't fix it?'

I shake my head. 'We tried. I'm struggling to accept it all really, because day to day it barely hurts now. That much.

But I don't have the mobility range needed for all the controls and panels. I can't do the job any more.'

'Hmm.' He rubs his lips with his fingers, drawing my eyes to them, and I watch his mouth form the words, 'I'm sorry.'

'Thanks. So that happened, and during a minor meltdown on my bedroom floor I realised that everything I was working for and living for and aiming for within my life has crumbled. I don't know who I am or what I want any more, so I ran away to New York.'

River blinks at me.

I blink back. 'And here I am. Until January. Late January.'

'After your birthday?'

He remembered. Good listener. 'Yes.' I smile.

'What are you going to do with yourself until then?' he asks after a few beats.

'That I don't really know,' I say slowly. 'I didn't exactly make a game plan before I leapt on the plane to come over here.' River lets out a laugh, a real one, and it makes his face sparkle, causing me to give a big, sparkling smile back. 'So we're both going through job problems and, apparently, I too am having relationship issues, though mine are more on the abstract side.'

'Yes, mine are clear cut. I am now . . . single.' His laughter stops and my heart pangs for the guy. Forty-eight hours ago he was happy, in love and on this big new adventure. Now he's back home, broken-hearted, and some woman's set up a blanket fort in his living room.

'Have you spoken to her, since you got back?' I ask him.

River shakes his head. 'I sent a text, saying I'd arrived, which she's read. But before I left she told me we should try to have a clean break.'

'But how can you go from living with someone to just never speaking to them?' But even though the words come out of *my* mouth, I don't really believe them. When Hugh and I split up he was pretty upset, and after a couple of weeks of me checking in he told me he needed to not hear from me for a while. Or again.

'We didn't live together,' River mumbles. 'I mean, I guess we did – briefly – over in Italy. But here in New York we didn't. Because we only got together after the Italy plan was in motion, it never occurred to us to try living together first here in the US.'

'Hmm,' I contribute.

He pushes a few crumbs around on his plate. 'She'll be back over early in the new year for a visit. I know because I booked the tickets. Unless she changes her plans, I guess.'

'Will you try to see her?'

'Yeah, I mean, I'd want to. Wouldn't you?'

'Yeah.' Would I? It's raw for him, whereas I'm trying to compare the situation to me and Hugh and at this moment in time I don't know if I really want to, or should, see Hugh ever again. I think I am kinda mad at him.

I want to pull River back from his maudlin thoughts, so I ask for his help. 'Where in New York City would you recommend someone go if they wanted to reinvent everything about themselves?'

He whistles. 'That's a big task. It's only a city.'

'It's not only a city! It's ... *the* city.'

'It is?'

I nod.

River exhales deeply, as if the assignment of finding something good in the place he's just been plonked back into is all too much. 'Everything?'

'Well, I need some new goals and a new career and maybe a better love life and a few hobbies. So ... yeah.'

'Bloomingdales?'

I laugh. 'What?'

'It's a start. You could buy a new, I don't know ...'

'Personality?'

'Or the New York Public Library? Get some self-help books out? You're talking to Mr Moving Backwards, remember? I'm not sure how much help I can be.'

'I don't know.' I meet his eyes. 'Maybe we could help each other. Take a few risks, try a few new things, together.'

River ponders this. Or is thinking of an excuse to leave. Either way, I sit back and watch the thoughts darting about on his face. Eventually, he utters the following rave review of my idea: 'Maybe.'

I push my coffee mug aside, so much of the stuff inside me now I'm going to burst if I don't go for a wee soon. But first, 'River, I've enjoyed getting to know you. You seem like a nice guy in a horrible situation with a great apartment, and I'm asking you again – one career failure to another – can I stay on your couch for a few days?'

'Until Thanksgiving?'

'Until just after Thanksgiving,' I clarify. 'Unless you have plans. I can make myself scarce for the day. Go and get those self-help books from the library or something.'

River shakes his head. 'I don't have any plans.'

'You won't spend it with family, now that you're back? Isn't that the big thing to do at Thanksgiving?'

'They're away, flying to Arizona to spend the holidays with my aunt and her family, and my two brothers are meeting them there.'

'Want some company, then?' Was I being too presumptuous here? Probably. Oh well. Too late now.

River looks at me as he seems to be weighing it all up. I know he wants the apartment to himself; I know it because if I were in his position I'd want to be in my own space and ripping through my old diaries and cutting off my own hair. Cough, cough. The last thing he probably wants is to have to go and stay on Hugh's bedroom floor, and that makes two of us.

'Give me one week,' I push, keeping my voice steady and gentle. My pilot voice, the one that says *I've got this*. 'In one week, I think I'll have won you over. We'll be madly in love, and you'll want me to stay. Kidding! But if in one week you're not feeling this new-found flatmate friendship, I'll go, no arguments, no excuses.'

'You sure you're all right with that sofa bed, though?'

Is that a yes? It's nearly a yes! 'Absolutely, I'm in love with that bed!'

'Because the least I could do would be take the couch and you take the bedroom.'

'I don't want to sleep in your and Delilah's love nest that's now soaked with your own tears.'

For a second I think I might have stepped a little too over the line, but River lets out a chuckle and then, I think, I *think*, says, 'Okay.'

'Did you say "okay"?'

'Yes, okay, come and live with me. For a week or so.'

'Yesssssss.' I pummel on the table like I'm watching sports and someone scored a something.

The waiter looks over at me. 'You want the check?' he calls out.

'Oh no, well, actually, yes.' I pull out my wallet. 'I'm buying breakfast,' I tell River.

'No, I told you it's on me.'

'Hush,' I say, like a British schoolmarm. 'You're buying Thanksgiving dinner.'

We step out of the diner and back onto the chilly, leaf-scattered streets of the Village and River pulls his coat around him and tenses his shoulders up towards his ears.

'Are you thinking about how you should be in Italy right now? Wearing a T-shirt, sipping an Aperol Spritz?' I ask, and we start a slow-paced stroll down the road back towards his place, comfortable side by side.

'I was there to work,' he reminds me, but with a smile. 'But no, actually. I was thinking about how you're in for a cold winter in New York.'

'Colder than usual?'

'Not necessarily, but come January I'd be surprised if we haven't seen a few inches of snow.'

125

'Do you think I should have had my midlife crisis in the summer months instead?'

We turn onto a pretty, tree-lined section of street. I see River glance at me, like he wants to say something, and then he mumbles, 'Um, so this is where Selena Gomez used to live.'

I stop and look up at the red-brick buildings, my eyes wide. 'Really?'

'Back when she was a wizard . . .'

'Huh?' I follow his pointing finger and spot a street sign that reads 'Waverly Place', and let out a laugh. That was kinda cute.

'Anyway,' River's saying, and we start walking again. 'I was actually thinking you came at the best time.'

'I did?'

'Well, it's beautiful here in the wintertime.' We turn onto another new street, strolling along like I totally know where we're going, too. 'But I'm sure you know that. You must have been here a lot, as a pilot.'

'Actually, I was short-haul, hoping to build enough flying hours to be long-haul if I felt like it, one day . . . But anyway, there's nothing quite like having your feet on solid ground for a change of perspective, you know.'

'I do know.'

We reach his door, and I double check. 'Are you sure you're okay with me staying a while?'

'Do I have much choice?'

'You do.' I smile. 'I really can go to a hotel. But I think you should give me one week.' River tips his head to the side like he's thinking about it, so I quickly jam my key in the door and scamper inside. 'I'm just going to take that as an, "Ashling, it would be my pleasure to have you stay with me. I think we're going to get on like a house on fire".'

# Chapter 16

Saturday plods along, with River heading off to run a few errands, like restocking his cupboards and doing laundry and other things that must seem extremely dull when you thought you'd be whizzing a Vespa along the Amalfi Coast with your girlfriend right about now. I spend a good hour on the phone with Mum and by the end I *think* I've convinced her that River is not going to murder me and that all is well. I don't mention I might be out on my own again in a week's time. I have full faith that won't happen.

On Sunday morning he emerges from his room, looking more chipper than I thought he would.

'How are you doing?' I ask, pressing buttons on his coffee machine until one of them causes steam to come out of the top, which I'll take as a win.

'Good,' River replies. He's in running gear and has those jet-lag eyebags I've been sporting for the past week and a half.

'Really?'

'Yes. Good. I need to get back on it. If I have to go back to the office again tomorrow, I need to be able to save face and show that a little set-back like my life being overturned isn't going to stop me from moving forwards.'

'You're just going to jump back in like it never happened?'

'What else can I do?' He shrugs.

He heads off for a long run, saying he's going to de-fog his mind a little. Perhaps I should join him. It would be good for him to witness me being as gung-ho as he is about my future, since I need him to see I'm serious about needing this place to stay in for the next two months . . .

And maybe this is a chance to try a new hobby? Oh— oops, well, he's gone now. I give up on the machine and make my way to the coffeehouse down the street to enjoy a morning drink with a morning paper, like a proper Sunday-morning person. A paper is a good place for career inspo, and apartment listings, and there's even a big, juicy crossword and wasn't one of my small goals from my journal to complete a crossword?

Besides – if I plough through as many of the mini-dreams I noted down as I can, maybe something there will ignite a spark of interest, like last time.

A long while later, with only an iota of very mild cheating, I complete the crossword and sit back in satisfaction. That felt good. I can't say that I suddenly feel inspired to enter the crossword championships or something though.

I've not been back in the apartment five minutes when the buzzer goes.

'Hello?' I say into the intercom.

'Oh. Hey. I'm looking for River?' says a male voice. 'It's his dad.'

'And his mom,' another voice says, further away from the microphone.

'He's not here at the moment,' I say. 'But, um, come on up.'

What else could I say? I'm not about to turn away his parents. They probably have more right to be here than I do.

I open the apartment door and hear the elevator clunking and whirring, and there's arguing coming from inside it.

'I told you, it's not fit for two people,' says River's mum as she cranks open the iron gate.

'We're up here, aren't we?' says his dad with a chuckle, before spotting me in the doorway and coming to a stop. 'You must be Ashley, hello, I'm sorry we stopped by without any notice—'

'We just had to see how River's doing, after, you know . . .' his mum says, peering at me.

I get it. I'm a stranger, squatting in their son's house. 'Come in,' I say.

They nod at me, a little tightly, and walk past me into the apartment. As his mum introduces herself as Meg, she takes in the little pile of my crap on the windowsill, the makeshift curtain draped off to the side. Then her eyes slide to the bookshelves where River's photo of him and Delilah is still displayed.

Meg is taller than her husband, her black hair in a claw clip and her nails a shiny, autumnal burgundy, which co-ordinates well with River's walls. His dad is called Ricky

130

and he's wearing a New York Jets jacket and a scarf so big it covers the whole of his neck.

I busy myself making them coffee (finally figured out the machine! Win!), and putting on a bit of a show of opening wrong cupboards and wiping the counter. I don't want them to think I'm *too* comfy and at home here, yet. 'River should be back soon.'

Ricky says, 'Ashley, tell us, how's he doing?'

'Oh, it's Ashling.' I smile. 'But I'll answer to whatever, really.'

'*Ashling*, I'm so sorry.' Meg reaches over and puts a hand on my arm.

'It's totally fine, I get it a lot.' Actually, I'm surprised they know about me at all. I wonder what River told them. 'To answer your question, I think he's . . . okay. I don't know him very well yet so it's hard to say. I don't think he's sleeping all that great, but it could be the jet-lag.'

'I never liked her,' Ricky says, shaking his head. 'Not you, honey – Delilah.'

'You absolutely liked her,' Meg argues. 'You only don't like her now because she broke up with River.' Meg turns to me again. 'Is he sad about being alone for Thanksgiving now? We can get him a ticket to Arizona if he wants to join us?'

I shrug. I'd love to get them on side by spilling all the details, but I just don't know what the details are. Thankfully, they exchange a glance and appear to agree to drop the subject of their son with me – the stranger.

'You're from the UK, am I right?' Ricky asks, sipping his coffee.

'Yep. Just here for a couple of months. My ex-boyfriend works with River and put us in contact. Sort of. And then, well, you know . . .'

'You don't work with them, then?' Meg sets down her cup, barely drunk. 'If you don't mind me asking, honey, what brings you to New York City? A vacation? Or are you planning to stay?'

'No.' I shake my head, quickly. 'I'm not here long term. Just temporarily. I'm a . . . I *was* a pilot. Until recently.'

'A pilot?' Ricky perks up. 'You know I nearly became a pilot?'

Meg tutted. 'You did not.'

'Well, it was between that or a railroad engineer, and I chose the trains.'

'Maybe trains will be my next career move,' I shrug, and before I know it, Meg and Ricky have warmed, my coffee's cooled, it's forty minutes later and I'm sitting in between the two of them on the sofa showing them my teenage journal.

'I guess I was thinking,' I say, 'back when I wrote this I was scribbling down everything, *everything*, I wanted to do and see and have out of life, then the real stand-out things kind of became my goals. What if I just go through it again and try a whole bunch of the other things?'

'Maybe one of them will stick?' Ricky is nodding away.

'Hopefully several of them,' I agree. 'I need a whole new plan, here, and I don't really know where to start.'

'You want my advice?' Meg asks.

'Yes, please.'

'The journal's great. But it's old news, and it's not relevant to the here and now. You need to let yourself have a bit of direction, a bit of help. Something to help you navigate this city while you're going through this difficult period.'

'Meg . . .' Ricky says, a hint of warning to his voice.

'I'm just saying, I know something that could help.'

Am I being pitched to, about something?

'It's not the same situation,' Ricky argues. 'And she's not River. And she said herself she has a lot of ideas of her own.'

'I'm open, though,' I interject. I don't know what they're referring to, but I'm happy to accept guidance. I think.

Meg stands and heads to River's bookshelf, plucking out a thin, glossy book with a blue spine, called *New YOLO: A Guide to Living Your Best Life in New York City*.

'Here.' She hands it to me.

Then I notice the names on the cover. 'You wrote this?'

Ricky nods. 'We published it ourselves, quite a long time ago, when the term YOLO was kinda buzzy. It was a gift to River and it's at least a couple o' years out of date, by now.'

'Our son has turned into such a workaholic over these past years,' Meg explains. 'But that's not him. Not really. He used to have this great work-life balance and we wanted him to get it back, put the brakes on from time to time, have some fun.'

'How did you feel about him going to Italy?'

'We loved the idea,' says Ricky. 'He wants to get out of the office and see the world.'

'There was a time he wanted to be a musician, and tour the world with his favourite rock bands.'

'Oh yeah?' I smile at Meg.

She nods. 'But life happens, you know? I just hope he doesn't fall back into that pattern again now he's home.'

I flip through the pages of the book and see there's faded highlighter circling some of the suggestions. 'You think I could use this?'

'What's the worst that could happen?' says Meg. 'You try a few new things, think outside of your own box, or journal. And before you know it, maybe you've found a little extra inspiration here in the city. Got some new glimmers in your mind for your career, locale, hobbies, travel—'

'Don't forget love life,' Ricky interjects, just as the door opens and River walks in.

Well, it's worth a go. I close the book as the three of them merge together in a group hug and a chorus of hellos.

'Oh, my boy.' Meg is cupping River's face. 'That job of yours is the worst, isn't it the worst, Ashling?'

My hesitation in whether I should agree or not is cut short by Ricky draping an arm around River's shoulders and declaring, 'I told you she was no good for you, didn't I tell you?'

'I thought you liked Delilah?' River glances over at me.

'He did,' Meg says. 'He thought she was a peach, he just doesn't any more.'

'Good run?' I ask River.

'Yeah.' He laughs.

'Meg, Ricky, it was great to meet you, and thanks for all your advice. You don't mind me borrowing this, River?' I hold the book up.

His eyes show recognition, a little flicker of happiness at the sight of the book his parents made for him. 'Of course.'

I smile. 'I'm going to leave you to visit with your son now.' There's a polite round of 'no, stay, join us' but I've taken up enough of their time. 'I've got a few errands to run, maybe get cracking with this.' I tap the book. 'Will you be around for dinner?'

Ricky shakes his head. 'We'll head back this afternoon. We're just here for the day.'

We all say goodbye and I head out into the late morning sunshine again, clasping the book. Is the key to my perfect future now in my paws? I dawdle on the spot, looking up and down the street. Hmm. Feels a bit real. Then I spot the local cinema is showing a double-bill of old black-and-white romantic comedies. How lovely! I'll just watch these first.

## Chapter 17

*Be a tourist in your own neighbourhood*
*Read Dracula*

River slopes into work on Monday with the reluctance of a kid going back to school after the summer holidays, but with a fake-it-until-you-make-it attitude that I'm envious of.

This makes me feel guilty, so I set out to do what I discussed with his parents. With a frankly admirable can-do mindset, I open up their book. Alrighty, time to seek out new opportunities.

In my mind, I'm reading Meg and Ricky's words like they're talking directly to me – I hear their voices and it's comforting. Now this one seems both easy and actually quite useful: 'Be a tourist in your own neighbourhood'.

I know I am a tourist in all of New York's neighbourhoods, but cementing myself here in Greenwich Village might just help me see what I like, what I don't like, what my 'vibe' is, so I know what to look for in a place to live, when I get home? It's a tenuous link, but what else do I have to go on?

My phone rings in my hand, as I'm swotting up on Google Maps for a good walking route around the West Village.

I frown at Hugh's name.

'Don't hang up,' he says when I answer.

'I wasn't going to.' Was I? I'm conflicted as to whether I should still be contrite for breaking his heart last year, or angry that he pretended we were still together to his US friends.

'Are you mad at me?' Hugh asks. 'You know, for the whole, telling people we were still a couple?'

'I don't know,' I tell him honestly. 'I was a little at first. Weirdo.'

He laughs at that.

'Why did you, though?' I ask, curious.

Instead of answering, he says, 'Can we talk? Can I come over?'

Um. I crinkle my nose. Not sure I really want to have 'a talk' right now. 'I was going to give myself a guided walk around Greenwich Village, get myself settled in.'

'Fancy a co-walker? I can point out a few things.'

'Aren't you at work?'

'I took the morning off. Well, I called in sick. I wanted to check in on you, after I heard River was unexpectedly back.'

'To check I wasn't furious?'

'No.' He chuckles. 'Just to make sure you're all right, with staying in the apartment with him. Not that you shouldn't be. But I just thought . . . no matter what happened between us . . .'

I smile down the phone. It's nice that he's checking in, I guess. 'Sure, come join me.'

A part of me is saying maybe this isn't a good idea, that we should keep our distance, but twenty minutes later, when he buzzes the doorbell and I meet him out on the street under a tree, his hands keeping warm in his pockets, the profile of his face sunlit from behind, a nostalgia sweeps over me for something that never happened.

This could have been our lives, out here. One day. If all had gone according to plan. To *my* plan.

But it isn't. And before I let the nostalgia slip its hand into mine, I say to Hugh, 'Talk. Why did you tell people we were a couple?'

'It was a misunderstanding, at the beginning.' He pauses, his usual brashness gone, his hands remaining deep in his pockets. 'I guess I mentioned you quite a bit. Maybe a lot. Our break-up still felt a little fresh, you know?'

'Mmm-hmm.' Awkward.

'And a few months in I realised my colleagues had got the impression – my fault – that we were still together. Long distance.'

'And you didn't correct them?'

'At the time I thought they'd think I was a right sad-sack if I admitted we weren't together, so I figured I'd keep it up for a bit, start bringing you up less, then drop in that we'd split. But suddenly here you were, in New York. And I never thought you'd actually meet River, at least not until January, so . . .'

I did understand, as ridiculous as this situation was.

'All right. I forgive you,' I tell him, and his shoulders drop with visible relief.

As the two of us stroll the streets, I tell him about what happened with my job, and he listens, keeping any judgements or simmering resentments very much in check behind a poker face. We pepper our conversation with facts about the area read aloud from my phone, and nuggets of information he has stored away in his brain.

'How do you know these things?' I ask, after he's pointed out where Taylor Swift once lived for a short while, on a lane that presumably inspired her song 'Cornelia Street'.

Hugh shrugs and stumbles over his words for a moment before looking me in the eye. 'I have a lot of time on my own. I don't have a group of friends here. Yet. So when I'm not working, I walk around the city and learn stuff.'

'Oh.' He never had those kinds of problems at home – he was always the sociable one. How sad. 'Hugh, I have to ask. Why did you come here, to New York, I mean, when you never wanted to . . . before. Why the change of heart?'

He begins to walk again. 'Didn't we already talk about this?'

'Briefly, when you gave me the keys. You just said you'd "grown" or something.'

'Yeah, well, that might not be as true as I would have liked to believe.' We shuffle along for a bit and finally he continues, not meeting my eye. 'When we split up, I was on the lookout for a big change, something drastic, something that would make people stop giving me the pitying "Oh, you've been dumped?" look.'

I'm not sure what to interject here, so I just stay silent.

Hugh sighs. 'My company at home had links with my company here and when I saw the New York opening come up, that fit the bill, even though it wasn't really the move I thought I wanted to make. To be honest though, there was part of me that wanted to make you jealous.'

He sneaks a look at me. 'That's very petty,' I scold. 'But also ... I kind of get it.'

Hugh exhales, a little light relief smoothing out his worry lines. 'Our break-up threw me off course a little, I guess, and working from home out in the countryside wasn't quite filling the, um, gap. I didn't really know what I wanted. I still don't. I thought I might as well do something out of my comfort zone to find out.'

So that's that. It's his life, his story, I can't begrudge him for decisions he makes without me, at least not any more.

By the time we're saying goodbye, and I'm back at the apartment, I'm very knowledgeable about all the history of the local jazz club scene, the tenement buildings, the food establishments that have been around for decades, the architecture of NYU and even more in the know about Hugh, which is nice. I can't decide if it feels more like a quiet bit of closure, or the soft opening of a window on a warm day.

Bringing it back to my *New YOLO* book, and the whole reason I'm being led by it – could I be a tour guide? I can be fun, engaging, impart my wisdom, but ... maybe I need to know where I want to live in the UK first, before I can become a pro about every street and moulding.

This thought sets me back a step, so for the rest of the day

I choose a goal from my own journal instead – that totally counts! – which is to 'Read *Dracula*'. Finally.

Downloading the book, I'm gripped right through until the end of the following day, lost in the atmosphere of reading such a dark book during my winter days. I reach the end, wide-eyed, just before River arrives back from work.

'Honey, you're home.' I greet River as he walks in the door, and before he's even said a word he blushes a little. Perhaps it's too soon for jokey familiarities? 'How was your day?'

'Uggghhhhh,' he replies, and sits down on the sofa. 'Sorry,' he says, standing.

'Oh my god, stop saying sorry for sitting on your own furniture. I told you, this is your living space in the daytime, it's only my bedroom at night. Something happen today?'

As River tells me about being back in the New York office again, I'm nodding along, asking questions like I know this group of people. I retrieve us both a beer out of the fridge, as if I've earned one as well, and keep listening. Eventually, he ends with, 'And so it all just feels so ... so ... fake, you know? Like everyone is almost pretending the five of us never left. Like if nobody mentions it and everyone just gets the same old workload they used to have we'll just forget about this big opportunity we were pulled from.'

'That sucks,' I sooth. It's part of the reason I baulked when Living In The Air offered to help relocate me to other positions after my accident. I can't bear the thought of everyone just pretending I was never a pilot, when that's all I knew myself to be. 'Did anyone mention Delilah?'

'Oh yeah, everyone mentioned Delilah,' River says, leaning his head on the back of the sofa and staring up at his ceiling. 'That was the one topic nobody felt they needed to avoid. It was all, "I heard about Delilah, are you okay? Do you want to talk about Delilah? I never liked Delilah anyway".'

'She wasn't very liked at your office?' I ask, surprised. River seems very likeable, to me, and I've built Delilah up in my head to be the personification of a Jo Malone candle. You know, fancy and sophisticated, nice-smelling and universally liked.

'I think she was; she *is*. I'm sure it's just people trying to be nice, like my dad did. In Italy the rest of them are all probably telling *her* they never liked *me*.'

We both take swigs of our beer. That is probably true.

'Did you miss her today?'

'Yeah.'

'I'm sorry.'

River swigs again. 'Well, 'tis what it 'tis, as people in Britain would say.'

'We say that all the time.'

'How's everything going with your "new you" plan?' he asks, turning his face to look at me.

'It's ... interesting.' I didn't tell him about seeing Hugh yesterday, considering Hugh had bunked off work under the guise of being ill. Instead, I pull out the *New YOLO* book and hand it to him. 'When I met your parents, I didn't know quite where to start, and, as you know, they suggested this.'

River takes it from me and smiles, flipping the pages.

'I haven't looked at this for ... I guess over a year, at least. When the Italy opening came up, I didn't think about it again.'

'Did you feel like you needed it before?'

'No. But my folks did. To be honest, I wasn't big on the idea of hitting up all the tourist traps, you know?' A tinge of something creeps out into his voice again – this small, misplaced resentment towards the Big Apple. He catches me studying him and gives a resigned smile. 'I mean, I guess some of the ideas were interesting, but I just didn't get time to do any of them. Like, well, I would have liked this ...' He hands the book to me, a circle drawn around a picture of a helicopter above the Manhattan skyline.

'Aren't these tours like, fifteen minutes?'

He takes the book back and shrugs. 'Let's call it motivation holding me back, then.'

I get what he's saying, I think. 'I haven't really tried anything new for a long time, you know. I've been very focused. And now ...'

'You have no focus?'

I clink my bottle against his. Spot on. 'When I flew out here earlier this month, I hadn't really thought beyond getting to New York. Now I'm here, what do I do? Take up writing? Take a class on woodwork? Go on a course? Learn to dance, like my gran?'

'Your gran was a dancer?'

'Yeah, she was a pro. She actually danced in New York for a while, when she was really young. Not for the Rockettes or anything, though she did love them.'

143

'That's pretty cool,' River said. 'Well, maybe you try all those things.'

'Yeah, maybe. I'm also using this ten-year-old journal of mine for inspo, though your parents did make the good point that I should try focusing on new opportunities instead. So far I've given myself a tour and decided I'm probably not tour-guide material at the moment, and I've read *Dracula* but I don't think I'm likely to take up writing or vampiring.'

He snorts into the top of his beer bottle, suddenly, reading something on his phone. 'Is there anything in *New YOLO* about joining a marching band?'

'I don't think so,' I say, reaching for it and fluttering through the pages. 'There's "take a ride on a parade float".' He's frowning at his screen, not quite listening to me, and I get up and move over to him. 'What is it?'

He hands me his phone so I can see what he's looking at. 'I just had an email from my old college in Massachusetts – the marching band are in town for the parade on Thanksgiving, and need extra participants.'

I hand the phone back, awe on my face. 'This is about the Macy's Thanksgiving Day Parade?'

'Yeah.' He sits up straighter, as if perturbed by the excitement in my voice.

'Would you do it?'

'No.' He laughs. 'I'm not ... I couldn't ... Not any more.'

'Were *you* in the marching band?'

'I was,' he admits. 'That's why they got in touch. They've had a couple of dropouts and have reached out to any band alumni who'll be around New York on Thursday to ask if they could step in.' I notice him light up a little from inside as he looks back at the email on his phone.

'What did you play?'

'Trumpet.' His smile is endearing.

'Are you going to do it? You're going to do it, right?' I coax.

'Absolutely not.'

'But they need you. What else are you doing this Thanksgiving? Everybody in the US has plans except for you.'

'Ouch.'

'Come on, River. We can both do it!' What am I saying, I don't play an instrument? I could march though, I guess. I laugh at the way he's trying to push down the smile from forming on his lips. 'I've not seen you look this excited since . . . well, I guess I never have because I've only known you four days and you've been under a dark cloud this whole time. Just go for it. March in that band.'

'You think this is me excited?' The smile breaks through.

'Close enough.'

But he shakes his head. 'Nobody wants to see a miserable thirty-five-year-old rusty trumpet player marching among a bunch of charismatic kids.'

'I would. It sounds hilarious.'

He studies me, but I think he's thinking about it. 'You would want to do it too? If I could get you in?'

Hell, maybe being a performer in some capacity is my destiny? Maybe I'm the best marcher this city's ever seen; I've just never tried it before. 'Absolutely. Let's do it. Let's New YOLO! But I'm going to have to fake playing an instrument.'

'I think I know what you could do, if my college don't mind.'

I punch the air with glee, which makes him roll his eyes, but the smile doesn't drop. 'If I do it, you'll do it?' I confirm.

River reaches out and shakes my hand, his palm cold from the bottle, but his skin warm. 'Deal.'

# Chapter 18

## Take part in a parade

'You know, I think this might be my future,' I say loudly, attempting to be heard over the tuba warming up beside me. I spin on the spot for River, who, like me, is dressed in his old college colours.

'What?' He leans in closer.

'This, being a performer, I think this is exactly what I needed to be doing. Maybe even what I should do. You know, my new dream. A "New YOLO", if you will.'

He gives me a thumbs-up but clearly hasn't heard a word.

It's eight-thirty in the morning and we're in the Upper West Side along with what feels like thousands of other Macy's Thanksgiving Day paraders who are getting ready for the nine a.m. start time. The sun is out, the temperature is cool but not freezing, the sky is blue and I've never heard so much noise in my life. And I've been in plenty of airport delays.

The whole atmosphere is as festive as Christmastime, with smiles in abundance. There's a whopping turkey float with a nodding head, whose name is Tom Turkey, Santa is wandering about, brass bands are warming up, giant inflated balloons are being carefully guided out from under their nets by teams of handlers, spiced hot drinks are being handed out from flasks and filling the air with their aroma, and people keep zooming up and down the block with last-minute costume fixes.

I can't believe I'm here. This is pretty once-in-a-lifetime.

River's college band are about halfway along the parade, and giant floats, and giant floating animals, characters and balloons, bob about every direction I turn.

I start to run over the simple steps I'll be doing for the next three hours, as one of the banner carriers who leads the band. I'll be on the right-hand side of one of the two university banners, holding the edge of one that reads '... wishes you a Happy Thanksgiving!'

A dancer rushes past, leaf costume wobbling in the wind. I see my gran in that moment, in my mind, dressed in her dancing get-up – perhaps her tap shoes, or her costume she wore for that Broadway show she was in briefly – flitting around the streets of New York City in the fifties. I imagine her pinning up her hair as she races to a rehearsal, applying her lipstick in the mirrors of streetcars (am I getting the era right?), practicing a pirouette or two as she waits for crossing lights to change. How big this city must have seemed to her back then, the same way it did for me the first time I came here. I remember her watching me, a smile on her face. She knew. She knew how this city buried itself into people's hearts. Everything was fast and big and exciting and full of dreams. And she made hers happen. I've got to make sure I make her proud.

Glancing back towards River, I catch his eye as he's just lowering his trumpet and mopping his forehead with the back of his sleeve. His face is painted a shade of nervous, his eyes down, and he chews at his bottom lip. Then he looks up, directly at me, and a quick beam passes from him to me, like I'm his best mate and not his annoying and unexpected roomie. I lift my hand in a wave.

'All right, band, I've just had word that the parade is about to begin,' says Max, the marching band director, as he edges behind the banner I'm holding and addresses the group. 'Who's ready to celebrate Thanksgiving?' The group cheers so I do the same even though there's a large part of me that doesn't really know what's going on. 'I said, who's ready to celebrate Thanksgiving?'

Our group roars and we all put our hats on. River and the band were outside Macy's before it was even light this morning, for their final performance rehearsal, so I know he'll be excited to get the show on the road. I face the front to see that way up ahead, the big, inflatable acorn and pumpkins have started their slow bob down the road.

I'm aware there's music playing up and down the parade line-up, but suddenly my ears are filled entirely with River's marching band's Rat Pack classic medley. Brass and drums

149

and stamping feet harmonise with whoops from onlookers, and I feel myself bursting with pride as we walk past all those people. Oh my god, is that Karamo giving an interview off to the side? I briefly wave and then clasp my hand back on my end of the banner in case my bad shoulder throws in a twang and my one hand can't hold it, it drops, the marching band stumbles over, there's a stampede and the parade is ruined and thus Thanksgiving, as New York knows it, is ruined.

Straining, I scan to see if anyone famous is gracing the float in front or behind us. I heard that Mariah Carey is here this year! But I don't think she's near me; there'd be more excitable screaming. And I would have to join in.

We come to a pause from time to time, and on one such occasion I turn back to look at River again. He's in his absolute element – if I can say that after barely knowing him for more than five seconds – trumpeting away, dressed in his neat uniform, his eyes concentrating hard. Whenever he pauses to take a breath, a smile seems desperate to jump onto his lips. He catches my eye and winks, then instantly blushes and looks away like he can't believe he winked. I chuckle and turn back to the front as we start moving again.

I kinda liked the wink, if I'm honest. It had an easy confidence, a playfulness. Are we on the edge of being Real Friends? Not just Accidental Flatmates?

A jaunty *Jingle Bells* is ringing out from our band (lol, 'our' band) and I step along in time, feeling small but important in this vast and world-famous parade. I'm dwarfed by the floating balloons. I'm drowned out by the voices and

150

instruments. And here I am, and it's something I never would have dreamed I'd be allowed to be a part of.

Overhead, like, way overhead, above the inflatables, above the top of the tall buildings, is a plane, and for the first time in a couple of weeks I find myself glad to be right here, on the ground, instead of high up there and missing it all. I'm sure it won't last, but ... it's a good thing, right? I'll tell Flo later and I'm sure she'll be proud of me.

Lowering my gaze back down I'm walloped with a dose of déjà vu. We've rounded the bottom end of Central Park West onto West 59th Street, with Central Park still on my left, Midtown Manhattan opening up on my right, and the beautiful, pointy Sherry-Netherland building rising into the morning sunshine in the distance, at the point which the road I'm on intersects with Fifth Avenue.

I've been here before. In this exact spot, I mean. Without my view being obscured by inflatable characters sailing along the sky, and maybe not in the centre of the street like I am now, but without a doubt I've stood here.

We walk on, the crowds waving colourful balloons beside us, and the feeling is subsiding while I try to cling to why it felt so familiar to me. Is it just because I've seen New York in so many movies? Have I just wandered along here, maybe already on this trip? No, no, it's something more. I can picture it so clearly, but in black and white. And then it hits me – I drew this spot. I sketched it, on that trip ten years previous, it's one of the pages of drawings in my journals that I've been skipping over to focus on the words. But I remember it now – walking along this road having just come out of Central Park a decade ago, and feeling like I had all the opportunities in the world before me. I loved the contrast of views from the different directions. I loved the architecture and the greens and the greys around me. So I made Grooms sit on the wall with me, level with where I am now, while I took out my journal and my biro, and drew this exact view.

It's funny to think that a past version of yourself stood in the same spot and saw the same things as you're seeing now, but with younger eyes. And I bet the me of back then never imagined that ten years later I'd be walking past here as part of the famous Macy's Thanksgiving Day Parade. Would Grooms have predicted this? I can well imagine her out there in the crowd, cheering me on, holding up a balloon.

We turn the corner onto Sixth Avenue; this is the last long stretch before we hit 34th Street and Macy's Herald Square where the parade finishes.

Behind me, River is still trumpeting his heart out, along with the rest of the marching bands in front and behind. And either side of the road there are crowds of people dressed in coats and scarves, waving at us all, photograph-ing the floats, sipping from coffee cups, pointing into the air at the big balloons. The atmosphere is wild and happy and it's as if everybody in New York is lining these streets today. I feel like a pumpkin pie, I'm so warm and toasty from the inside.

We keep marching, and the music keeps booming and the floats keep floating and before I know it, we've reached Macy's. We wait our turn, and then while I stand off to the side, River and the band rush onto the big green carpet and perform their medley for the TV cameras, confetti raining on them.

Remnants of confetti are still falling like snowflakes from the sky as the band moves aside for the next performers, which will continue until the balloons and floats take their final bows and retire until next year's holiday.

I pocket a piece of red confetti. I'm going to keep it as memorabilia of this amazing thing I just did. Now, where'd River go? I spot him, embracing Max, the band director, and laughing, his face pink and puffed. Then he searches the crowd for me, I think, so I stand on tiptoes and give him a wave.

Striding over, River throws his arms around me. Oh! Well, okay then. Let's do this. His exhilarated breath is in my hair and he's taller than I realised, now he's all up close and everything.

'Hey.' He grins, letting me go and standing back, his wavy hair a little wild, a red stripe across his forehead from the hat, which I probably have too. 'That was amazing, wasn't it? What did you think?'

He seems genuinely interested, his eyes focused only on me, despite everything still going on around us. Not distracted by his instrument, or his bandmates, or the task at hand. On me.

Oh my. Hello, heartbeat, what are you doing picking up your rhythm? Must be the uniform.

My throat is parched from the walking and smiling and I can't seem to find the right words. 'It was ... intoxicating.'

'Yeah?'

'Yeah.' I laugh.

'And that's coming from a pilot.'

I like that he still calls me a pilot. 'It was such an awesome experience. You slipped into that march like you'd never left – you were fantastic! The music! The crowds! The ...' I'm not sure what I'm trying to say here. Telling River I'm proud of him seems a bit weird, doesn't it? 'I've never been a part of something like that, ever. Thank you.'

'Oh, you're welcome,' River says, glancing at the ground, scuffing his shoes over the confetti.

'And you had a good time?' I press.

He nods. 'I loved it. It's been a long time since I was part of a band.'

'You never play any more?'

'I don't have a lot of time any more. It was a college thing, really. But it was fun to rediscover it.'

I nod, and for a moment we're lost for words. Confetti is stuck to my trainers, and the music of the bands and performances still arriving in front of Macy's reverberates in my ears. 'So ... I guess everyone just gets on with the rest of their Thanksgivings now, when they're done?'

'I guess so.'

'Are you going to hang out with the band? I presume they aren't heading all the way home this afternoon?'

River accepts two bottles of water from a passing bandmate and gives one of them to me. 'I think they're staying around, but, as fun as this was, I don't know any of them. They're all current students, and I am old.'

I let out a laugh. 'Fair point. You know the director guy, though? He was the same one as when you went there?'

'Yes, but he's chaperoning these guys. I'll just say bye and then leave them to it.'

River darts over to the group and I watch him. He seems alive, like he's surrounded by his people, and I like that for him.

My phone bleeps with a message from Hugh wishing me a 'Happy Thanksgiving', which I wish back at him in a quick, typed return. I wonder if I have the same look of fond familiarity on my face as River does right now.

And then, my roommate is back in front of me, screwing the lid back on the water bottle. 'You want to just hang out, have the rest of Thanksgiving together? Sometimes over here we call it "Friendsgiving".'

'You don't have to do that with me,' I say. But I guess he has no other option, really. He already said his friends are pretty much all at their parents' homes for the holidays, his girlfriend ditched him, and I'm squatting in *his* home. So, he's kinda stuck with me. To avoid him retracting the offer, I add, 'But that would be great, actually, thank you.'

We head into the restrooms of a nearby hotel to change out of the band uniforms and back into regular clothes, and then after a lot of goodbyes and thank yous and photos with the band, it's just River and I again.

'The subway might be super-busy. How do you feel about walking back to ours?' he asks as we head south away from Herald Square.

'Love that you called it "ours",' I comment.

155

'Good point, I should say *mine*,' he corrects himself, but with a smile thrown in my direction. 'Or have you had enough of walking for one day?'

My legs are a little wobbly. 'How long will it take?'

He considers it for a moment, taking stock of where we are. 'Maybe a half hour?'

'Oh, that's fine.' I stop and stand on the spot, and pull him to a stop beside me. 'Ready, and, march.' Off I go, singing 'Santa Claus is Coming to Town' and marching in time, until River jogs after me and tugs on my coat sleeve.

'Stop, stop, stop, no more marching,' he says, laughing. 'We can just walk now.'

'Just walk? How boring.'

# Chapter 19

A thirty-minute walk and two hot showers later, and I'm stepping back out of the apartment building into Greenwich Village once again. But this time, I'm just going to a mini-mart a couple of streets over.

Because River is more in the know than I, he's taken off to a nearby deli that he knows does great Thanksgiving sandwiches, and I'm picking up a bottle of wine and some sweet treats.

As we walk out of the door, he says, 'Sorry. I should have cooked or something. Or booked to take you out, as a thank you for helping today. You should have had a proper American Thanksgiving.'

My stomach growls up a thunderstorm and I give him a gentle shove in the direction of the deli. 'This is going to be just perfect. And you've had a lot on your mind the past week, so who cares about trying to ram a bloody great turkey into your tiny oven, anyway?'

We split up and I totter on achy legs to the store, where I peruse the aisles for a while before selecting a Californian red. Do East Coasters have a 'thing' about West-Coast wine? No idea, but I guess I'll find out. I grab a bag of monster marshmallows too – I'm sure I've heard that Americans put marshmallows on yams during Thanksgiving dinner.

Heading back to the apartment, the street seems quiet, almost serene, especially compared to the loudness and festivities of the morning. Now it's just me, and a couple of others, and the crunching of leaves beneath my feet.

And I guess it's only a little over four weeks to Christmas. I'm going to be spending Christmastime in New York City. I feel a glow like somebody's wrapped a string of multicoloured lights around me.

I love living in Greenwich Village. I know it's only been for a week, but I'll miss it when I have to move out of River's apartment. I've been lazy this past week, or perhaps living in hope is a better way of putting it, my attention held by being in the New York minute rather than focusing on finding a new home. I have nothing lined up, though it's totally possible River's going to want his living room back once this holiday is over.

I reach the apartment again and head up the six flights of stairs. By the top I *know* I'm not imagining it – these stairs are getting easier. I started out feeling so puffed, now I'm only mostly puffed. My legs could sure use a rest though, to be honest.

I'm the first to arrive back, so I stick the red wine bottle in a sink full of warm water to warm it a little after the chilly air outside, and light some candles.

Then I blow out the candles, because that's a bit romantic, isn't it? Wine, candles, sandwiches ... I don't want River to think I'm seducing him into letting me stay.

But it's the holidays, candles are festive. I light them again, but also turn on all the lamps and fairy lights and overhead lights so there's atmosphere but also loads of bright, I'm-not-trying-to-snog-you lighting. Then I throw on River's TV and turn it to football, the volume low, rather than risk putting on music that might shuffle its way to a love song.

Oh god, the LAST thing he would need right now is love songs! Poor guy is spending the holidays without any of his loved ones, while trying to get over his heartbreak. This morning was a great distraction, and now I have to make sure the afternoon is as well. As a ... friend? We're friends now, right?

The door opens and in comes River, surrounded by a waft of delicious aromas. He grins and holds a bulging paper bag aloft, and I pull some plates from the cupboard while he sets about decanting two absolutely ginormous turkey sandwiches, positively dripping with stuffing and gravy and vegetables, and possibly even some of those marshmallowy yams in there too.

I fish the wine out of its hot tub and unscrew the lid, and within minutes the whole apartment smells like herbs, spices, cooking and Christmas. Or, I guess, Thanksgiving.

'This looks amazing,' I say, waving a glass of red

somewhere towards River since I can't take my eyes off the sandwiches.

'They are good,' he says. 'I've never had them *on* Thanksgiving before, but the deli I got them from usually does them for a couple of weeks around this time of year. In lieu of a proper Thanksgiving dinner, this is just as tasty. In my opinion.'

'Well, if the smell is anything to go by, I trust that opinion.'

We take our plates to the sofa, and I instantly curl up on the side nearest the window, with the view of the Empire State Building, and we clink our glasses. 'Happy Thanksgiving,' River says.

'Happy Thanksgiving.' I grin. 'Thank you to my gracious host.'

'Thank you to my unexpected guest.'

'Shut up now, I can't wait any more.' I pick up half of the sandwich and bite down, the warm, salty, sweet, oily, tangy flavours and crispy, soft, squidgy textures causing a big smile on my face even as I chew. I try to say something along the lines of 'Delicious!' but it won't come – I'll wait until I've completed my gobful.

The two of us watch the football side by side, and I'm pretty sure neither of us fully get what's happening, but we're entertained nonetheless. I take my time over my sandwich, and afterwards refill our wines and grab the marshmallows, which we stuff into our mouths until we're both feeling a little sick.

When someone does a touchdown (maybe . . . ) on the screen, I let out a 'yay' then glance over to River since he's made no reaction. He's gazing at the bookshelf, his mind in another place as he stares at the photo of him and the girl at the canyon (who I've now gathered is definitely Delilah).

I'm about to say something awkward like 'penny for your thoughts' in a Dickensian cockney accent, but River speaks first.

'Delilah and I were going to host Thanksgiving this year, in Italy.'

'Yeah?' I say, plucking out another marshmallow.

'Just a small one, for the group that went out there together, in the apartment the two of us were sharing.'

'Is she still in that flat?'

'I think so,' he replies, not taking his eyes off the photo. I place a marshmallow in his hand for him. 'I wonder if she's still hosting, whether they're doing anything as a group still.'

'Would you get in touch and ask her, do you think?'

'No.' He shakes his head. 'That feels like a bit of a lame excuse to call.' He breaks his gaze to peep at me. 'I might check all of their Instagrams though.'

'Obviously.' I chuckle, gently. 'Sorry you didn't get a proper Thanksgiving this year.'

He shrugs. 'It is what it is. At least I can be home for Christmas, now.'

'That's true. You were going to be away, weren't you? Did you say you planned to come back in January?'

'For a visit. Which means Delilah *should* be back then too.'

'Will you try and see her?'

'I'd like to. Do you think I should?' He asks me this

just as I've stuffed the entire massive marshmallow in my mouth, but at least it gives me a bit of time to think of a tactful answer.

Finally, swallowing, I settle on, 'Do you want to?' which I think we can all agree is a very helpful and insightful response.

'Yeah.' He nods. 'Yes, of course. I don't want to just never see her again. But . . .'

'But what?' I pull out another marshmallow from the packet, god help me.

'I guess . . .' He trails off, shifting a clump of his hair to the side, then fiddling with the drapey makeshift sofa curtains. 'I guess I want to have a few things figured out by the time she comes back.'

Oh. 'Did she ask that of you?'

'No, but in my company, it's kind of expected that you're all work and no play. I feel like I need to be onto the next project or promotion or rung in the ladder before the momentum slips away.'

'Might it? Slip away?'

He nods, slowly. 'I have ambition. But I know I need to push myself to keep up with the crowd in this career.'

'Tell me about your job.'

'It's . . . I'm . . .' He laughs suddenly. 'It's so boring I don't even want to talk about it.'

I laugh at that. 'Why are you busting your ass so much if it's too boring to even talk about?'

He chuckles harder. 'I don't know!' Then he leans forwards, resting his chin in his hands and staring towards the

TV, the green of the field reflecting in his eyes. He lapses into his thoughts.

'Delilah. Do you want to win her back?' I ask.

'No,' he says, his voice hesitant. 'I don't really believe in winning people back. I think if Delilah changed her mind about the long-distance thing and wanted to be with me, she would, and if she doesn't, I want to be the guy that respects that. But . . .'

'But?'

'But at the same time, I don't want her to see me as this guy who doesn't have a plan. Who doesn't have his shit together. So I think I need to become that person, that guy, the guy with ambition like the one she fell for. And when Delilah comes home and we meet up then . . . we just see what happens.'

He's still in love with her, of course he is.

I trickle the last of the red wine into the bottoms of both our glasses, and River immediately gets up to pluck another bottle from a cupboard. 'All right,' I say. 'You want to get your life together. I can relate to this, River. We're a couple of sorry sacks.'

River turns from the TV towards me. 'Sorry sacks?'

'Yes.' Is that even a phrase? Whatever.

'It's a good job we're together then.'

'Yes, we're in this together!' I say a little too loudly, and clink my glass against his. 'To recap, for you, getting your life together means working your arse off at work and finding something that makes the Italy debacle feel like kismet. Right?'

'I guess so. And for you it's reinventing yourself?'

'And everything I've ever been.' I nod. River laughs, and I'm glad to see he's pulled himself from the pity party he was about to enter. 'Anyway. This is a holiday. Shall we stop talking about work?'

'Yes,' he says with gusto. 'All right, we have to do this Thanksgiving tradition.'

'Another one? We already paraded and footballed and turkeyed.'

'One more.' He faces me fully now, giving me his attention. 'Ashling.'

'So serious,' I comment, then shush.

'This Thanksgiving, what are you thankful for?'

Oh *yes*, I've always seen this tradition in movies and TV and now I'm getting to do it IRL. I think for a moment. 'I am thankful that you let me stay.' He starts to protest but I cut him off. 'I'm not saying I would have made it easy on you if you'd tried to kick me out – you and I are in a real grey area regarding subletter and landlord rights. But I like that it didn't come to that. You let me stay, at a time I'm sure you didn't need a stranger taking up your space, and it can't have been easy considering everything you had going on. I've loved living here. Thank you for giving me this experience.'

Was that a little gushy? Maybe. Oh well, that's what a morning of festive marching-band music and two-and-a-bit glasses of wine get ya.

River looks down at the sofa, a small blush on his face. His eyelashes twitch as his eyes roam the cushion while he thinks.

'And what are you thankful for?' I ask. 'Considering the circumstances.'

He chuckles. 'I am thankful for you.'

'Shut up.' I sit back. 'No, you aren't, you just feel like you have to say that.'

'No, really. I admit when I first got home that night, I wanted nothing more than to be alone. And even the next day I thought, really? Hugh's ex-girlfriend wants to stay on my couch? This is all a bit much.'

I nodded. It was a bit awkward for him, working with Hugh. Because of me. Not (just) because Hugh can be a bit of bell-end at times.

'But actually, you've been a good distraction.'

'Thank you.' I laugh.

'Not in a bad way. I know I would have wallowed a lot more if you weren't here hanging out in my living room, stopping me from just lying on the couch watching TV all day. And I definitely wouldn't have pulled myself out to be part of the parade this morning.'

'But you loved it.'

'I really did.' He smiles. 'You know I studied music at college? That band, that life, was everything.'

'What the hell made you pivot to IT?'

'Sometimes, I have no idea.'

We run out of things to say so turn back to the TV and watch the chaps legging it about holding their balls for a while.

I drain my glass of wine and notice he has too, and so I reach over him to fill them both up. I am getting just a teeny bit fuzzy in the head, and I don't mind one bit.

165

A tiny drop splashes onto my journal, which I've left on a side table, and I pick it up, licking the blob of wine off and wincing at the musty taste. Why did I do that instead of getting a tissue like a normal human?

'Is that the journal you mentioned? Where you keep all your hidden desires?'

'They're hardly hidden.' I chortle. 'And I wouldn't call them desires. More, dreams.'

'Can I see?' He reaches over.

'Can you read my journal?'

'Yeah.' River puts his wine down and leans over to me, but I put it behind my back with a shriek.

'No!'

'Just one page?' He's grinning, his arm reaching behind my back and we lock eyes for a millisecond, the unanticipated closeness seeming to hit us both like a static shock, before he sits back on the sofa and lifts his hands in the air. 'I'm sorry, I was kidding. I would never try to read your journal, I promise.'

I pull myself up, smiling, a little dazed from the flirty exchange. And the wine. 'There's actually nothing secret in here anyway. But thank you.'

We fall quiet again. What's he thinking? Is he thinking about me?

A fluttering in my chest has me leaning forwards, not wanting the conversation to end. Actually, I *want* to talk to someone – him – about my list. He's been so open about Delilah and his job, and I've only been vague, in a 'I guess the sky is falling!' kind of way.

I turn to face him and put my feet up on the sofa. 'I can read you my list,' I declare.

'Your list?' He raises his eyebrows at me in question.

'The list of five big goals – the ones I'm trying to replace. My reason for being in New York.'

'All right.' He nods, angling his body towards me too and placing a hand on my socked foot for a second before, perhaps, thinking it seems a little too intimate and removing it again.

It's not too intimate for *me*, but whatever.

I start reading. 'The first one was to get this Young Artists' Residency thing, but I am now too old and haggard.'

'You draw?'

'A little.' I smile. 'Um, there's one about taking my gran on a big trip, but she passed away before I got round to it.'

River gently places his hand back on my foot, and this time he leaves it there.

I continue. 'Marry Hugh.'

'Oh.'

'Yeah.' I look up and meet his eyes, then shrug, before moving on. 'Be a pilot. You know what happened with that. And live in New York. Which is why I'm here, doing the next best thing, lest that one slip from my grasp also.'

River brings his glass back to his lips, before blurting out, 'Do you want to just stay?'

I cough on the marshmallow I sneaked into my gob. Then I compose myself enough to ask, 'What?'

'Do you want to just stay, here, with me, while you're in New York?'

I forget the journal, the feet-touching, the football, all in an instant. 'You mean live in this apartment?'

He nods, just once. 'If you want to. I'm sure you want to find your own place though, and even if you didn't, you don't want to spend your time here with miserable me.'

'Yes, I do – we're Team Miserable,' I protest. What a great duo name.

'I'm just saying, you don't have to leave, and if you stay you can take my bedroom and I'll move onto the sofa.'

'No,' I say, putting a protective hand on the window, which I've grown to love sleeping beside.

'No, you want to go?' I think he looks a bit sad.

'No, I want to stay, but I want to sleep in here. Get out of *my* bedroom.'

'You want to stay?'

'Are you sure *you* want me to stay? What will Hugh think?' I recalibrate. 'Who cares what Hugh thinks! What will Delilah think?'

River looks away, like he hadn't thought about that, and I kick myself, literally – I kick my own ankle and wish I hadn't put that thought in his head. But ... 'She's not my girlfriend any more, so, I guess it doesn't matter. But also, you're just a lodger.'

'Exactly,' I agree. 'The Artful Lodger.'

'What?'

'Nothing. River. If you'll have me, I would be honoured to be your roommate for the next couple of months. I promise not to cause a mess, never to take too long in the bathroom, I won't invite Danny the Pizza Guy over

168

without leaving a sock on the door handle, and I'll always pay rent on time.'

'I promise all those things too,' River says, and we shake hands. 'Welcome to the Village. Officially.'

# Chapter 20

Try stand-up comedy
Play chess in Bryant Park
Drink a Long Island iced tea on Long Island

Now I'm staying, I allow myself to properly settle into River's Greenwich Village flat. I even take advantage of the Black Friday sales the following day and treat myself to some bedding of my own to see me through the winter. And that night, I curl up under my silky soft sheets and marshmallow duvet and gaze out at the Empire State Building. Phew. That was a whopper of a meltdown I had up there in my first week. How embarrassing. But I like that I can look up at her every night. She can remind me why I'm here, what I need to do. My dreams are just out of reach, but they're going to be as big as she is. I know it.

Early in the morning, my phone bleeps with a message from Rebecca, my pilot pal from Living In The Air.

Hey friend. Just checking in – we're all thinking of you. How's life treating you?

I smile. That's nice of her. I'm doing okay thanks, I text back. New York is wonderful!

That's great to hear! All pleasure or any business?

A bit of both. Pleasure, but trying to figure out my next business move.

Rebecca starts typing and then stops, as if she's having a good think about what to say. Eventually, another message pops up:

HQ keeps asking me if you're okay. If there's anything they can do to help, I know they'd want to.

I know, I type. Thank you.

In actual fact, 'HQ' (meaning the HR department of Living In The Air) sent me an email a couple of days ago, but although my heart leapt when I first saw it – perhaps the medical exam had been wrong! – I saw from the preview it was just checking on my wellbeing. Kind, but I didn't know how to answer now, so I left it, unread.

Over the next few days, as November waves goodbye with a few final, fluttering leaves and the festivities of December descend upon the city, I set to work.

I need to be a little more strategic here, if I'm serious about replacing my five goals. River's *New YOLO* book has a whole page of hobbies to try out in the city. A new hobby goal seems a good place to kick things off, a good substitution to my artist-residency dream. A perfect future needs some perfect ways to spend your free time, right? But what else am I into?

And why is that question so surprisingly hard?

With a fantasy that quickly rolls itself into me being asked to be the newest cast member on *SNL*, I rock up to a club down the road from our apartment building to try a stand-up comedy class. How did it go? I don't want to talk about it. And now I have to move.

Perhaps a more silent hobby would suit me better, so the next day I chess-board hop the tables at Bryant Park, my fingers freezing as they move the pieces in haphazard and irritating ways. I don't think I'm going to be the next *Queen's Gambit*.

My hobby could be trying drinks from the place they originated from? And it just so happens that in my journal I have a decade-long goal of sipping a Long Island iced tea in actual Long Island. I sit on a series of trains for over an hour each way, the gentle rhythm, the rolling views expanding my heart and mind, only to find I loved the adventure out of Manhattan, but the cocktail was a little *too* easy to drink for my tastes, so I was super sensible and stopped at one. Okay, two.

I'm flipping through the book again a couple of nights later when River walks in from work, late.

'I'm going to put a pin in the hobby thing,' I tell him. 'Nothing is *me*. But I've been thinking about my "move to New York" goal. I don't know if that's ever going to happen – properly – but I do know I like adventure and travel. Seeing the world was one of the things I loved about being a pilot, but it was also fun exploring Long Island by train. I should have some kind of dream around that, right?'

'Right.' River nods, kicking off his shoes and flopping down on the end of the sofa, immediately pulling out his work phone, which he seems to need to be glued to, even when he's just got in. 'If that's what you want.'

I hold the book aloft. 'Your parents say that visiting new places, even just outside the city, can bring new perspectives. I'm wondering if I need a new place to set my sights on, or live in. Or to do one of those huge treks across a continent that takes three years or something.'

'You've seen a lot of the world, right? Where appeals?'

Hmm. 'I don't know. I do a lot of cities. Perhaps I need to get off the beaten track to find what I want.'

'On that note, I have to go to Vermont for couple of days,' River says. 'It's a work thing.'

'That's positive,' I say, looking up. 'That they've got you going out on work trips again.'

'It's not like that – it's a team-building conference thing, they do it every year when the snow season starts.'

'Nice. Why do you sound like they're making you go to prison?'

He laughs. 'They're just *a lot*. Competitive, showy. I know that sounds ungrateful, and the place – and the state – is gorgeous, but . . .'

River trails off and I ask, 'Is it compulsory?'

'No, but I feel like I should go, if I want to make a good impression. Show I'm still a team player and all that.'

'What's Vermont like?' I'm picturing New England charm coated in icing-sugar snow and maple-syrup dripping from the trees.

'You wanna come?' he asks, looking up at me over his phone. I can't tell if his tone is slightly amused or slightly hopeful.

'On your work trip? With my ex?' I guffaw at the thought. I know Hugh and I have reconnected, to a small extent, but still. Can you imagine how awkward that would be?

But River shrugs at my outburst and looks back down. 'If it's a place you'd like to visit, I don't think you should let Hugh being there stop you.' When I don't respond, he adds, 'But I get it. I'm just saying, you've got a free ride up there if you change your mind.'

'You'd drive? Isn't it a billion miles north?'

'It's about a five- or six-hour drive,' he replies, basically confirming what I said.

'That's a wildly long way for a work trip. Can't they fly you all?'

'They are,' he says, and shuffles in his seat. 'But I want to drive.'

'Why? Are all the seats booked up?' I'm guessing he's a late addition to the trip, due to, you know, getting sent back from Italy and all. 'Does that mean all of you that came back from overseas are driving?'

'No, I'm the only one driving. I just . . .' I see him blush. 'You of all people are going to think this is pathetic.'

'What?'

'I just, well, I don't really like planes.'

'Oh, you have a fear of flying?' I ask.

River squirms. 'I guess.'

'I don't think that's pathetic at all. I see that every day in my job. *Saw* it every day,' I correct myself.

174

He glances into my eyes. 'Thanks.'

'Did you struggle going to Italy?'

'I didn't love it,' he admits. 'But I got through it. I wasn't really expecting to have to do the journey again so quickly.'

'Of course.' I think of him getting back to his flat that evening and how frazzled he was anyway. Now I know he was dealing with a fear of flying on top of everything else. Poor guy. 'So, we're driving to Vermont.' I don't phrase it as a question.

'You're coming?' A smile forms on his lips, his blush fading.

I hesitate. Maybe this isn't a great idea. 'I don't know, you're probably looking forward to a break from me, let's be honest.' Then I remember something else. 'Also, don't you think word will get back to Delilah that two weeks after you split up you snuck a new girl on your work trip and into your room with you.'

Now he's definitely trying to push down an amused smile. 'I wasn't actually planning to sneak you anywhere. And as much as I'm enjoying this arrangement of ours, you know we don't have to share a room?' He holds his phone over to me, a website open on a page showing a snowy vista dotted with little log chalets. 'The hotel, where I'll be staying, has a few cabins on the grounds. You could stay in one of those. They have their own kitchens, their own nature-walk trails. The main hotel building itself is huge – you probably wouldn't even see us the whole weekend. Including Hugh.'

'A bit of space to myself? Hallelujah!' I smirk up at him to show I'm kidding. These do look beautiful though, and I have always wanted to go to Vermont, and I bet there's just a shit ton of maple-syrup everywhere and that sounds like heaven.

But, I don't know. Shouldn't I try and stay focused? I mean, am I likely to decide I want to be a hiker or a log-cabin builder? I reach for my journal and start hunting for any mention of wanting to camp in the wilderness or some such thing, but River interrupts me.

'It's okay if it's something you hadn't yet dreamed up.' He shrugs. 'Maybe that's a good thing. We'll be driving right by the Ben & Jerry's factory, if that sways you in any way?'

I throw my journal to the ground. Why didn't he lead with that? 'I'll get packing.'

## *Chapter 21*

Visit a new place

River and I have been on the road for nearly five hours now, since picking up a hire car at Newark airport. We've eaten two big bags of crisps, ploughed through most of a family-size bag of peanut butter M&M's, I've fallen asleep twice and we've talked about everything from current affairs to celebrity gossip to what our favourite foods were as children.

It's getting dark, being late afternoon, and, outside the window, houses appear between the trees, their porches lit up with Christmas lights, wreaths on the doors. There's a dusting of snow here that reflects the car headlights, and I'm glad we drove.

River's been quiet for a while and into the silence of the car I say, 'You didn't ask, but just to say, if you ever want to talk about your fear of flying, I might be able to help.

Sometimes hearing from a pilot about what all the processes and noises are can be beneficial.' I glance over at River to see his reaction.

He smiles, and nods. 'Thanks. I'll bear that in mind.'

'There's got to be some use to having an ex-pilot living on your sofa, hey? Speaking of which, can't wait to have a cabin by myself for the next two nights.'

I've booked one of the hotel's smallest cabins – a one-bedroom beside a lake, behind the big main hotel where River, Hugh and all of the other work-trippers are going to be staying.

'How are you feeling about the team-building expedition?' I ask River.

'Meh …' he says. 'It's nice to get out of the city, and Vermont kinda reminds me of where I grew up. The countryside, the lakes, the views, the trees. It's good to get away. But it's not the same as getting away on my own. Present company excluded.'

'Feel free to just leave me at the ice-cream factory, if you'd rather.'

'Have you settled on what you're going to do with yourself while I'm team-bonding for forty-eight hours?' River asks, ignoring my comment.

'Yes,' I say, patting the bag of food I bought when we stopped at a supermarket earlier on the drive. 'Tonight, I'm making a big bowl of pasta, I'm going to drink a glass of a wine and I'm hoping to watch the film *White Christmas* if they have it.'

'A classic Vermont movie.' River nods.

'You like it?'

'It's actually my mom's all-time favourite. We used to watch it every Christmas when I was growing up, and I was nearly, so nearly, named Bing after Bing Crosby.'

'No way,' I say, immediately thinking of Chandler Bing from *Friends*. I can just see Meg being a Bing Crosby fan.

He continues. 'I had this whole surprise plan for her fiftieth birthday. We were going to visit Pine Tree in Vermont, stay in the inn from the movie, see where it was filmed, everything. I was this close to booking trains when I realised the whole thing was filmed in LA and the town and inn were fictional.'

'Oh no!' I cry. 'How did you realise?'

'My mom told me. She was like, "Why do you keep talking about Pine Tree, Vermont like it's a real place, honey?"'

'So what did you do?'

'We went to Vermont anyway, got the whole family up and stayed in a B&B outside a small town called Woodstock. It was a great time.' He smiles at the memory. River's a nostalgic chap when he leaves the city, I am discovering. 'Sorry, I interrupted. Just jealous, I guess, that you get to watch *White Christmas* while I'm making small talk over a buffet with everyone I see at the office every single day.'

'The gala dinner isn't until tomorrow night, is it?' I ask, referring to a sit-down meal in the hotel's ballroom where River tells me they'll be handing out awards and free booze. It doesn't sound too bad to me.

'Yep,' he says, taking a right. 'What are you doing tomorrow?'

I dial my seat-heater up a notch. 'I'm going on one of the hotel tours to a maple-syrup farm and I'm going to learn how it's made. Who knows? Perhaps there's maple-syrup farming in my future.'

'Are there a lot of maple trees in the UK?'

'No idea. But regardless, my plan then for the remainder of tomorrow is to come back to my lovely cabin and eat, or drink, my body weight in maple-syrup.'

River laughs. 'Sounds perfect.'

I grow quiet. It's not exactly a step forward though, is it?

'You okay?' he asks.

'Yes ... yes, I am.'

'Tell me.'

'I just have little moments where I worry I'm never going to land on a future as good as the one I had in my head.'

Peeping over, I see his thoughtful eyes on the road. 'I get that,' he says, finally.

'I hope I'm not wasting my trip.'

'I don't think you are. Not at all. I think ...' A passing car's headlights illuminate his face for a moment, his hands on the steering wheel, his knitted sweater sleeves pulled to his knuckles. My heartrate slows knowing he's thinking about me right now. 'It's cool that you were a pilot,' he says, his voice that low, coffee drip that I'm starting to really like. 'You're brave, and adventurous. And those qualities are going to make sure you land on something right. I'm excited to see what you'll do next.'

River's eyes don't leave the road, and mine don't leave his face. How did he know exactly what I needed to hear, right now?

'Thank you,' I say, and I see him smile. Wow, this guy ...

I check Google Maps on my phone and we aren't far from the Ben & Jerry's factory now. Plucking the *New YOLO* book from the side pocket, I flip to the next section, which causes me to shriek.

'What?' River says with a twitch of his lips, glancing my way.

'Did you know your parents wrote date ideas in here?'

He nods, his eyes back on the road, but amused lines crinkling the edges of them. 'I sure did.'

I turn a couple of pages further and gasp. 'And wedding venues? *"Hell Yeah I Do's"*,' I read aloud. I put the book down and turn in my seat towards him. 'Wow.'

'Right?'

After a moment, I ask, 'Do you think your parents wanted you to marry Delilah?'

It's possible I've asked too personal a question (so unlike me!) but River answers. 'I think they just wanted me to be happy. I expect they expected it, what with us moving to Italy and all.'

'She probably did too,' I murmur. 'Sorry, I just mean, Italy being such a country full of *amore* and all that.' I'm on a roll, so I dare to ask the question that's been playing on my mind. 'Is it weird for you coming to this, without her?'

He doesn't take his eyes off the road, and instead just says a simple, 'Yeah.' And a minute or so later he adds, 'But everything is still a little weird without her, to be honest.'

Yeah. I shift the focus of the conversation, bringing it back to me in case he doesn't really want to talk about this. 'I guess I need to replace my "Marry Hugh" goal with something else, come to think of it.'

'Or someone else.'

'I don't know. When I was nineteen it seemed like such an obvious goal, but I've been single for over a year now. I don't know if getting married is, actually, *me* any more.' I've never said this aloud to anyone before. But with River, I'm not afraid. 'But maybe it is! I just don't know.'

'Do you need to know? Right now? Does it have to be set in stone?'

'Well, that's kind of the point of my whole exercise.' I frown, then spot a sign in the darkness. 'Ooh, Ben & Jerry's factory tour, up ahead!'

We follow a winding road until we come to a car park in front of a large building with a big, pink ice-cream cone above the door. It's late, the factory only being open for another hour, and there's no queue to get inside.

Forgetting the slightly serious turn our conversation took, I get so excited I nearly run right past one of those big wooden photo stand-in structures you can put your face through, but spot it at the last minute and force River to tag team with me to get some pics. I've never passed one of those and not stuck my face in, and I wasn't about to start now. Perhaps *that* could be a new goal? Getting a photo in every single one in the world. Something to think about.

River and I follow the thirty-minute guided tour past glimmering machinery, colourful décor and sweet aromas scenting the air. I am more than happy to sample a dollop of delicious ice cream that's offered to us, but on the way out I also buy a loaded sundae, which has ice cream, bits of brownie and cookie and banana swirled in, some hot fudge sauce, some whipped cream, and a host of toppings. A good appetiser before my pasta tonight, I think.

'Want some?' I offer, jabbing my ice cream towards River just as he reaches forwards and says,

'Can I try a bite?'

Our hands knock together clumsily, a blob of deliciousness plopping down onto our digits as we try to hand the cup off from me to him. For a moment, our sticky, cold fingers become entwined, which sounds disgusting, but something about it causes my breath to catch.

All right, just going to wipe my hands with this napkin, busy, busy, nothing to see here.

Back in the car, my breath back to behaving itself, I hold my happy tummy. 'That was perfection.' I smile, in a daze.

'I'm glad,' says River. 'And now we'll be at the hotel really soon.'

He was right. In no time at all – and I don't think I fell asleep again but the clock *is* now showing half an hour later – River is parking the car. We've pulled up in front of a multi-storey building of brown and green, surrounded by pine trees, the hotel and the tree trunks all lit from below so they can be seen in the dark. There are also gas lamps dotted about the car park, and signs pointing towards two different receptions.

River pulls our bags from the trunk. 'I check in inside the main building, and over there is the reception for the cabin.' He points off to the side where a porched log chalet with all its lights on glows with a welcoming warmth. 'I'll come in with you,' he says, zoning his eyes in on mine for what feels like the first time since we hit the road in the morning. It feels intimate, after everything we spoke about in the car, after all the hours we spent together in a confined space.

'No, I've got this.' I wave him away. Perhaps it's time for a little space. 'You go and settle in, and try and enjoy the next couple of days. I'll be just fine.'

'All right.' He hesitates beside the car.

'Thanks for all the driving. And the ice-cream stop.'

'Oh, no problem. Thanks for the company.'

He's dawdling again and it's cold out, chillier up here than it was back in the city. 'Go,' I say with a laugh. 'Eat, shower, schmooze the big bosses, get that life back on track.'

River chuckles out an exhale of cold air, and then we do an awkward one-armed hug, which feels a bit like it's meant to be a reassuring pat on the back, and then I turn and walk towards the cabin reception, without looking back.

My boots clop-clop on the frosted ground as I stride across the tarmac, alongside a verge dusted with a thin sweep of snow, blades of grass poking up through.

Opening the door of the cabin there's a tinkle of what sounds like sleigh bells overhead, and I'm met with the warmth of a heater facing me, and an upside-down view of a polar bear in a hammock. Oh no, it's a Samoyed dog – same thing.

The dog blinks at me, flips over, falls out of his hammock, and plods over to sniff my bag, which I've put down in front of the reception desk.

A woman bustles out from a back room, wiping her hands, and greets me with a huge smile. 'Hey, welcome to Vermont, are you staying with us tonight? No wait, don't tell me.' She looks me over. 'Ashling from the UK?'

'How did you know?' I say, as the Samoyed settles down on my feet.

'You look like an Ashling.'

'Oh.'

'I'm kidding. You're our last guest to check in today so I guessed it was you.' She chuckles and moves towards a beverage vending machine. 'What would you like to drink? Hot cocoa? Cider? A cup of tea?'

'Is it hot cider?' I ask.

'Sure is. Here you go, honey, on the house.'

'Thank you!' The scent of apple and cinnamon fills my nose, and as the reception woman clicks about on her computer, I look around the chalet as best I can, seeing as my feet are trapped in place.

There's a small amount of merch for sale, and a big shelf full of well-loved books, begging to be borrowed. There are net bags containing logs in one corner and a table covered in local leaflets above it.

'I'm booked on the maple-syrup farm tour tomorrow,' I tell her, and she smiles at me.

'That one is so popular. I hope you have a sweet tooth!'

'I definitely do. What time do we go?'

She hands me some paperwork. 'The minibus will leave here at ten-thirty, so you can have a lie-in. Breakfast is either in the main hotel from seven until eleven, or you can buy some pastries from me here sometime after eight. Here's a map with all of the walks you can do straight from your cabin, and you'll be in number five, which is, in my opinion, the best one for real private views over the lake. Which you'll see in the morning. Maybe don't try to explore in the dark this evening.'

'Good plan.' I grin. I definitely won't be heading to the hotel for brekkie. Even though River insists it isn't a secret that he's brought his roommate along with him, I don't fancy chewing on bacon with a view of Hugh lording it up in front of the fruit platters. Nor do I expect he would be keen on seeing me with all his workmates around.

Anyway, I'll be eating my way through those fresh pastries in the morning, thanks.

Reception Lady gets me to sign a few bits and bobs while I sip on my cider, then loads me up with a packet of fresh coffee, the maps, some leaflets, an extra blanket and a bag of logs, and then walks me over to my cabin. Unlocking the door for me, and then calling for the Samoyed (whose name is Cookie Dough) to come back outside, she bids me goodnight.

The cabin smells of cedar and woodsmoke and the flooring creaks as I step through the living space and put down my bags. Lamps and faux candles light the cosy space, and thick, burgundy curtains – already drawn – hang from ceiling to floor, covering windows on either side of the door. A wood burner sits in the corner, with a welcome bottle of wine and wine glass on top of it, together with user instructions. For the wood burner, not the wine. There's a kitchenette, a small bathroom, and a separate bedroom also decorated in the colours of berries.

I stop moving for a second and hear ... nothing. Absolute silence. It's the first time I've heard silence since leaving the UK, I think. Here there are no city sirens, background chatter, flight paths, distant music. I can't hear the main hotel, nor the other guests. But don't get me wrong, it's not eerie. It's serene. The perfect place to get some thinking done.

Or, to curl up in front of a movie.

The wood burner fires up without too much effort, and I'm chuffed to bits to find *White Christmas* available on the TV, as hoped. Despite still being a little full of ice cream, I can't wait, so I unpack, get my pasta on to boil, WhatsApp a quick pic of the cabin to River, change into my pyjamas, and settle down on the soft, soft, soft sofa.

Mmmm. Every muscle relaxes and I am a happy puddle within the cushions.

With only fifteen minutes to go before the closing credits, I feel myself drifting off, the long day and big bowl of pasta getting the better of me. I stretch and squeeze my eyes open and shut a few times to try to wake them up. I'd better put out the fire, just in case. And finish off my glass of wine.

Settling back down again and rubbing my full belly, I focus on the fabulous finale, and then zonk.

Sometime in the night I manage to drag myself into the bedroom and by the morning, as the daylight begins to creep in around those big curtains, I'm curled up, under a pile of duvets in the very centre of the double bed, snoozing like a woodland mouse.

# Chapter 22

I'm circling the lake and eating a bear claw. This is not a grim meaty breakfast, for those not in the know, it's a type of Danish pastry that tastes sweet and almondy, and is frankly perfect paired with a creamy coffee and taken for a walk around an icy lake.

Morning frost coats everything I crunch past – the edges of the red leaves, the scattering of wooden benches, the blades of grass, the iron fences. The snow is a light dusting, just enough, combined with the frost, to paint the scenery a duck-egg blue.

I woke at dawn feeling as soft and supple and rested as someone who'd had an eight-hour massage. Sleeping in a proper bed again, not an albeit-comfy sofa bed, or a dorm bunk, felt like heaven.

River texted this morning, just a quick hello. Later, they're heading off to the slopes in small groups for their day of skiing and snowboarding. I told him to enjoy himself!

Make some new connections! Who knows where that could lead! Switching to a new department could get him past this feeling of having stepped backwards.

But also, what did I know? I know sweet FA about the inner workings of his company, beyond the fact their team-bonding trips are a far cry from an afternoon of crazy golf under the British rain.

Maybe I'll end up in an office. It could be nice. Having my own desk, with a mug that says something quirky about my personality. Maybe a fake plant and a perfectly adjusted swivel chair. Or an office of my own, perhaps, where I can shut the door and secretly catch up on *Selling Sunset* under the guise of being in a super-important virtual meeting.

But picturing it, I just don't quite feel that *thing* you know, that tingle, when an idea clicks with your soul and you think, *that's what I want to do*.

I check the time on my phone and pick up my stride. All right, I've got to pack a bag, throw on a few more layers, and pee at least twice before it's time to head back towards the reception for the tour bus.

'Good morning, folks, how are we all today?' says a mousta-chioed man into a microphone at the front of the minibus.

I'm in the first seat, like a right keen bean, so I have the full view of the countryside we'll be driving through out of the front windscreen. What can I say, you can take the pilot out of the cockpit but you can't . . . take the . . . I don't know, but you get why sitting here appeals to me.

The bus is warm and half full, about seven other people

sitting on the blue velvet seats. I'm on my own, as is a woman about my mum's age. A family of four are pressing their noses against the window and waving at Cookie Dough, who is showing off and rolling in the frost on the verge beside the bus. Then there's a young couple snogging on the back seat like they meant to get on a school bus instead but were too busy snogging to realise.

'Fine, thank you!' I say to the tour guide. 'How are you?'

He smiles at me and answers in a lovely soft American accent. 'I'm good thank you, ma'am. Alrighty, folks, today we're heading east for about a thirty-minute drive through some beautiful countryside and then we'll reach our maple-syrup farm. The kind folks there're going to show you how maple-syrup is made and then how it's turned into all sorts of produce, and they'll give you plenty of samples to try, too.'

'Yes!' I whoop, a little too loudly.

'Afterwards we'll take a drive to some other beautiful spots so you can get out and see a little more of what makes Vermont so picture perfect, before we make our way back here to your hotel sometime in the afternoon.'

The guide, whose name is Jim, sits down in the driver's seat. He's about to pull away from the car park when, beyond the glass, I see a familiar walk, a man who strides with confidence in red salopettes, his hands wrapped around a pair of skis.

*Hugh!*

I duck down in my seat just as he looks over, and I know he's seen me and my fading, but still obvious, peach hair, before I even slide back up and meet his eye. He tilts his head at me from across the car park, a smirk on his face, and I have no defence so just wave as the bus pulls away.

Crap. Crappity crap. He probably thinks I'm stalking him, that I've followed him to Vermont. Okay, Ashling, focus on the scenery. Look at all those nice trees. What lovely thick rows of them.

Hugh wouldn't think I was here for him.

The roads are lightly snow-rimmed. Very nice. And look at that pretty pointy steeple!

Maybe I'll turn my phone off, just in case he tries to ring. Nope. He hasn't yet. Maybe he didn't even see me?

All right. I fidget in my seat and brush thoughts of Hugh away. I'm here to enjoy myself; it doesn't really matter what he thinks. Anyway, River might have already told him I'm here. So what?

Beside the bus window, bright red barns, large and small, match the hues of the leaves fluttering to the ground. I thought it was beautiful last night, seeing the wood-slatted homes decorated for Christmas and illuminated with tiny golden lights, but this is just lovely too.

Who knew this whole world was right outside my door?

With my ex's face fading away from my mind, we dip into a valley and make our way down towards a cluster of red buildings and I feel like I'm entering Sleepy Hollow, although I think that's in New York and actually looks nothing like this. We pass a hand-painted sign stating 'Vermont loves maple-syrup, and you'll love it too! Tasters inside, come on in.'

'Here we are, ladies and gentleman,' Jim says, pulling the

minibus to a stop and standing up. Even the couple stop snogging for three seconds to join in as we all grab our things and put our cameras away, then step out onto the farm.

Is that the scent of maple-syrup on the air, or just wishful thinking?

We're greeted by two women, dressed warmly, who introduce themselves as the owners of both the farm and the maple-syrup business they'll be talking to us about today. They start things off with a bang by asking if anyone wants to sample some maple-candy lollies while they talk, which we all grab at greedily. This maybe is a way to stop us asking questions until the end, since we all stay silent and round-eyed as they talk to us about the perfect sapping environment and harvest time, and take us to see what the trees and the spikey things they shove in them to get the sap out look like.

'Conditions need to be just right – below freezing overnight and above freezing in the daytime – for us to harvest the sap,' says Carly, one of the owners. 'So we usually harvest in the springtime, from February onwards.'

'But don't worry,' chimes in Sam, her wife and co-owner. 'We have plenty of this year's syrup for y'all to try while you're here.'

A relieved chuckle spreads through the group, which is then followed by the continuation of lollipop slurping.

The tour takes us from the woodland into one of the barns, or the 'sugarhouse', where Carly and Sam show us the machines that'll be used in the spring, and sit us down in front of a video about how maple-syrup is made.

'Would anybody like to try some more maple-syrup?' Sam asks, appearing at the end of the video with a tray full of shot glasses filled with amber liquid.

This is so tasty. I might actually be in heaven as we sample a selection of syrups of different grades. I lick every last drop out of each of my shot glasses, before scampering after the others into the shop area, where Carly and Sam make themselves available for questions and help but aren't pushy in the slightest. I buy a big amber-coloured bottle of maple-syrup whisky to give to River as a thank you for driving us up here (and in the hope he'll open it while I'm around because I want some too), and some maple candy to post home to Mum.

Sam approaches me while the family of four are still deciding between maple cookies or maple candy or some of each. 'Anything else I can getcha?' she asks.

'No, this has been just perfect,' I rave, my lips sweet and sticky from the sampling. 'Thank you for having us.'

'Thank you for coming and supporting us.'

'How did you know this is what you wanted?' I ask, as she starts to walk away. 'To run this business, I mean? If you don't mind me asking.'

Sam turns back to me. 'Of course, I don't mind you asking. As a matter of fact, though, neither Carly nor I did know this was what we wanted.' I tilt my head in interest and she continues. 'My father owned this farm and I grew up here, and then I left for college, well, a few years ago.' She smiles. 'Then I moved around a bit, mostly East Coast, I lived in DC for a while, and that's where I met Carly. I brought her home to meet my family and she fell in love with here as much as they did with her.'

'Honestly, it was love at first sight all around, I think Sam was even a little jealous,' Carly says, walking over and giving me another maple-syrup lollipop, which I stick straight into my over-sugared mouth without a second thought.

'Seeing it again but through her eyes make me rethink everything I'd told myself, about how I wanted to live somewhere big and amazing. That was always what I wanted. Then I realised, this is just as big and amazing. We have big trees, big skies, amazing people come visit us. Turns out, this was what I wanted.'

'What we wanted.' Carly smiles then adds, 'Sorry, that couldn't have been cheesier if I tried.'

'Maybe you could make maple-syrup cheese, too.' I laugh with her.

'What made you ask that question?' asks Sam, tilting her head at me this time.

'I'm having a kind of midlife crisis,' I explain. 'Just some things to sort out.'

'You want to run a maple-syrup farm?' Carly says.

'Maybe. That might be a little trickier in the UK.'

At that point, Jim starts to round us up. The family make a snap decision to just buy everything, the snogging couple pack up their PDA and head back towards the minibus, and the other single tourer and myself begin to make our way outside.

'Thank you,' I say to Sam and Carly. 'For the tour and the chat.'

Sam nods, her face warm and rosy against the cold air. 'You'll find your thing, don't worry about it. Just maybe don't assume it's not already in front of you.'

Carly groans. 'This young lady is right, we're going to need to add cheese to our produce, as soon as possible.'

Back on the bus, we trundle away from the farm, our paws brimming with tasty treats to take home. As promised, Jim takes us on a windy, meandering route from the farm to the hotel, stopping by pretty towns and under classic, covered bridges for photo ops.

I don't know if it's the slow pace, the gentle weather or the sugar comedown, but I'm extremely relaxed, my breathing slower, my shoulders soft, my brain very in the here and now. By the time we get back to the hotel and I've said hello to the fluff ball that is Cookie Dough, I lumber my way back to my cabin, where I'm intending to sit with my journal out on the porch and make some plans for the next couple of weeks. But I don't do that. I lie down on my bed FOR A SECOND and fall into a slumber. When I wake, it's twilight, the views from the cabin fading and the frost settling itself back down for the night.

With a stretch, I make myself a cup of the fresh coffee and take a box of crackers and two of the big wool blankets out onto the porch, where I let my imagination see fireflies dancing on the surface of the lake. My journal is already out there, icy cold, a pen beside it whose ink I'm surprised hasn't frozen solid.

I pick it up and open it near the back, where there's a dozen or so blank pages. I haven't added anything to this journal in a decade. But before the coffee's even fully seeped into my soul, I begin sketching in biro the evanescent view before me. The lake, the trees, a line of chimneys with woodsmoke still visible against the darkening air. I use shadow and shading as best I can to add the tiny glows of fireflies.

Drawing used to relax me. This time it feels like it's waking me up.

# Chapter 23

All right, Vermont, you're getting a little too chilly for me now, even under all these blankets. I scoop up my stuff and head back into the cabin to fire up the wood burner, and notice the time. It's soon after six, which means the gala dinner will be swinging away over in the hotel (poor River) and also that Flo won't have gone to bed yet back home in London.

'Howdy, partner!' I greet her, in my best American accent. River really must find me infuriating. 'You weren't sleeping, were you?'

'Of course not,' Flo replies. 'I just got in from dinner.'

'With who?'

'Just a date; it wasn't brilliant. He pulled the whole "you're not like other girls" line and it was downhill from there. I just sent him a PayPal for half the dinner bill and a link to the YouTube video of Hailee Steinfeld's song 'Most Girls'. The sushi was nice though.'

'Oh, you went for sushi?'

'No, we went for a pub meal but that was crap, so I got sushi on my way home and ate it on the bus while I chatted to a group of girls who'd been to see *Hamilton*. Anyway, how are you?' she asks. 'How's *Noo Yoik*? Any good sushi and-or dates?'

'Actually, I'm in Vermont,' I declare. 'On a mini-break.'

'A mini break from your break?'

'Kind of. I'm just here for two nights. This is my second night.'

'How'd you get up to Vermont – isn't it quite far from New York City?'

Erm. Flo knows about my interesting living situation, but she's a very sensible gal and I can't imagine—

'Oh my god, have you taken off on a romantic weekend with Lake?'

'River,' I corrected. 'And no. Well, yes. Well, no.'

'Ashling, yes or no?'

'I came up here with River, but not for any romantic reason. He's here on a work trip. His whole workplace gets taken for a weekend skiing every year, can you believe it? Team building.'

'Nice team building,' Flo agrees.

'So I hitched a ride up and I'm doing my own thing, then will hitch a ride back. We're not even in the same ... accommodation.' That wasn't strictly a lie so it's fine.

'You sound disappointed.'

'No, I don't!'

'I know you, and you do. Are you getting a crush on River?'

198

'Not at all. Besides, I think he's completely hung up on his ex, which is fair enough because they only split up less than a month ago.' I don't have a crush on him. I just like him . . . He's sweet and kind, and he keeps wearing these sweaters that make me want to climb inside. But I won't. 'He's here with work,' I reiterate, to Flo, and maybe a little to myself.

'Wait a minute,' she says, being a wily one. 'His whole workplace? Hugh's on this romantic getaway too? Ashliiiiiing.'

'It's not romantic, and I haven't even run into Hugh yet.' Technically true. 'It's not like I'm trying to be closer to him, it's just . . . circumstances.'

Flo sighs so loudly it's like a gale's whipped past her end of the line. 'I know that, and you know that, but what do you think it looks like to him?'

'It doesn't look like anything,' I say in my most reassuring tone, as silky as today's maple-syrup. 'Neither of us are in that place any more.' I am *not* going to tell her the thing about Hugh pretending to his workmates that he and I were still together.

'Well, just be careful, okay?'

'I will. Now, tell me about you. How's work? How's life?'

'How's your hair?' she asks me, suddenly.

I look in the mirror. 'Right now it's curled and frizzed a bit because of the cold air. And the peach has faded a bit. But,' I shake my hair from side to side, 'I think it's still très chic.'

'Good. When we're off the phone I'm going to tag you in few New York hair-salon accounts I follow that I think'll do a nice job refreshing the colour for you.'

'Thank yooooou.'

199

'All right. My life . . .' I hear her take a seat on her battered old floral armchair, the tell-tale creak of the springs making me smile three thousand miles away.

We chat for a lovely long time and when we're done, I can't summon the energy to go over to the main hotel to find something for dinner, so I make another pasta and whip up a simple sauce out of the olive oil and lemons left for me in the cabin, and take my time over it in front of some sitcom reruns. It's nice to feel like I'm living on my own again. I do kinda miss bouncing thoughts on the TV shows off River though. But no, Flo, that doesn't mean I fancy him.

I'm mid-way through a *Seinfeld* when there's a quiet tap on my cabin door. A tree branch? With the TV muted, I stay still and listen. *Knock-knock-knock.* This time it's louder – a burglar, perhaps? Do they knock? But then comes a soft, 'Ashling?'

'River!' I grin, opening the door. He stands on my porch in the dark, shivering in a dark suit, a tie loose around his neck. His hands are in his pockets and his hair wavy in the frosty night air, like mine. My eyes run over him in his suit, they can't help themselves, and I croak, 'Come in.'

'Thanks,' he says, stepping in through the doorway.

*Pull yourself together, Ashling.* 'Not to sound like a mum, but where's your coat?'

'Back in my room. I just got to the point where I wanted to get out of the gala and so I walked straight out the front door.'

'And came here,' I finished. We blink at each other,

200

perhaps both wondering why he didn't just go up to his own room. 'Warm up.' I jump into action, shoving him towards the wood burner and moving my pasta bowl to the kitchenette. 'You want a drink? Coffee? Wine? I have whisky, but it's, well, it's a present for you, actually. A thank you.'

I hand him the bottle of maple-syrup whisky I bought earlier. 'You got this today?' he says with a smile.

'I did. Congratulations, River, this is your award for being best chauffeur on the East Coast.'

'Thank you, but no more awards.' He groans and unscrews the lid of the whisky to smell it. 'You'll have a glass with me?'

'Sure,' I say. No harm in that, right? 'Did you win many awards? How was tonight? And how was your day on the slopes?'

'The slopes were fun. Tonight was ... it was *nice*. The hotel is great and the food was delicious. And the setting is really beautiful ...'

'But?'

'I could just have done without this one-upmanship atmosphere, which has been going on all day.' He rolls his shoulders and they make a satisfying crack.

'Your work is whoppingly competitive, huh?' I feel a flash of gratitude for my airline.

I've taken a couple of short glasses from one of the cupboards and placed them on the coffee table in front of River, who is perched on the arm of the two-seater sofa. I mirror him on the other arm. It feels a little less ... snuggly ... this way.

'So competitive. And I did win one award, thank you very

much.' He cheers me and we both take a sip, holding eye contact for a second. Because you're supposed to.

The amber liquid, thick and warm and sweet and fiery, burns my throat as it slips down. 'What was the award?'

'Myself and the four other chumps sent back from Italy were given this year's "most accommodating" awards.'

I laugh and then cough on my whisky for a full minute. 'Most accommodating?'

'I know. As if we had any choice in the matter.'

'But also, is accommodating always a compliment? I'm not sure it is.'

'Not when everyone else is getting "biggest money-maker" and "future CEO".'

'Damn.' I shake my head. 'They're not making it easy on you, are they? But ... why are you here with me?'

'I'm exhausted,' River answers, reaching over to splash a little more whisky in my glass before topping up his own. As he does so, our eyes meet again and all I can hear is the crackling of the wood on the fire, and our synced breathing. 'I don't know,' he answers, his voice crackling a little also, and he sits back. 'I think I just prefer spending time with you.'

We both look away and drink from our glasses. Dammit, whisky, you always do this to me. It puts me in a hazy place of confidence and romance and low lighting and slow dances. Must. Not. Start. Slow. Dancing. It doesn't help that River's there all handsome and dishevelled in a suit, swirling his glass, bringing it to his lips.

Seriously, though. I'm reading too much into this. And

even if I wasn't, there's no need to try to move this to something we can't come back from just because of a bit of alcohol and a little goading from Flo and a crackly fire just begging for a make-out session to be held in front of it. I stand up, intending to put some extra lights on when there's another knock on my door. This one is harder than River's, more demanding.

I freeze, and River stands, taking a step towards the door, and I'm caught momentarily by how things have changed. Only a couple of weeks ago he was the one trying to barge into what I now know to be his own apartment, and now he's unconsciously stepping into the role of chivalrous protector, should that burglar from earlier be the one banging on the door this time.

Oh no, it's not a burglar, it's bloody Hugh.

'Ashy,' he slurs through the door. I know Hugh like the back of my hand and he only calls me that when he's a bit pissed.

I roll my eyes at River. 'It's Hugh.'

River puts a hand on my arm as I start to move to open the door, and hisses, 'Do we have to let him in?'

His touch is warm now, like the fire, through my sleeve, and I wish I knew exactly what he meant by that. But my brain can't catch up with the analysis before Hugh wails another, 'Ashyyyyyyy, it's Huge.' Ah, yes, he also calls himself 'Huge' when pissed. 'Let me in, it's freezing out here.'

'I can't leave him out there. You remember how cold it was.' I smile.

But River is glancing around him, a hand tugging at his

203

hair. 'All right. I've gotta . . . I'm gonna just hide.'

'Hide?'

'If that's okay? Is that weird?'

'It's a little weird,' I reply, but then realisation settles on me, my shoulders drooping a little. He doesn't want this getting back to Delilah, and her getting the wrong impression that he's already moved on. He's still in love with her, he wants her back in his life, and we are nothing more than roommates. Despite what this syrupy whisky is having me believe.

'Okay, go in there,' I say, pointing towards the bedroom. God, I hope I haven't left any undies strewn about. 'I'll get rid of him.'

River tucks himself behind the doorframe of the bedroom and I open the cabin door. 'Hi.' I chuckle as I greet Hugh, who's having a little dance to the music inside his head.

He stops and grins at me. 'Just trying to keep warm.'

'What are you dancing to, there?'

'Our song.'

'Adele?'

'No, the Coldplay one.'

Oh, one of *his* favourite songs. I lean against the doorframe, 'Can I help you with something?'

'What are you doing here, Ashling?'

He doesn't ask it with hostility, more with a hint of smugness. Like he knows my game and he's willing to play it. Ah, shit. Have I led him to believe this is something it isn't? I just wanted us to be friends again. 'I'm just visiting Vermont.'

'I think you might be following me,' Hugh stage-whispers.

'I'm honestly not,' I say gently. I notice the porch light come on in the next-door cabin, and a curtain is twitching. 'Come inside, for a second.'

Letting Hugh in, I glance towards the bedroom door but River is well out of sight, and not making a sound.

'This is nice,' Hugh says with a whistle. 'Did River get you this?'

The mention of River nearly throws me. 'Of course not. I paid for it myself.'

'Sorry, I'm only joking.' He softens then and looks bashful for the implication. 'It *is* weird seeing each other again, isn't it? We're an ocean away from where we had our lives together, but here we are. Together. It's just . . . weird.'

'It is weird,' I agree. He's not wrong. He was everything, for many years. And then he was gone. My choice, but still. I couldn't agree more that being back in the same vicinity is a wild old ride.

Hugh's eyes are scanning the inside of the cabin, and his gaze rests on the coffee table. 'Is he here?'

The two whisky glasses. *Dammit.* 'No,' I lie.

'Is he here? I haven't seen him for a while at the gala. Did he come and see you?' His playful smile has drooped.

'Kinda none of your business either way,' I warn him. 'But no, he's not here and he never was.' River doesn't want me to tell, so I won't.

'Who are you drinking with?' Hugh is looking me straight in the eye, and I feel like I've cheated on him or something. It was the same look he gave me when I broke up with him:

incredulous, confused, angry, sad. I feel bad lying to him, but I don't owe him all my thoughts.

'One is an older glass. One is a fresh glass. I just haven't cleared up today. I'm on holiday.'

He's not buying it, and he starts to walk towards the bedroom. Now he's going too far.

'Stop,' I say, moving into the doorframe space in the nick of time. From around the corner, in the darkness, I feel River reach for my hand, which feels both alien and comforting inside my own. I squeeze his to let him know everything is okay, but in my heart, and my head, it's anything but. The connection of our skin pulses with the breakdown of my defences. Oh, man. I think I like him.

Dragging my mind back to the problem in front of me, I say, 'Hugh. I think you should go back to the party. You shouldn't be storming around my cabin. You know that. We aren't together any more, and it's weird, really weird, and I'm sorry I've stirred up all this crap by coming to New York—' not actually sorry about that, tbh '—and then maybe being here on your work trip wasn't the best decision.' That was true, though. 'Now, I *don't*, but if I did have an entire ice-hockey team waiting for me in my bedroom, it really wouldn't be any of your business.'

Hugh seems to consider this, even smiles a small smile, and after a moment backs away. 'Yeah, okay. Sorry. I didn't mean to get all macho man. I actually just wanted to say hi.'

I smile at him. 'Hi, Hugh.'

'Actually, it's *Huge*.'

That makes me laugh. I stay beside the bedroom, my

hand in River's, until Hugh has waved goodbye and shut the door behind him.

River drops my hand, slowly, waiting a heartbeat before he does so, but I can still feel the imprint of his fingers against mine. He comes out of my bedroom, standing close to me, and I'm level with the top of his loose tie.

'Thanks,' he says, in barely a whisper.

'That didn't feel good,' I say. I mean the lying to Hugh part. The hand-holding felt ... well, I don't think I can lie to myself any more about that feeling.

'I know. I'm sorry. I just, shouldn't really be here, I guess.'

'But we're friends,' I counter. Nice cover-up. 'And your party sucks. So, we know it's okay.'

'We do.' River nods. 'And it does. But maybe I should get back to it before I'm missed.'

'Mr Accommodating,' I say with a tut, and I'm relieved when he laughs.

River heads towards the cabin door. 'I didn't ask you about your day.'

'I can tell you all about it in the car tomorrow. You get six more hours of me, then.'

'Looking forward to it,' River says and before I know it, he's disappeared back into the night, leaving a blast of cold air from the door, and a fire in my fingertips.

# Chapter 24

Me and Cookie Dough are having a moment in the car park when River emerges from the hotel the following morning. I'm sure it's just the mountain air and this big scrummy dog that's giving me high doses of dopamine, and the fact he and I are surrounded by the bubble of this Christmas snow-globe of a town, but I can't help but feel a fizz of happiness at seeing my flatmate.

Who am I kidding?

After years of packing, unpacking, repacking and flight times at all hours of the day, I've become a master at gathering my belongings together with military efficiency, and so my rucksack and the remainder of my food are packed neatly and waiting beside our rental car, along with two cups of fresh coffee, courtesy of the lovely receptionist.

'Ready to go?' I ask River with a big grin.

'Ready, set, go,' he confirms. He looks surprisingly upbeat considering the miserable time he was having at the gala last night, back in his casual clothing instead of a suit. Maybe the party picked up after he got back. I ask him about it as we climb into the car (after we've both had some elongated goodbye ruffles of Cookie Dough's snowy white ears). 'The gala was messy and loud and I went to bed early, but I am now happy to be heading home.'

'Poor guy,' I say with a laugh. 'It is horrible of your company to take all of you on an all-expenses-paid ski trip to this horrendous place.' I gesture out of the car window at some of the most beautiful, frosty, piney scenery I've ever laid eyes on. 'Ugh. Wankers.'

'Fair point, you're right, I really can't complain.'

'I'm kidding.' I pull my shades over my eyes. 'Complain all you like. Complaining is a good thing – you need to let out your frustrations so they don't eat away at you and affect your ambitions at the company.' I sound so damned wise right now.

'Was your old company like this? The airline, I mean?'

'No.' I shake my head. 'I'm all talk and actually can't relate, to be honest. Living In The Air is, was . . . a dream to work for.' My words fade out for a moment and I watch the white countryside slide by from behind my darkened lenses. 'A company that really tries to look after you, you know? Even when things get in the way.'

We're quiet until River says, 'Good for you. I mean that, not in a sarcastic way.'

Let's move on to something else. 'So that was Vermont,' I say.

'You liked it?'

'I absolutely loved it. It's over too quickly.'

'Nothing stopping you going back,' he says.

We talk for a while longer, until I think River's heard enough about the nuanced differences between everything maple-syrup that I tasted, and he suggests we put on the radio. I spend the remainder of the journey lulled by a mix of current hits and Christmas music, but something has changed. Not necessarily for him, but I can certainly feel it. A shift in the atmosphere, a delicate snowflake born out of what happened last night. I can't stop glancing at his hand as he drives – the one that held mine.

Was he right, when he said that a new love goal didn't need to be set in stone right now? But love is such a huge part of life. Surely I need to know what I'm aiming for . . .

Maybe I'm just horny right now. Maybe I do need to call Danny the Pizza Guy.

Eventually, we roll into New Jersey and navigate to the Newark airport car-rental depot. From there, we slog back across Manhattan to our home, where I settle in on my sofa bed, draw the drapes, and fall asleep to the now familiar sounds of New York City at night.

I wake early the next morning. Like, wide awake. Might be all those coffees I drank on the long journey home. Might be the nightmare I was having about the Statue of Liberty peering in the window at me as I slept.

Regardless, here I am, pre-six a.m., sitting bolt upright and ready to start the day.

Outside the window, on the still-dark streets of the

Village, is *not* the Statue of Liberty's looming green eyeball, thankfully, but instead are Christmas lights. Twinkling frames around windows, scatterings of bulbs in trees, a twist of string lights surrounding a stoop. I think now might be a great time to start embracing a New York Yuletide.

I get up quietly, changing from my PJs into some toasty clothing, and slip out of the door. Padding down the stairs, I exit into the cold early morning air without seeing a soul.

A brisk walk to the subway and I'm zooming up to Midtown, where I exit at 50th Street Station and walk the couple of blocks towards Rockefeller Plaza.

I see the Rockefeller Center Christmas Tree before I see anything else. Standing at over eighty feet tall and adorned in thousands and thousands of multicoloured lights, she's absolutely breathtaking.

At this time in the morning, I'm one of the only ones here, and I circle the tree in awe for a while, before walking around the edge of the ice rink and taking photos in between the two rows of angels that hold their trumpets aloft towards the tree.

New York's hum and horns and noise seem to be resting at this hour. The soft glow from all the little lights against the black of the sky, combined with the cold air I feel on my lips and cheeks have me singing 'Silent Night' in my head. One of Grooms' favourite songs. That and 'Gangnam Style'.

Oh, Grooms, were these angels here when you lived in New York? I wish I could ask you.

It's late morning at home, in the UK, so as I sit here among the fairy lights and darkness and with a view of the biggest and most beautiful Christmas tree I've ever seen, I give my mum a ring.

'Hi, Mum!' I say as soon as she picks up.

'Hello, sweetheart.' Her voice fills my ear and warms my heart. 'This is a lovely surprise; you must be up early?'

'I am,' I say. 'It's just gone six a.m. and it's freezing but I've come to see the big Christmas tree at Rockefeller all lit up.'

Mum gasps. 'Oh, how magical, I remember seeing that in *Home Alone 2*.'

I pull the phone away from my ear and send her a quick snap of it in all its glory. 'It looks just like your one at home,' I joke. 'Minus a few dodgy homemade decorations from yours truly. So how are you? Merry December!'

'Merry December,' Mum answers and I hear the smile in her voice. 'I'm quite all right, keeping busy. But tell me about you – you're the one living your dream in the Big Apple.'

*I am living my dream.*

I breathe in the icy air, looking up towards the star atop the Christmas tree, the blue-lit façade of Rockefeller Center behind it. 'It's just brilliant. It's brilliant here, Mum. I think I made the right decision.'

'Does that mean you've figured out a few things already?'

'Well, no. But I have been having a lovely time.'

'And is it all very Christmassy?'

'It is. I forgot to tell you – I actually just spent a couple of nights up in Vermont! River took me.'

'River, your flatmate? The one who's friends with Hugh?'

'Yeah, but it was nothing weird,' I insist. 'He was going anyway for a work do and I wanted to see Vermont. Which, by the way, is gorgeous, and I'll be putting some maple candy in the post for you shortly. Anyway ...' Time to move the convo on from River, and from Hugh. 'New York is absolutely beautiful with all of the Christmas lights on. And the ice rinks. And all the shop windows, and shop fronts themselves, are decorated, but I haven't had a good look around yet. How long did Grooms live out here? Was she here over Christmas?'

Mum thinks for a moment. 'I think she was there for a year or so, so, yes, probably. I doubt she would have had the means to be travelling backwards and forwards to the UK so probably just stayed put once she was out there.'

'Do you have any photos of her out here?'

'Just the ones in that old album you used to ask her to bring out. Nothing you haven't seen.'

'Could you do me a massive favour and snap a pic of a few of them and email them to me? No rush. I just want to see them again. It can be your Christmas present to me!'

'Of course, no problem,' Mum agrees.

We chatter for a while as the sun slowly rises and the sky turns from ink to indigo and then brightens, and then I let her go because she's meeting her crush, Madeline, for a festive coffee date, and I can tell she's excited. Since they met at the library about six months ago, and talked for so long they got kicked out, Mum's had a thing for Madeline. Madeline absolutely feels the same.

I amble back to the flat, taking my time, admiring the holiday-themed shop windows along Fifth Avenue while there are no crowds. I think I'm going to enjoy Christmas in this city.

# Chapter 25

*Climb the Statue of Liberty*
*Take inspiration from the past*
*Discover the holidays in the City*

In the run-up to Christmas, New York City is decking all of her halls and ringing every silver bell. The streets are getting busier every day, and festive music pours out of shopfronts, street-corner brass bands and probably even from the steam that rises up from grates over the subway.

I keep myself busy by spending my days searching high and low for my future. Using the *New YOLO* book as a guide, I explore parts of the city I wouldn't have thought of. I look for it in the couples I see getting engaged in front of a Manhattan winter wonderland (do I even want to get married any more?). I seek out exact spots from my old drawings (did I leave any wisps of inspiration behind all

214

those years ago?). I follow in my gran's footsteps, literally, using the beautifully time-distressed photographs of Really Young Grooms that my mum sent through (can I channel her determination and drive for myself?). I climb to the top of the Statue of Liberty and cram myself into her crown and look out for as long as I can, but I can't see my future from there, either.

One day, I'm standing by a crossing, in a spot similar to one in Grooms' photos, though the street signs are blurred in hers. I just stand there with my eyes closed and then someone asks if I'm lost and tbh I'm not sure what to say.

I'm searching all over, dammit; why can't I find myself?

Living In The Air gets in touch from time to time, checking in. HQ have requested a phone call at some point, when I'm ready, to see if I want to discuss any alternative jobs with them. But . . . I know I need to get something else lined up for when I get back. The thought of sitting on a video call and seeing them tilt their heads with pity while they list off a ream of desk jobs that keep me tethered to the ground just feels . . . I sigh at the thought, blowing the image out to get lost among the jungle of skyscrapers.

You know who else keeps getting in touch? Hugh. Just little bits here and there. A hello text, sharing a photo from our past that he 'just came across'. My heart wonders each time if I shouldn't have reopened that door, given how he behaved in Vermont. But also, can't people be friends after they split up? It doesn't have to be all or nothing.

River is keeping busy too. He's got it into his head that he needs to move up in his company, fast, before he ends up just stuck in his old job again for another however many years. He applied for one internal role during Vermont, and didn't get it, and now he's gunning for a promotion and putting in all hours to ensure it's his.

'Will you tell Delilah?' I ask one evening as we're sharing some Friday night take-out, the week after Vermont. 'If you get it?'

'Do you think I should?'

'Definitely. If you want her to know. Do you want her to know?'

Now, I know exactly what I'm doing, even if River doesn't. Ever since Vermont, it's tightened my chest whenever I think of Delilah jetting back to New York for a visit in the new year. What does he feel about her? Could there be a chance, a little, Ashling-shaped chance, that he might be magically over her? And ever since Vermont, every time our paths cross in the kitchen, every time he makes me a coffee in the morning, every time I see him with a loose tie, every time he makes some small joke and catches my eye, every time I imagine our hands touching in the dark of that cabin bedroom, it reminds me that there's a little glimmer inside me that's smouldering away for him.

But he's keeping me at arm's length – I don't know if it's subconscious or not – or whether it's to do with Delilah or his work or just because he's not interested in anything beyond temporary friendship.

'Yeah, I'd want her to know,' River says now.

Booooo.

He continues. 'Just so, you know, she knows I haven't

216

just given up after Italy.'

I nod. 'That sounds like a good idea. It'll be good for her to see you thriving. Maybe you need a fake girlfriend to make her jealous!' *What the actual hell?* I could stab myself with my chopstick for letting that slip out of my mouth. I backtrack. 'No, that's not a good idea to play mind games. Besides, you didn't want to try and *win* her back, did you? Sorry. Also, who would you even use? No, forget that, hahaha.'

River laughs but looks confused at what just happened. 'She actually got in touch yesterday, just to say hi, and to ask about a couple of bill-related things.'

'Oh yeah?' I ask, eager to wallpaper over my weird outburst.

'Yep. I told her about Vermont, and my award.' He chuckles and catches my eye and bloody hell, there's that eye contact again *combined* with a reminder of Vermont. Does he even know what he's doing to me? 'I didn't tell her about the internal job I didn't get. But this promotion could be really good, I think. It has travel around the US, a bit more responsibility, it's a bit more creative, and I'm the most qualified for it.'

'Well then, fingers and toes crossed.'

Maybe my digits weren't crossed enough, because by the end of the weekend, River gets his lump of coal.

'What did they say to you?' I ask, handing over a couple of notes to the vendor for the hot cider I'm buying us. It's a bitterly cold evening but the skies are clear and River returned home after a Sunday of putting in hours at the office with a frown the size of the Grand Canyon. I'd suggested we take a walk to see the world's largest menorah being lit, near Central Park, for the first night of Hanukkah.

'They told me they needed me too much in my current department. That I'm so good at my job and they'd miss me too much to want me to move elsewhere in the company.'

'Oh my god,' I scoff. 'So you're just never allowed to progress because they'd miss you?'

'I think they thought I'd be flattered. I don't know whether they're just trying to sweeten the blow and it's all words, or they really just want me to stay where I am. For ever.'

'And that's not what you want? Just to be totally clear?'

He shakes his head and sips his drink. At that moment, the first candle is lit on the giant menorah, causing a warm, happy celebration through the crowd of onlookers. We soak in the music and dancing for a while, before River asks, 'What would you do, if you were me?'

As I think, I cup my hands around my cup and feel the warmth percolate through my gloves to my palms. 'I don't know. Maybe it's not your problem if your work would "miss you". Maybe that's not your responsibility. So ... maybe if you want to pull your life together you need to let it fall apart first. Speaking as a pro at this.' I wink at him.

River laughs, blowing the steam away from the top of his cup with his breath, and gazing off in thought towards the holiday lights outside the Plaza. 'Maybe,' he says, but

I don't think he's taking the suggestion seriously. 'Thanks, Ashling. You're ... a good roommate.'

Hmm. Not exactly an invite to join him under the mistletoe, is it?

## Chapter 26

*See the skyline from a new perspective*

I'm standing outside Lincoln Center for the Performing Arts, home of the New York City Ballet, which is lit up for Christmas. And I'm wondering if they have an adult ballet class I could take. Something for beginners.

I feel like I can hear the Sugar Plum Fairy music on repeat, seeping out of every window and drifting from under doorways. But I might be imagining that just because of all the Nutcracker posters around. I also don't really know what exactly the Sugar Plum Fairy music is, so it's possibly something else altogether.

My gran is on my mind this morning. Christmas is now only days away, and I'm away from any kind of family, but also my wandering mind is back thinking about finding a new hobby.

*New YOLO* suggested trying a dance class, and something

clicked. Of course! I made jokes about following in Grooms'
footsteps, but what if I, quite literally, am supposed to?

Grooms had big dreams. It can't have been easy for her.
Especially back then. A single young filly (she would hate
me for calling her that) out in the Big Apple, on a quest to
make those big dreams come true. I needed Hugh to help
me out this time, and I couldn't have done it without my gran
herself the time before, but I'm pretty sure she arrived across
the Atlantic all on her own. Standing at Lincoln Center, I rub
my brow as if Grooms' hazy stories will come back to me in
clear colour, as if I'll remember what she told me about her
journey to making it as a dancer in this city.

I know she must have worked hard. I know she must
have been brave as hell. She made her dreams happen, no
matter what, and I want to be able to say I've done the same
with my life.

I'm hesitating beside the fountain in the huge forecourt,
wondering if my gran was a big ol' bag of nerves before her
first-ever class too, and mopping the tiny little tears that have
sidled out through my eyelashes at the thought of Grooms
perhaps hesitating exactly where I stand now, when my
phone rings.

I hold it up to my ear while shielding my eyes from the
winter sunshine above. 'Hello?' I say, without clocking
the caller.

'Where are you?'

It's River. I like that I know that just from three words in
his voice. 'The Upper West Side. Where are you and why
are you calling in the middle of a workday?'

221

'I've got something to tell you. Can we meet?'

He sounds excited, jubilant even. For a moment my heart starts bouncing in my chest. This is it – the movie moment! He's walked out of work and wants to cross the city and run into my arms and tell me he *loves me*. But then I remember he doesn't love me, he most likely still loves Delilah. In fact ... she could be why he's calling with such glee. She's coming home. Or at least back in town. And he wants to meet up to give me notice to get out of his, now their, flat.

'Ashling?'

'Sorry, yeah, sure. I could jump on the subway and see you at, um, Bryant Park? Fifteen minutes?' I'll revisit the dance class idea another day.

'Great, see you there.'

Fifteen minutes later, I'm watching the ice skaters in the sunshine, carving their way around the white-covered rink at Bryant Park's Winter Village, and trying to banish thoughts of Delilah. Look, it's probably something to do with that promotion. Maybe they changed their minds and he got it after all?

'Hey.' I hear River's voice and turn to see him grinning and holding his arms wide.

Are we hugging? What's happening? I don't wait for clarification and jump at the chance to be embraced by him, squashing myself against his chest for a happy moment. 'Hi!' I emerge, looking around for Delilah just in case. I'd only recognise her from one photo and that brief glimpse at the airport, but I don't think it's the nearby brunette with two kids who looks like she's about to scream at the pile of freshly dropped s'mores.

'Guess what?'

Here it comes. I haven't seen him this animated since he finished the Macy's Thanksgiving Day Parade with his old marching band. 'What?'

'I just quit my job.'

'You *didn't!*' I take off my glove and slap him on his outstretched arm with it. 'You quit?'

River laughs. 'Yep. How's that for getting your life together?'

'Well, it's ... it's better than feeling shitty every day.' We look at each other for a moment, and I take in his giddy face, the fact he just walked out of his whole life and wanted to come and tell *me*. 'Congratulations!'

We share another hug and I squeeze him tight. I don't know what possessed him to do this today but ever since I've lived here that job has brought him nothing but misery.

Breaking apart, I point at a structure behind the rink and in front of the New York Public Library called The Lodge. 'Seeing as we're both just pissing about in the middle of the workday now, can I buy you a midday festive drink?'

Once we've navigated the queues and crowds and found an end of a wooden table with a heater to huddle under, I ask River, 'Start at the beginning. What happened today to make you quit, right before Christmas?'

'After that promotion fell through, I'd just had enough.' He takes a sip of his mulled wine and I watch the steam curl up around him, exploring his face. 'Then, you know how I'm going home for the holidays?'

'Of course. You're looking forward to it.'

'Exactly. But today at work, three days before Christmas, my boss says that he needs me and a couple of others to work.'

'Surely that's not ... legal ... or something?'

'Well, it's not a *requirement*, he said, but he made it very clear that those who made themselves available would be looked at favourably for some new project.'

'Oh, what a prick. As if. They're just stringing you along now. You already know this, sorry, carry on.'

He's grinning at me unlike a man who just lost it all, but like someone who just found clarity and a way forward. Thank god. And good for him. And good for me because I like him looking at me like that. 'I was thinking about what you said, the other night, and I just quit. And walked out. Right before Christmas.'

I laugh. 'When you gotta quit, you gotta quit.' I cheers my cup against his. 'So ... what do you want to do now?'

'I don't really know,' River replies. He looks at me a little bashfully. 'Sorry for interrupting your day, I just thought you'd, you know, *get it.*'

'Because my life is a big mess too?' I tease.

He looks panicked. 'No, not at all.'

'I'm kidding.'

'It's because you're going after your own happiness, which is what I want to do, I think.'

'No more "I thinks",' I say. 'Today is a day for "I wills". So let me ask you again, River.' I sit up straight, cock my head at him, and slide a certain book across the table. 'What do you want to do today instead of working at your shitty job?'

River nods, taking in the title and tracing the words *New*

*YOLO* with his fingers. He inhales a deep breath, and says, 'I want to go in a helicopter.'

'Okay, jumping straight in there.'

But that excited look is back, that adrenaline-fuelled, seize-the-day look is in his eyes, and he reaches across the table and grabs both of my hands in his, grinning. 'I'm completely serious.'

Holy crap, he's holding my hands and he's inches from my face. His look is wild and confident. Imagine if he just swooped our drinks out of the way and planted a kiss on me, right in front of all the ice skaters. Calm down, imagination. 'But you said you hate flying.'

'I know, but I've always wanted to do a helicopter flight over New York, and I've always been too nervous. But today I don't feel nervous.'

'Okay . . .'

'Maybe a little nervous.'

I smile and extract one of my hands from under his to take out my phone and start googling. 'All right, so it seems you can get helicopters from down the bottom of Manhattan or over in New Jersey. Any preference?' I've left one hand under his and am playing it extremely cool considering there are fireworks exploding inside me.

Bollocks, he removes his hands to take out his phone, too. 'I found one. It's a company my parents used for their wedding anniversary a few years ago, and I know they're good. They depart from Manhattan, and if we can get there in forty minutes there's space for two. Must be a cancellation.'

I laugh. 'I'm not going.'

'Why not?'

'River, it's at least a couple of hundred dollars per person, and not to sound big-headed, but I've flown planes in and out of cities many times.'

'But you've never done this, right? Besides, it's on me.'

'You're not my sugar daddy.'

He's still smiling, and it's infectious. 'Please come with me,' he says, and leans a little closer. 'I need you there to help keep me calm, Captain.'

Goddamnit, River. Say it again! 'Fine. But I'm not letting you pay.'

'No deal. I want to. I pulled you away from your day of peace, and I'm also going to make you run for the subway.' He leaps up.

'What? Oh!' He's already taken my hand and I don't want to let go again, so with my free one I reach back and swig the last of my mulled wine, and before I can blink, the two of us are racing hand-in-hand down 41$^{st}$ Street to the nearest subway station.

On the train, River tells me a little more about the events of the morning, and how he reached bursting point. His speech is peppered with chuckles, his eyes bright, but the closer we get to the heliport, the more I can sense his nerves kicking in.

'Have you ever flown a helicopter?' he asks me as we speed-walk out of the subway and towards the tour company building. He keeps putting his hands in and out of his pockets, doing up his jacket, undoing it again, tugging on the front waves of his hair.

'Nope.' I shake my head. 'So I don't know how much I can help you with any kind of insider knowledge.'

'I trust you.'

'Thanks, that's a nice compliment.'

'Was it hard being a pilot, as a female?'

'I mean ... not with Living In The Air – they're amazing to work for. But yes, in the wider world it's hard. I'm so proud of what I do ... did ... but I often felt like I had to prove I'm just as capable as the male pilots. Just as able to be in command of a plane. Just as worthy of being there.'

River nods, taking it in. 'That sucks. I'm sorry you dealt with that.'

I smile at him, and at that moment we spin into the heliport. We check in and are ushered to a waiting area where we're directed straight towards four other soon-to-be passengers just in time for the start of the safety briefing. River keeps glancing out of the windows towards the helicopters, but as much as I can tell he's a little jittery, he hasn't lost that determined, excited sparkle either.

We're seated inside the helicopter in a formation determined by the staff, and I'm glad that River is by a window, with me opposite him. Before we put on our headsets, I lean over and talk into his ear, so he can hear me over the whirr of the propellers.

This close, I can smell his aftershave, I could count his eyelashes, but no. Stop it. I push all of that aside and feel the pilot in me wake up, ready to do her job.

I'm good at making people feel at ease in the sky, I know I am. I'm not patronising and I'm always calm. I've even been invited to speak at a few fear-of-flying events in my time. I've got this, and I've got him.

I speak to him quietly, telling him how the helicopter works, nutshelling some of the things I've learned over my years that can help someone like him. As I talk, he smiles, raising his eyes first to the window, then to mine, then to my lips as they talk. Which of course makes me stumble over the last of my words.

We're then directed to put on our headsets, which include huge earphones and a mic, and off we go.

Rising into the air, I do the opposite of probably what all their other passengers do – I close my eyes. Just for a moment. I just want to feel the sensation of being lifted above the world for a minute. My breathing slows, my heart relaxes.

When I flutter open my lashes, we're swooping in a deep curve around the Statue of Liberty and across from me, River is glued to the window. His fingertips touch the glass, his breathing shallow, and as the helicopter levels his hand shoots out to take mine.

I lace my fingers in his; maybe my own heartbeat can travel between us, to calm his. He keeps his gaze beyond the glass, with New York's skyline reflecting in his eyes. His lips curve into a smile, and, without looking at me, he strokes his thumb over mine.

We glide alongside Lower Manhattan, the helicopter humming rhythmically, and the tall slopes and angles of One World Trade Center glint in the sunlight.

As we edge up the island, River leans to me and points

to the streets below. What's he trying to show me? My eyes dart about – I don't want to miss it.

River's fingertips cup my face and move it, so gently, to the direction he wants me to look. Chill out, lips, he's not going in for a kiss. Do. Not. Pucker.

Ohhh! I finally land on what he's gesturing at – it's Greenwich Village, with its irregular and small streets. It's our home. I lift my eyes and beam as he points to me, then himself, then down to the Village below. And then he takes my hand back in his, only this time, it doesn't seem like it's because of nerves.

The flight is fifteen minutes of swooping and sightseeing at its finest. We soar alongside the Empire State Building and although I can't see them from over here in our position above the Hudson River, I know there are people, just like me, atop it right now. Watching the world below, wondering what's next for them.

Central Park stretches itself beside us, long and wintery, before the helicopter turns and makes its way back down the Hudson again.

When we come back down to earth, literally and meta-phorically, River is wide-eyed. After we're led back into the heliport building and have handed back our life vests, he and I exit out into the cold and shelter from the breeze by the side of the building. I approach with caution, touching his arm. 'River, you okay?'

'That was amazing.' He exhales, and I let out the breath I was holding too.

River envelops me in his arms, blocking out the wind, taking my own breath away and pushing my back softly against the building. 'Thank you,' he says into my hair, pulling back and soaking me into him for a moment.

'Thank *you*.' I exhale. We're pressed together, adrenaline having replaced his blood, and the whole of New York City's skyline has disappeared from my thoughts and all I can think about is kissing him.

But the blood returns, his breathing relaxes, he straightens up, releases me, chuckles bashfully, and asks, 'Did you enjoy it? It was all right for you, being up there?'

'I loved it,' I choke out. Did I? I think I did. Where are we? Who am I?

'You were so ... calm up there.' He points to the sky, gathering his words. 'I couldn't have done this without you. Any of this, today.'

'That's sweet of you. But you could have. Of course you could have.' I was calm. Calm and in control, at my most centred.

'I wish I'd flown with you as a pilot,' he says, and he looks completely serious. 'I imagine you were one of the best.'

'Stop it. Or carry on, if you want.'

River laughs, and I mentally shake myself as we head off for a bite to eat while he tells me all about everything we just saw.

After we're done, strolling back up Broadway, River says to me, 'Your turn now.'

'What?'

'Name something you've always wanted to do. Anything. And we'll do it.'

'Oh, I have a whole list of them I've been working on.'

I start to check off a bunch on my fingers. 'Where to start? Get a tattoo, go to university, have a painting in a gallery, get a dog . . .'

I pause in front of a building, which has its door propped open, despite the cold, and a large sandwich board outside, and a smile creeps over my face. 'You'll do anything?' I ask River.

## Chapter 27

Take a dance class

'I want to try dancing, just in case it runs in the family. Maybe all this time I've been destined to be a dancer, like my gran?' I'm chattering to River as we ascend the stairs to the dance studio on the second floor of this small arts centre. 'I was up at Lincoln Center when you called, actually, trying to see if there was a class I could take. I don't know what kind of dancing I might be amazingly gifted in, but this is a start, right?'

'Got to trot before you can gallop.' River sighs, then does a little chuckle at his own joke.

We walked by the studio just in time to join a beginner's foxtrot workshop and though I was instantly obsessed with the idea, River needed a little convincing. But just as I was about to go full-scale guilt trip on him, and remind him he had nowhere else to be, he relented, shrugged, and said, 'New YOLO, I guess.'

Though I'm probably dressed inappropriately for ballroom in my leggings and massive jumper rather than a glittering gown, River looks quite the part in his smart work clothes.

On the polished wooden floor of the studio, those doing male steps and those doing female steps are separated into two lines facing each other. I stand opposite River with a beam on my face. What if I'm such a natural the studio hires me to teach and that's my ticket to living in New York after all?

The instructor starts by demonstrating the male steps, and I watch River concentrate on what she's saying, his feet tapping to the rhythm she's clapping out with her hands. River's line then performs the basic steps three times in a row and then the teacher puts the music on for them. Immediately, River messes up a box step and ends up facing the other way to the rest of his line, but he just laughs at himself, catching my eye and carrying on.

When it's time for the female steps, I feel him watching me. I wish I could read his mind, and know if he's just watching me because I'm his partner in the class, or whether he's watching me for the same reason I was watching him: I can't take my eyes off him.

'Put your hand behind her back,' the dance teacher is saying and I pull my thoughts back to the present moment as River advances towards me. He does as she says, and then slips his other hand into mine.

'Is this okay on your shoulder?' he asks as he lifts my arm into the air.

'Yeah, fine.' I nod. Like I can feel my shoulder right now. God, he's handsome.

Does the foxtrot involve kissing, by any chance? Lots and lots of kissing? With his hand on my back and our bodies close and the music beginning to swell I think it would be a really welcome add-on. A crowd pleaser.

There's little time for talking over the next forty minutes, as we work up a sweat perfecting a series of steps until we can, kind of, dance our way through a whole rendition of *Winter Wonderland*.

I'm loving every second of this, not just because of the now skin-on-skin contact with River thanks to us removing a few winter layers in the process, and him rolling his shirt sleeves up to his elbows. But also, it's fun and light and challenging. However . . . I'm not sure it's my destiny, unfortunately. River and I, collectively, are perhaps the least coordinated in the class, to the point that when the teacher asks everyone to switch partners, she just leaves the two of us together. At first, I convince myself that maybe she thinks we're super cute, then I realise she just doesn't want to inflict us on anyone else.

Oh, but we laughed and we rose and fell and we dipped and we stumbled and we stood on each other's toes and we hid our chuckles in each other's shoulders. For those reasons, I'm glad we gave it a go and knowing my gran, she still would have been proud of us.

After the class, we head back out onto Broadway, pink-cheeked in the cold air, and River says, 'Are we getting tattoos now?'

'No!' I cry, giddy from all the dancing. 'Unless you want

to? Shall we do it? What would we get? Would we get matching ones? No, that would be weird. Weird *good*? Actually, I think I need a drink.'

We agree to shelve the tattoo idea for now and instead hit a bar for a couple of late-afternoon beers, which are much needed, while we recap the day and get our breath back.

Ahhhh. That hits the spot. I gulp my beer and watch him talk. Why does he have to be so easy to get on with? I could talk with him for hours.

When we emerge back onto the streets, it's dark now. The Christmas lights are on all over the city. New York is ready for the holidays in every window, every sidewalk and every awestruck face. And it's cold, it's gone so cold.

'You doing okay?' River asks me after a couple of blocks, and I try to chatter a 'yeah, fine' but it doesn't come out as I become muffled against his chest when he pulls me close to him.

He's so deliciously warm. His chest, at least, the fabric of his wool jacket. But his hands are cold through my sleeves, and I say, 'You're freezing too,' into him.

I'm in trouble. I have fallen for River like a snowflake drifting from the sky, but I know I'll just hit the ground and melt away because I'm leaving in a month, and I'm not the one for him. I know it, even though it makes me sad. I think he's tempted, I think he has a warmth for me, but there have been multiple times now we could have taken this further and he always cuts things short, always. What's holding him back? Is it the ghost of his Christmas past, Delilah, haunting us? Or are we too different, are our lives just too distant?

River pulls back, keeping his arms around me, and I see the Christmas lights reflecting on his face. 'It's been a day, huh?'

'Especially for you. How're you feeling?'

'Free,' he answers immediately, and his eyes click into place with mine again.

But free from what? Just his job, or something – someone – else? I'm about to just come out and ask him what he means, but then he lets me go and starts jiggling on the spot.

'You look like you've just had another idea,' I say. 'What do you want to do?'

'It's two things, actually. Do you ... do you want to ...' He stops and I breathe as quietly as I can in case I miss what he's about to say. 'Do you want to come to mine for Christmas?'

Oh! That wasn't quite what I hoped, but actually ... 'With your parents? And brothers?'

'Yeah, in Saratoga.'

I don't even need to think about it. 'I'd love to.'

'You would? It's just that I thought, you know, otherwise you're alone. Not that that's the only reason, it's not a pity invite, I like your company. I appreciate that I've now ruined it.'

I smile and shush his babbling. 'If you don't think your family would mind, that would be lovely.' Holy crap, this has to mean something, right? 'Um, what's the other thing?'

'The other thing?'

'You said there were two things, that you wanted to do?' Kissssssss meeeeeeee please.

'Have you ever done a marathon?'

'No.' I laugh at the thought. 'Have you?'

He shakes his head. 'I always wanted to do the New York Marathon.'

'Why didn't you?'

'Who knows?' He shrugs. 'I was just thinking that running would be a good way to warm up right now.'

'Where would we run?'

'Home?' he replies, and I try – I swear, I really try – to not read anything into it. 'Where we can order pizza.'

I'm in a heavy coat. He's in his suit. 'Well, we're very much dressed for a run. About as well attired as we were for the ballroom dancing.'

His eyes are glinting and I don't think it's the Christmas lights. 'If we cut over to Sixth all the way up we'd be there in ten minutes, I reckon.'

'Basically a marathon.' I nod. 'Are we racing?'

'No! Yes! Um . . .'

You snooze, you lose, mister. I take advantage of his dithering and go for it, taking off, running up Sixth Avenue. The cold air makes my eyes water, and my coat flaps behind me, but I'm grinning, warming from the inside. I laugh into the night at this euphoric feeling of being free. But I hope nobody thinks River is chasing me and trying to attack me. Just in case I let out a happy 'whoop' and turn my head slightly to see River right behind me.

'Come on, slowcoach!' I shout, my words floating up between the buildings, and his hand grabs mine from behind. We run together, as fast as we can, weaving between other pedestrians, on the busy sidewalks, and sometimes

I'm pulling him along and sometimes he's guiding me, but we're in this together.

We round a corner soon after reaching Greenwich Village, causing me to swing into him with a bump. I was so busy looking at the firefly lights of planes and helicopters up above that I didn't spot that we were changing direction.

We untangle ourselves and River asks, panting, 'What's up?'

'Just looking at the aircraft,' I say, breathing hard, holding a stitch in my side.

'You okay?'

I don't know if he means my side, or am I okay seeing the planes. Either way, I'm okay. I'm better than okay. I'm alive. It feels great to be looking up again. 'Come on,' I say, grabbing his hand again and squeezing it. 'We're near the finish line.'

We run, frozen air filling our lungs, pinking our cheeks, hands clasped, grins wide.

You know that feeling when you've been laughing so hard it's like you're flooded with chemical happiness for a moment? It's the same feeling when you're dancing to your favourite song, or swimming in the sea, or flying a plane, or moments before a kiss.

We tumble into our building, laughing, out of breath, our clothes a mess, wild hair. River heads towards the staircase but nope, I need to catch my breath, not climb Mount Everest. I shake my head, unable to speak, and push him into the elevator.

We have no choice but to stand close in here, his face only

inches from mine as I close the elevator door and push the button for floor six.

The floor underneath me moves and the lift begins its slow and creaky ascent. I close my eyes and let the endorphins and adrenaline soak through my body. I never thought I could feel this way again after my last flight, but, in a small way, running with River this evening, perhaps everything that led to this moment today, woke something in me, like a whispered reminder that maybe joy can be found in all sorts of ways.

I open my eyes and he's looking at me, his eyelashes flickering as his gaze traces my face. His lips are slightly parted and I raise my chin, just a fraction.

We're still catching our breath, our breathing deep, but I feel mine grow slower with his eyes on me.

The elevator reaches and passes the second floor.

I shift so I'm no longer side on to him, and now we're face to face, our lips so close that his breath is on my eyelashes.

We pass floor three.

I reach up to move my hair from my face and when I lower my hand, he takes my fingertips in his. It's different from when we ran holding hands. It's different from when we danced. This feels like when he held my hand the first time, back in the cabin in Vermont, when he was just inside the bedroom door and I was just outside. This is unmistakable. This is electricity.

The fourth floor glides past.

I'm aching in my whole body for him to make a move, for him to be the one to reach for me. I need to know he wants this like I do.

River shifts in the tiny space, his movement causing my back to press against the wall of the elevator. He swallows and it's like slow-motion as his fingers entwine more with mine, tightening our grip together.

He looks at my lips as if he's being drawn to them, and we pass the fifth floor.

River brings his other hand up and places it on the elevator wall behind my head. I use my free hand to tug on the edge of his coat softly, asking him to lean in.

He leans in. And the lift judders to a stop.

Our lips, which were so close, are momentarily jerked away from each other but River moves his hand from the wall to my neck and in his dark eyes I know this is about to be it.

Finally. I want this. He wants this.

Until our bubbled silence is punctured with the lift door grinding open and laughter echoing down the hallway. Laughter that I know.

River drops the hand of his that's touching my neck but with his other hand keeps hold of mine, and leans out of the elevator to look down the corridor.

'Hi!' he says, his voice cracking. He clears his throat, lets go of me, and steps out from the lift.

## Chapter 28

'Hey, is Ashling with you?'

I hear Hugh's faux-jolly voice before I've even come
back down to earth and stepped out of the elevator. I take
a breath and tuck my hair behind my ears, before following
River out into the hallway a second later. 'Here I am,' I say,
and then my eyes move to who's standing beside him, and
I yelp. 'Mum!'

'Hi, honey!' my mum says, here in my hallway, rushing
towards me and catching me in a hug.

'Mum,' I repeat, my heart still thumping, my cheeks still
pink, my fingers still tingling. I yank myself back to the
present and a huge smile takes over my face while I say
'Mum' for the third time, and hug her back. 'What are you
doing here?'

Mum steps back, her hands on my arms, and smiles.
She looks cosy, bundled up in what looks like a brand-new
puffer jacket and walking boots, a midnight-blue woollen hat

dotted with sequins and a matching pair of gloves. 'I thought I'd surprise you for Christmas.'

'Oh my god,' I say. 'I can't believe you're here.'

A flicker of worry suddenly clouds her face and she looks from me to River to Hugh. 'I hope you don't mind. I assumed you'd be by yourself, but maybe I should have asked—'

'No, Mum, this is the best present ever!' I squeal. I turn to River. 'Mum, this is River, my, um, he's the guy who owns this flat and he's letting me stay. River, this is my mum, Joanie.'

I meet River's eyes for a second and try to convey everything to him all at once: *I can't come to yours for Christmas, I don't know why Hugh's here, I wish we kissed.*

Maybe it's wishful thinking, but the eyes that meet mine are warm and understanding, and then they focus on my mum.

'Hi, good to meet you,' he says, taking her hand and shaking it in both of his.

'I hope my daughter's not too messy around your flat?' Mum asks.

River laughs. 'Not at all, I've really enjoyed having her stay.'

'Let me guess, she transformed your whole flat to better suit her within the first twenty-four hours?' she teases.

'Of course I did,' I say. 'Come in and see what I've done with the place.'

'Ooh, yes, please,' says Mum.

River steps between Mum and Hugh and pulls out his key, and I see Hugh tense.

'Where's all your stuff?' I ask, looking around for suitcases.

'Well, I'm actually staying in a hotel up by Central Park. It's a gorgeous big room with two queen beds, and I thought maybe you could come and stay there with me over Christmas? A little holiday for both of us? Or if you'd rather not we can just do things together in the daytime.'

'When did you arrive?' I ask, and all four of us step in through the door of the flat.

Mum looks around, her face happy. 'This afternoon. I did try to call but didn't get an answer.'

Shit, I've been so on-the-go with River today I haven't even looked at my phone since before the helicopter ride.

Mum continues, 'So I got some directions from the hotel, hopped on the Underground and here I am. A nice lady from downstairs let me into the building and when I realised nobody was home, I called Hugh, just to check in case he knew if you'd actually gone away for a few days or something.'

I bite my tongue to stop myself from correcting Mum that even if I was, Hugh and I aren't in regular enough contact that I would have told him.

'You navigated across the city on the subway by yourself? You've never even been to New York before, Mum.'

'I managed just fine,' she says with a shrug. I am so bloody proud of her.

Hugh jumps in at this point. 'I wasn't going to let your mum wait around on her own, and I'd finished work for the day, so I came to keep her company. It's so nice to have a catch-up, and I've been telling her all the things she should do while she's in town.'

'Oh, it's been lovely,' Mum coos.

'Speaking of work,' Hugh faces River, who's lost in thought beside the door, 'heard you got fired today, River, mate.'

'Oh!' Mum's eyebrows whoosh up her forehead.

'I didn't get f-fired,' River stutters. 'I quit.' He looks at my mum as if he should offer an explanation. 'I've been at the job a long time and it wasn't for me any more.'

'Okay, well, good for you,' Mum answers.

'Let me take you for a drink,' Hugh says to River, and it sounds more like a statement than an offer. 'Let's leave Ash and Joanie to catch up.'

'Sure.' River nods. He hasn't even taken his coat off so he opens the door and gestures for Hugh to go ahead, but turns to me first, his eyes locking with mine. 'Are you ... will you be ... I'll be heading to my folks in the morning so shall I say Merry Christmas now?'

'I'll stay here tonight,' I rush to say. 'Mum, if that's okay? Then I can gather a bag together and come to the hotel in the morning?'

'Perfect.' Mum beams.

'So I'll see you later,' I say to River.

'See you later.' He nods. 'Pleasure to meet you, Mrs Avalyn. If you're not here when I get back, Merry Christmas. I hope you have a great stay.'

'Thank you,' Mum says, touched.

Hugh leans back into the room. 'Bye, Joanie. So good to see you. Shout if you want a coffee or anything while you're here.'

'Bye, Hugh.' She waves. When the door closes behind the two men, Mum says, 'What a lovely, handsome chap.'

244

'Hugh?' I query, furrowing my brows.

'No, River. Hugh's a bit of a kiss-arse.'

That makes me laugh and I let confused thoughts of near kisses with River melt to the side to focus on the fact my mum came to New York to spend Christmas with me!

'Fancy a mulled wine?' I say, picking a bottle I bought earlier in the week off the side.

'Yes, please,' she says.

'Or do you want to go out? Are you hungry? I know a nice pizza guy?'

'I am absolutely exhausted. All I want to do is stay in, spend time in your New York apartment, share a bottle of mulled wine and hear all about how things are going. Most importantly, hear what's really going on with your "flat-mate".' She uses air quotes on the final word.

I'm just going to slide along like I didn't hear that last part. I busy myself pouring the wine into a saucepan and turning on the tiny hob, finding a couple of mugs, getting the pizza menu up on my phone.

'Ashling?' Mum prompts.

I hand my phone to her. 'I don't know what you mean!'

She peers at the menu. 'All right, I suppose I have a few days to get all the information out of you.'

'How long are you here for?'

'I leave very early in the morning on the twenty-seventh.'

'You're here right through Boxing Day!' As the wine starts to warm, I motion for Mum to sit down on my sofa bed and I join her, tucking my feet under her legs to keep them warm, like I always have. We spend a few moments chopping and

changing our minds over the pizza menu, and I end up order-
ing three – a four-cheese and a barbecue chicken for me and
Mum to share, and a Hawaiian for River, in case he's hungry
when he gets home later.

I climb back off the sofa and head to the stove, sloshing
steaming mulled wine into two big mugs, the aroma of cinnamon and spices filling the cosy space. I bring them back
over to Mum, who's shuffled down the end of the sofa and
is leaning forward, looking out the window.

'Look, I think that's the Empire State Building.' Mum
points. 'It's all lit up in blue and white!'

'It is, and it's lit that way in celebration of Chanukkah
this week. I sleep out here and I get to look at that building
every night before I drift off.' I pat the sofa. 'This turns into
a bed, and look, I strung up bedcurtains.'

'You sleep in the living room?' Mum's brow creases.

'I promise it was my decision,' I explain. 'River was insist-
ent I took the bedroom but I just loved sleeping beside
this view too much. And I won the argument, of course.'
Mum chuckles, and I clink my mug against hers. 'Merry
Christmas, Mum. Thanks so much for coming out.'

'It's my pleasure,' she says, and her face is lit up like the
Rockefeller tree. 'It's quite exciting, isn't it? New York City.'

'Especially at Christmastime. I've just . . .' I trail off, looking for my words. My heart is still bouncing from today, from
this evening, from River, from Mum surprising me. 'It's the
most magical place I could be right now.'

Mum is studying me, the steam from her mulled wine
misting the window beside her. 'I think you might be right.

You seem content. Do you feel like you're figuring out a few things?'

'Oh, sure,' I say, waving my hand. 'Kind of. I'm sure everything will click into place; I've just been keeping myself so busy.'

With a nod, Mum takes a sip and briefly closes her eyes. I take the moment to Bluetooth my phone to River's speaker and start a soft Christmas playlist for the background. Mum opens her eyes at the sound of Judy Garland singing 'Have Yourself a Merry Little Christmas'.

'Tell me about some of your favourite adventures since you got here,' she says.

Time slips by as my mum and I chat into the evening over mulled wine and hot, mozzarella-stringy pizzas. She even met Danny the Pizza Guy! She thought he had lovely hair.

I prattle on, reliving Vermont, Macy's Thanksgiving Day Parade, how I watched *You've Got Mail* on a rooftop, the time I looked out of Lady Liberty's crown. I sprinkle in details I omitted over the phone, and add descriptions of the people I've met so she gets the full flavour. She then talks to me about life at home and when she decided to come out here to the US, which was after I called her from beside the Rockefeller Christmas tree.

'I dithered about for a couple of days, of course.' Mum laughs, cheeks and lips maroon from the warm wine.

'Of course.'

'It's not exactly my comfort zone to leap on a plane with only a couple of weeks' notice. But Eric told me to stop being so stupid and "be more like our daughter".'

'I will send extra festive vibes over to Eric.' I grin. Well done to my brave mum. 'What do you want to do while you're here?'

'Everything they do in the Christmas movies,' Mum says, her smile bashful.

'You want a full-on New York City Christmas?'

'With bells on.' She nods, and then the biggest yawn in the universe pops out of her mouth.

'Oh, Mum, you're all jet-lagged and it's so late for you; I didn't think!' I stand up and start gathering together her coat and gloves. 'Let's get you back to your hotel and we can start fresh and festive in the morning.'

Mum gets up and rolls her shoulders. 'That sounds like a good plan. Remind me which direction I walk for the subway?'

'Absolutely not, you're not going on your own.'

'I got here on my own, didn't I?' she answers, pulling on her woolly hat.

'Yes, but I'm here now, plus it's late. I shall escort you. And we'll treat ourselves to a taxi.'

'A yellow taxi?'

'Why not?' I laugh, and climb back into my own coat, a memory of running through the dark streets with River flashing into my mind. I send him a quick text to let him know I haven't left for the night, that I'm just taking Mum to her hotel, and then we head out the door.

'Does Carrie Bradshaw live around here?' Mum asks as we descend the stairs.

'You know who Carrie Bradshaw is?'

'Of course, I've been watching *Sex and the City* since you came to New York.'

We exit the building into the frosty night air, and New York, like us, isn't sleeping. I hail a passing cab and say, 'In the show she lives in the Upper East Side, but her apartment building they filmed in front of is near here.'

In the taxi ride towards Central Park, I see my mum's eyelids drooping, even though she keeps forcing them back open to watch the Christmas lights whizz past the windows. I drop her off with a hug and a promise to be back in the morning to take her to breakfast.

'Night, Mum.'

'Goodnight, honey.'

I hold her tightly. 'Thank you.'

She whispers, 'Merry Christmas.'

As the taxi back to the Village nears my apartment block, I'm glowing inside at the thought of seeing River. He'll be home by now, surely. Will we pick up where we left off? Will we have tonight together before we spend Christmas apart?

It would have been lovely to have gone to Saratoga with River for the holidays. To see his parents again, to meet his brothers, to see somewhere new and to spend more time with him. But I wouldn't change my mum being here for the world. At least he and I have tonight.

'Thank you,' I say, paying the driver, and I take off up the stairs.

Entering the apartment, all is quiet. I stand for a moment, and check the time on my phone. Ten. Maybe River is still at the pub.

Then I see the pizza box on the side and lift the lid, to see just a quarter of the Hawaiian pizza remaining, and a note beside it that says 'Thank you' together with a tiny heart. I step towards River's bedroom door.

'River?' I whisper, then whisper just a little louder in case he's only a little bit asleep. 'River?'

There's no answer and I step back, disappointed.

He has had a huge day – quitting his job, flying in a helicopter, learning to foxtrot, having to endure drinks with Hugh. He's probably shattered. Still, though, couldn't he have stayed awake long enough to kiss me goodnight?

# Chapter 29

'River?' I wake with a start to a pale blue dawn outside the window and a rustling outside my bedcurtains.

'Sorry,' he whispers.

I pull the curtain back to see him dressed, already in jeans and a knitted jumper, his coat over the top (the coat I pulled in towards me), stuffing a couple of books from the bookshelf into a holdall. 'You're leaving already?'

He stops and straightens, looking at me, in all my half-asleep, crumpled glory. 'Yeah. I have to get to Grand Central for my first train; it's an early one.'

'But, what about . . .' What about what? Us? 'How was the pub, with Hugh?'

River studies his open bag. 'Fine,' he answers. 'How's your mom?'

'Great.' I rub my eyes and step off the sofa bed. I bet my morning breath would be a massive turn-on right now, perfect for a first kiss. 'Can I make you a coffee or something? To go?'

'No, it's okay.' He zips up his holdall and turns for the door. 'Thanks for yesterday, for the pizza. And for, you know, the fun day.'

He's not looking at me. 'It was fun, wasn't it?' I smile, and move into his eyeline.

'Alrighty, Merry Christmas. I'll be back in a few days.'

What the hell? 'Merry Christmas, then.' Dammit. I meant that to come out sharp, feisty, a voice that would snap him out of it, but instead my forlorn voice snuck in at the last second. But he finally looks directly at me. I square my jaw and meet his eye. I want him to know that I didn't imagine what nearly happened between us last night.

Seconds pass until something struggling in him seems to resign itself. With a sigh and a tilt of his head, there's an unspoken beg to let it go, and he reaches for the door handle. 'I have to catch my train.'

'Okay.' I nod. 'I'm sorry I'm not going with you.'

'Don't be sorry about that. Have a great time with your mom.'

I take the door from him and hold it open and as he passes me, his knuckles graze my bare arm and he gives me a final look out of the corner of his eye.

I lean back against the closed door. Where was the free, happy, daring guy of yesterday who came this close to kissing me up against the wall of the elevator? Or even, where was the shy friend from before who made silly jokes and held my hand in the dark in Vermont?

Maybe I'll find out by New Year's. Right now, he's getting on a train, and all I can do is let him go.

'All right,' I say into the silence of the apartment. 'Forget about him. Time to show Mum the merriest Manhattan Christmas.'

Sliding my sofa bed back into place, taking a quick shower, getting dressed, packing a few things into my rucksack, taking the rubbish out to the rubbish shoot, and I'm ready to leave the flat for the holidays. On my way out of the door I pause to look at one of the photos of River.

'Bye,' I whisper, picturing him boarding his train. My gaze flicks to the photo with Delilah in. I wonder if she knows she still has a hold on his heart.

I meet Mum in her hotel lobby, where I'm trying to get an artsy photo of the big gold Christmas tree's baubles without my nose or fingers fisheye-lensed in their reflection.

'Happy Christmas Eve-Eve!' she says behind me. She looks as fresh as a daisy, or maybe as fresh as a sprig of holly, to be more festive. I clock that we've both worn jeans and bright red sweaters today, so we look a bit like a walking holiday card, but I don't mind one bit.

'Good morning.' I hug her. 'How did you sleep?'

'Like a million bucks,' she says with a laugh. 'Come see our room.'

She bustles me towards a lift, which is about four times larger than the one in my apartment block, and snow white. It also doesn't crank and groan its way between floors and instead pipes a nice *swishhhh* sound as it rises up the building, which is very lovely but doesn't give much time for if you have a suitor in there whom you're trying to canoodle with, should you want to. I'm feeling a little fond of the crappy old lift in the Village now, despite what happened this morning with River.

When we reach the eighteenth floor, the lift doors open to a long white and cream corridor, where very quiet seasonal music is being played out of speakers I can't even see, and bright red poinsettia plants decorate side tables between every few doors.

Mum swings open the door to her room with pride, and I'm faced with a view of Central Park. The window is narrow and tall, and Mum's pulled the curtains right back so the space is flooded with yellowy morning light. The queen bed closest to the window has crumpled sheets pulled back over, an open copy of the *New York Times* lying in the centre, and a used coffee cup sitting on a saucer on the bedside table. The other bed is neat and tidy, its covers still tightly tucked in, and Mum takes my rucksack from my hand and places it atop.

'I hope you don't mind that I've got the window bed,' she says. 'I've been awake since five so a nice lady from Reception brought me a drink and the morning paper. I've been just lying here and watching all the morning colours over the park.'

'It's beautiful,' I say, spotting the frost coating the grass down below, giving the park an almost minty hue from way up here. 'Besides, my bed's closer to the loo and I wee more in the night than you do.'

'Well, I didn't want to say . . .'

I clap my hands together and grin at my mum, ready to begin our festive fun. 'Hungry?'

She smiles back at me. 'Starving.'

*

254

Half an hour later, we're sat in a pretty café near the edge of the park. Mum's practically ordered one of everything on the menu.

'Do you think I ought to get a bagel?' she asks as she's pouring maple-syrup on her pancake stack, one eye on the table next to ours who are being brought their plates.

'No, I think you're good,' I say, cutting a wedge off my French toast. 'You're here for a few days, we'll make sure you sample everything you want. Any thoughts on what you want to do today, or shall I simply whisk you off on a tour?'

'I'd love to go ice skating,' Mum answers without even pausing for breath. 'If that's okay. That's the only thing I really, *really* want to do. Everything else I'll leave in your hands. Apart from Christmas Day – I've got that sorted.'

'You have?'

'Yes. But today, and Christmas Eve, and Boxing Day you can take the reins.'

'Except for ice skating.'

'Yes, please.'

I was not expecting Mum to want to ice skate. I don't think I've ever heard her mention skating before in my life. Even when I used to go as a teen, she'd always want to sit at the side and watch.

'You're wondering where my love of skating has risen from,' Mum says, pronging some banana from her açai bowl onto her fork. 'I'll tell you. *Dancing on Ice.*'

'The TV show?'

'This winter I want to be able to watch it and think, yes, I know exactly what that feels like.'

That's my kinda logic. I nod my head. 'Skating it is. We've got Rockefeller, Bryant Park, Central Park—'

'That one, Central Park, the big one with the trees all around and the skyscrapers watching you.'

'Central Park's Wollman Rink it is.' I gesture at the table-ful of food still in front of us. 'Get your skates on.'

## Chapter 30

Mum's a bloody natural, whereas I, who has spent a fair amount of time on ice skates during my nearly thirty years on this earth, am flailing about like I've had seven G&Ts (I haven't).

My mum glides past me as I move, sloth-like, around the circumference with my knees bent into right angles and my arms stretched out in front of me as if I'm reaching for the light at the end of the tunnel. She keeps twirling her hands and wrists in time to the Mariah Carey Christmas mix playing over the speakers like she's putting on a show for the *Dancing on Ice* judges, and I'm a little bit jealous, but mostly impressed.

'I know what you're doing,' Mum says the next time she passes me, and I have to wait until she laps back around again to call after her,

'What do you mean?'

She curves around the rink again, her short hair tickled

by the breeze she's creating, a vista of New York skyscrapers behind her, and her lipstick matching her red sweater in a way that would make Mrs Claus proud.

Mum comes to a stylish T-stop beside me and we take a break, her perching with her hand on her hip, me draped over the wall with my legs spread apart under me.

'You're thinking so hard about getting to an end goal that you're letting the whole experience pass you by.'

'End goal?' This feels pointed, and Mum is quiet for a while, letting her point sink in.

I listen to the whooshes of the other skaters, the chatter and laughter filling the cold air. But isn't the end goal the whole point?

I'm about to ask as much when Mum continues, 'You want to be "A Good Skater" again, and you want to get there now. But the reality is, you've forgotten a few moves. It's not going as planned. You aren't perfect. Does that mean you can't enjoy it?'

'No . . .' I say after a pause.

'Maybe it isn't all about the end result. Maybe it's just about falling in love with something, or someone, and living it. Now hold my hands, and just relax. And don't be afraid to fall.'

'That's very easy for you to say, you're out there looking like Michelle Kwan. How'd you pick it up so quickly?'

Mum shrugs. 'Maybe the arts are just in my genes.'

I smile and take her hands, and we laugh like Christmas bells as Mum guides me around the ice, acting like one of those plastic penguin aids they have for kids on skating rinks.

If Grooms were here, she'd be doing exactly what Mum's doing – relaxing into it, not trying to be perfect, and then ultimately having fun.

Standing up straight, ish, I force myself to let go of Mum, move a little faster, and to breathe. In truth, I am worried about falling, about hurting my shoulder again. But what am I going to do? Wrap myself in cotton wool and never travel faster than walking pace? That's not me.

Mum appears again and takes my hand, which makes me shriek and wobble about for a few moments, but I catch myself and all is well. Before I know it, we're singing our heads off to Wham! and having a merry old time. Mum's definitely going slower than she needs for me though.

Once we've had enough, we hobble on blistered feet back across the road to the hotel to shower off our sweaty bodies and freshen up before the next adventure.

'Feeling festive yet?' I ask Mum as we lie on the top of our respective beds, our limbs akimbo.

'So festive,' Mum says. 'That was a lot of fun this morning.'

'Thanks for the idea. And thanks for helping me.'

'What are mums for?'

I wonder about River at that moment, if he's made it home yet and is with his mum and dad, or whether he's still sat on a train, looking out the window, waiting to reach the place he grew up, somewhere near Saratoga Springs, perhaps thinking about me?

Making myself sit up before I fall asleep on this heavenly bed, I turn to Mum. 'Do you want to do any shopping while you're here? I would have thought things would be open over the holidays, except maybe Christmas Day, but perhaps we should go this afternoon if you want to?'

'That would be fun,' says Mum. 'I don't need to buy much but I like looking at Christmas windows. Does New York do Christmas window displays?'

A happy laugh escapes me. 'Yep, I think I can find us one or two ...'

We spend the rest of the daylight hours joining the masses doing their last-minute Christmas shopping. To be honest, most of the time nowadays I do my Christmas shopping online, avoiding the rush of the stores. But this year I'm not minding the bustle of people on the pavements, the *dingalingalings* of cash registers, the dazzling decorations inside every store. It makes me want to carry my own armful of brightly coloured shopping bags and spend two hours deciding between a crystal ornament or a copper lamp for second cousin Fanny.

'Do they have the gloves in extra-large?' somebody calls out to a person the next concession over in Saks Fifth Avenue, hollering in my ear as I pass.

'I don't know if she was really saying she liked the earrings, or just wanted me to shut up,' says another voice, leaning over a jewellery counter in Tiffany's.

'Archie, *be careful with the gifts*,' hisses a woman whose little boy nearly clobbers Mum with his giant brown Bloomingdale's bag.

Mum is pressing her face against so many festive window displays she's probably leaving her nose prints all across

Manhattan. The bigger and more extravagant the better, and if they have light-up bits or moving parts, she's in heaven. And I get an idea for what to do that evening.

'This place is famous for its Christmas lights,' I explain to Mum as we board the coach outside our hotel. My breath is visible, white puffs against the cold night air. 'It's called Dyker Heights, in Brooklyn, and it's an area where the residents go all out. I've heard it's amazing.'

'It must be pretty special if they do tours there,' says Mum, climbing into a soft seat and murmuring hellos and merry Christmases to our fellow passengers.

The drive to Brooklyn takes a while, and New York at night passes us while we watch out the window. We roll through the suburbs, passing tree-lined streets and houses with porches with wreaths on their doors. Where would I have lived, if I'd fulfilled my 'moving to New York' dream properly? If I'd packed up my life in the UK, not been on a time limit, employed by someone sponsoring me to live here? Would I have stuck to finding a home in Manhattan, an apartment in one of the neighbourhoods I now know well, or would I have chosen somewhere like Brooklyn, accessible to the city but quieter, with a little more space, maybe a garden?

This sliding-doors version of my life plays out in my mind and thoughts of River float back in. Would he and I have ever met? Bumped into each other at a diner? Caught eyes at Macy's Thanksgiving Day Parade? What if he'd done a Dyker Heights tour and stopped to take a photo of the choir of inflatable singing Santas on my front porch right as I stepped out the door?

'Here we go, ladies and gentlemen, get your cameras ready,' says our tour guide. 'We'll cruise some of the streets for a bit, slowly, then there'll be an opportunity for you to get out and have a walk around. Please respect the properties, these are people's homes, and enjoy.'

The coach glides up and down the avenues and now we're all creating nose prints, blinded by the magical mix of a million lights strung up and over roofs, threaded through trees, coating walls and porches, circling windows. Illuminated animals frolic on lawns, lit-up Santas dangle from chimneys, ten-foot nutcrackers and singing angels wave mechanically at the passers-by. Oh my god, it's brilliant.

We step out of the warmth of the coach onto the street and though I swear the houses are radiating enough heat from the bulbs that I can feel it, Mum and I do snuggle into our coats, hats and scarves to shelter us from the wintery evening.

'What do you think?' I ask Mum, as we stop for a full five minutes outside one place just so we have enough time to take in the multitude of decorations.

'I think it's wonderful, a real winter wonderland, isn't it?' she replies. 'You know who would have loved this?'

'Grooms?' I smile. 'She would have absolutely flipping loved it.'

As we continue strolling, taking photos, taking it all in, I link Mum's arm, keeping her close, and tell her, 'I'm glad to be seeing this with you.'

# Chapter 31

Mum is snoring in the other bed. It's gentle, like a soundscape on a sleeping app, and it's quite nice to hear her beside me, peaceful.

It's sometime in the night, around two-thirty, I think, and I don't know why I'm awake. The room is quiet, except for the snoring. The curtains are thick, but there's a pale blue illumination thanks to the power light on the TV.

And I'm just lying here trying to focus on Christmastime and not think about the fact that I go home in a month and have yet to come up with any kind of plan with regards to what happens when I get there.

Where do I live?

What job do I get?

Why do I have to keep thinking about River when I won't even see him again in just a short number of weeks?

Why didn't I spend more time with my gran while I had the chance?

What does my future even look like?

Am I lonely?

Over in the bed my mum shuffles and props herself up to take a sip of water from her bedside table and I keep as still as a contestant on *Squid Game*. Mum's snores crescendo again within minutes and I smile – she deserves to sleep well. Jet-lag will have her awake in just a couple more hours anyway.

Her words from skating slide about my mind. Am I trying *too* hard to make a perfect future for myself? Is that not possible? Or is it just not predictable?

I squeeze and shuffle the position of my pillow. All right, let's just tally everything up. What have I found while being in New York that could translate into new dreams?

Hobbies. I could take up some kind of performing art that involves marching in parades or dancing foxtrot. But I'm not sure I exactly excelled at either.

Career. I could open a maple-syrup farm, but I googled it, and it looks like our climate would make it tricky for me to be able to produce much of the stuff.

Love.

My phone lights up with a notification and I grab it off the bedside table so it doesn't wake Mum. River! What's he doing, awake and texting me in the middle of the night?

Squirreling under the bedcovers with my phone, I open WhatsApp and see he's forwarded me something. A link for the *Christmas Spectacular Starring the Radio City Rockettes* show at Radio City Music Hall.

'What the . . .?' I whisper into my duvet cave and type a message.

What's this? And how come you're awake? I type and send, and then remember to add, Hello by the way. Merry Christmas Eve! Was your journey home okay?

He's typing a reply and as I wait, I go to the link but it's just telling me the show is sold out.

Did I wake you? I'm sorry.

No, I was just lying here trying to resolve every life problem. The usual. What's with the link?

Some friends of my parents can't make it into the city like they'd planned and want to sell their tickets for the Rockettes tonight. I thought you and your mom might like them, if you don't have plans? They're in California – I can pass you their number if you want to be in touch with them? Or I can pay for them now. I didn't want to wake you, but thought I should jump on them before someone else did.

I put my hand over my mouth and curl up in a happy little ball under the soft cotton sheet. The Rockettes! Mum would love it.

He sends another message: Jump on the tickets, I mean, not my parents' friends.

Yes! Yes please! Send me their info and I'll sort out payment for them right now. Mum is going to be ecstatic. *I* am ecstatic.

Thank you, I type, then delete it. That isn't enough. But where else could I start? I write it again and press send. That is the nicest surprise anyone's ever given me. Thank you for thinking of us.

It's no problem. Merry Christmas.

It's very late evening on the West Coast and I want to catch the ticket sellers before they go to bed for the night, if possible, just so I know for sure that we're going when I tell Mum. I stay under the covers, typing messages, awaiting responses, then checking the forwarded tickets and sending money via the power in the internetz. When the transaction is complete, and the lovely lady in California has wished me and my mum a Happy Holidays and asked me to give 'that little darling River' a hug from her, I text him again.

Are you still awake?

A message comes back not long after. Yep. You got the tickets?

I got the tickets. Thank you again. Then, You can't sleep?

Just ... thinking.

I hesitate for a second, and then go for it. About what?

Then he pulls the whole typing and stopping and typing and stopping and typing and stopping, and just when I think my eyes are in danger of drooping closed for some extra zees, he replies.

I don't know.

You bloody do know! I know you know, and you know you know!

Goodnight, Ashling, he adds, and I do a little, quiet sigh.

Night, River.


By the time Mum wakes up I've already crept to the bathroom twice, done my morning skincare, googled everything there is to know about the history of the Rockettes and made a plan for our Christmas Eve.

'Morning, sunshine,' I say to her as she awakes. It's still dark out, but the sun is on its way up: I can see it in the way the greys of the towers are beginning to form in front of the deep purple sky.

I fetch us both a coffee from the lobby, which is quiet at this hour, luckily, since I padded down in my PJs, and bring it back up to her in bed.

'Here's the plan,' I say, propping up beside her. 'I thought we could start the day with a little sightseeing, getting the subway right down to the bottom of Manhattan and taking a morning ferry to and from Staten Island so you can see the Statue of Liberty. Then we'll grab lunch somewhere, and in the afternoon do Top of the Rock – the observation deck at the top of Rockefeller Center, cross the road and visit St Patrick's Cathedral for Christmas Eve Mass, and then . . . we have tickets to the Rockettes in the evening!'

Mum's eyes widen. 'Wow, what a day! Boats and observation decks and cathedrals and dancing! What should I wear?'

'Well, *we* won't be dancing, so just go with comfy and warm, because we'll be outside a fair amount.'

Once the sun has reached a point in the sky just high enough to see over the skyscrapers, Mum and I board the orange Staten Island Ferry and stand by the railings. The morning Manhattan skyline drifts by and Lady Liberty stretches up into the new day.

'There's so much to see, isn't there?' Mum comments, speaking loudly so her words can be heard over the hum of the ferry and splashing of the water below us. 'In New York, I mean.'

'We'll see as much as we can while you're here,' I reply, and watch the sunlight on her smile.

Mum links my arm and we huddle in close, and it feels just like Grooms is here with us. Mum has the same sense of wonder today that my gran always had in the world, the same desire in her face to soak in every drop of what's in front of her. This is why I wanted to take Grooms on the big Orient Express trip, to see that look one more time.

It's comforting to know it's something she passed down to her daughter, even if it's taken Mum a while to let it show. I hope I have it too.

Once we've sailed to the Island and back, and enjoyed some hot sandwiches for lunch that dripped barbecue sauce all down my jumper so I had to dive into the nearest American Eagle store and buy a new one, we make our way back up to the Rockefeller Plaza. Here, Mum pops in and out of all the shops, buys us both a Banana Pudding Cup from the Magnolia Bakery, asks me to take photos of her with the angels, and points out somebody she thinks is Miranda from *Sex and the City* but is actually just a tall redhead.

'Look, there's Central Park.' Mum whoops with joy as we stand together on the Top of the Rock. The clouds have rolled in, far overhead, and the park is earthy in tone – muted browns and greens. From here, it's so clear just how huge the area is, and I trail my eyes around all the areas I've visited since arriving. The Macy's Thanksgiving Day Parade went down that side. And my hostel was right up there, near Columbia University. I point these things out to Mum.

'You've done so much,' she says. 'You've made the most of your time here, haven't you?'

I'm toying with whether to divulge that I was having just

the opposite thought in the middle of the night when some-one behind us says, 'It's snowing!'

There's a collective shuffle as every observer looks upwards instead of outwards, and, sure enough, tiny flakes are falling from the clouds. They kiss my eyelids as I blink into them. 'Merry Christmas Eve!' I laugh to Mum.

'Did you put this on just for me?' She steps back and twirls, her arms out, and I snap a quick photo.

'Of course I did, only the most festive weather for my mum,' I say.

She watches me for a minute, my face turned towards the clouds; I can feel her. And then she says softly, 'Ashling's got her head in the clouds again . . .' I look at her, and she adds, 'It's nice to see.'

Arm in arm, we make our way to the other side of the observation deck and take a million photos of the view of the Empire State Building with the snow confetti-ing past, in case it suddenly stops. And once our hands are frozen solid and our hair frizzed from the snowflakes, and every angle of the view has been captured for posterity, we make our way back down and have some warmed eggnogs from one of the cafés to defrost our palms.

The snow continues to fall, light and gentle, directionless and with flakes of different sizes, as the sky darkens behind the clouds, and now Christmas is only hours away. There's a magical sensation in the air; Mum and I can feel it in every fairy light, every excited face, every melody of festive music that drifts out of stores upon wafts of heated air when the doors open.

We skip across the road and into St Patrick's Cathedral and, with closed eyes, let the music sprinkle over us like it's indoor snowfall. When we emerge back into the night and head straight down the block to join the queue over at Radio City Music Hall, I ask Mum, 'Ready for the Rockettes?'

Inside, we take our seats. The house lights dim, and Mum whispers to me, 'Your gran auditioned to be a Rockette, you know, while she lived in New York.'

'She did?' Why did I not know this?

Mum nods. 'She always liked to try her hand at a lot of things. I don't think she made the cut, though.'

I sit back and imagine Grooms as a high-kicking, cherry-lipped Rockette, and it brings a smile to my face. Good for her for trying. I wonder if she ever gave the foxtrot a go.

My thoughts are drowned by the swelling of the music, and spotlights appear on the stage as we sit back to enjoy a true Christmas Spectacular.

When the curtain lowers for the final time, and my ears are ringing with music, and I'm shuffling out of the aisles along with six thousand other people, I drop a message to River.

It was amazing. Thank you. Hope you're having a very merry Christmas Eve?

A reply comes almost instantly. I am now, glad you liked it.

He is now. Because I texted him? Or because he's pleased we had a nice time? I wish I could read his mind all the way upstate.

Mum declares we should have a nightcap before retiring for the night (Mum has *never* been one for nightcaps but she's really letting herself enjoy this holiday), so we treat

270

ourselves to some bulbous glasses of brandy and let the warm liquor lay itself over the excitement of the day.

We're both snoozy by the time we get back to the hotel and that night, Santa gives me what I needed for Christmas: a peaceful mind, and a peaceful sleep.

## Chapter 32

I'm sleeping so soundly that Mum's awake first this Christmas morning, and I flutter open my eyes to see her placing a red-wrapped parcel on the foot of my bed. The curtains have been drawn and bright sunrise light is coming in, and a thin layer of snow rests on the window frame.

'Merry Christmas!' Mum smiles and takes a photo of me, bleary eyed and double-chinned.

'Merry Christmas,' I croak in reply, sitting up. 'What's this?'

'It's silly, and it's only half of your present. I know you probably don't have much space in your suitcase so I can take it home with me again if you like and you can have it back when you fly home at the end of January.'

My sleepy brain can't keep up with what she's on about, but my hands' muscle memory kicks in and I reach for the parcel, beginning to rip open the paper before I've barely got a 'Thank you' out.

Inside is a plush red dressing gown, soft and thick, with my initials embroidered on the top left side. 'Mum! I love it!' I say, stepping from the bed and enveloping myself in the soft fabric. When I look up, Mum is wrapped in a matching one, with her initials, and she grins at me sheepishly.

'I bought one for myself, too.'

I bounce over to Mum, my grogginess long gone, and we squish ourselves together in a big, robey bear hug.

'Come on,' Mum says. 'I'm in charge today, and the first order for Christmas morning is that we're going for a walk.' She pulls me to the window by the hand. 'Out there.'

My eyes and mouth widen at the view. Below us, Central Park has been icing sugared, a soft dusting of snow covering the whole ground. 'It's a White Christmas,' I say, stating the obvious. 'Can I wear my robe?'

'No,' Mum says. 'But later this morning, it can go back on . . .'

We stroll over the bridges and around the icy lakes of Central Park for at least an hour, admiring the scenery, wishing a merry Christmas to the dog walkers and joggers. I veer off the path from time to time to step on the snowy verge and feel the crunch of the coated grass under my boots.

The park twinkles in the sunlight, the white of the snow glistening and appearing the colour of soft spearmint under the pale blue of the Christmas Day sky.

'Heard from River this morning?' Mum asks, super nonchalantly.

'We exchanged a couple of Merry Christmas texts.' I

shrug back, also super nonchalantly. We are the most stoic ladies in New York.

Until Mum snickers, ruining it. 'I'm sorry he's not waiting for you under a Christmas tree.'

'Mother.' I laugh. 'I don't, that's not . . . shut up.' In truth, I've been over-analysing a kiss River had put at the end of his text this morning like I'm a lovesick teen. Argh, we were *this close* to that being a real, live kiss!

'Can you tell me the plan for today?' I ask Mum as we stop on a pretty bridge and look back at the city, the Christmas-morning ice skaters on the Wollman rink in the foreground.

'All right, so the second part of your present, the main part, really—'

'Mum, you don't need to give me anything, you came to New York!'

She shushes me. 'We've had a wonderful but busy couple of days, and I think you've had a busy couple of months here. So as much as I know there's a million things we could go off and see and do around the city, even today, I wanted us to just *be*. Just enjoy the day for what it already is.'

'That sounds brilliant,' I say, not sure what she's getting at.

'What I'm getting at is, I've booked us into the hotel spa, and we're going to spend a good few hours wallowing in warm water, getting massages and lying back with cups of herbal tea.'

I accidentally make a face at that and Mum corrects herself. 'Or something you like – hot chocolates. What do you think?'

'I think …' I struggle for the words. 'I think it sounds perfect, Mum. Absolutely perfect. Thank you.'

'I just wanted to give you the gift of time. A bit of space to just be with yourself and give yourself a rest. Whether you use that time to think or not think is up to you. Just step off the treadmill, you know?'

She's watching me closely, seeing me, seeing the tiredness in my face, and I know she's right. I haven't stopped, really stopped, in weeks. And I'm not complaining, I'm basically on a long holiday so what do I have the right to complain about? But the constant running in the dark to try to find myself, attempting to uncover meaning I may have missed in decade-old diaries or 'you only live once' guidebooks, searching every corner of the city for what comes next … 'I am tired,' I admit.

'I know,' Mum says, and pulls me in close. 'And I know you've dealt with a lot, and I know you're lost, but you're also going to carry on having a fabulous life with wonderful memories and some of them are being made right here. So, let's just recharge those batteries for a few hours, okay?'

'Okay.'

'Merry Christmas, honey.'

'Merry Christmas, Mum.'

Back at the hotel, Mum tells me that after the spa we're booked in for the hotel restaurant's Christmas dinner, which is served mid-afternoon, and that after that she'd like us to sit in our robes and watch Christmas movies on the TV until we fall asleep. Knowing we're calling it a day on the streets of Manhattan gets me all giddy and I vow to wear nothing but slippers as footwear for the rest of the day to pad around the hotel.

My breathing is long and deep, my eyes closed, my ears soaking in the spa music, and as the masseuse presses on my upper back with some orange-and-cinnamon-scented oils, a few unexpected tears are squeezed out. Ouch, my shoulder. I grit my teeth. I'm not thinking about that today. I refuse. Then some more tears pool out, yet these are straight from my heart, and they don't feel as bad, strangely enough.

Later, when I meet Mum in the large, warm soaking tub, which overlooks the still-snowy park, she tells me about another spa setting she'd like to visit.

'It's not a specific one, but I'd just really like to go to one of those hot springs one day. Somewhere with magnificent scenery and you float about like this.' She lies back and her feet bob up to the surface. 'And it's all warm and milky and maybe cold outside.'

'Like Blue Lagoon in Iceland?' I ask.

'Yes, that would be nice. Have you been there?'

I shake my head. 'I've flown to and from Reykjavik a handful of times, but I've never stayed over long enough to go out there. Maybe we could go together sometime?'

Mum smiles at me. 'That would be nice. We are having quite a lot of fun, aren't we?'

'It's the best,' I say, sinking my mellow shoulders down into the water. It would be nice to explore some new places, or visit some of the locations properly that I've only ever stopped by for a layover. I'm so lucky to have seen so much of the world, and I know I'm not a pilot any more, but that doesn't need to stop, I suppose.

Now hang the hell on, did I just have that thought without the accompanying pity party?

Beside me, Mum starts humming along to the slow, twinkly piano melodies of Christmas classics that are playing quietly over the spa speaker system.

I pull myself out of the water, wrap my new red robe around me and pad soggy footprints across the tiles, fetching us both a glass of iced, lemony water from a cooler.

Glancing at the clock on the wall, I can't believe we've wiled away over three hours in the spa so far, dotting between the treatment rooms and the facilities. It's been a truc gift – one I didn't know I needed – just to give my racing mind a bit of a break. When Mum told me this was what we'd be doing, part of me thought that by the end I'd have used the time to stop and conjure up that new life plan. But I didn't.

I'm really happy right now, though. My mum is here, living her merriest life, and beyond her my snow-coated Manhattan stretches into the distance, and I know that no matter what the past or future have to say, right now I wouldn't want to be anywhere other than my perfect Christmas present.

# Chapter 33

'Stand right there, that's it, right there, and put your left hand on the railing,' I instruct Mum. 'Now look out to the left. Wistfully. But also laughing a bit.'

'What am I laughing at?'

'Um ... how about that scene from *Happiest Season* that had you in stitches yesterday evening?' I say, naming one of our Christmas movie marathon films from the night before.

Mum's mouth immediately curls into an unstoppable chuckle at the memory and I take the photo. It's perfect.

We're on the Brooklyn Bridge and it's Boxing Day, Mum's last day in the city. Behind her is the New York skyline and the snow is falling again, piling thin mounds of white on the railings and benches of the bridge.

'Look at this.' I step over to her and pull another photo up on my phone. It's of Grooms, standing exactly where Mum is standing now, her left hand on the railing, her face wistful and laughing. 'Like mother, like daughter.'

'Oh, I'd forgotten about that photo,' Mum says, taking my phone and peering closely at the screen. 'That's nice. But we'd better take a third-generation version, too.' She steps aside and guides me into frame, and I do my best to copy the poses of my gran and my mum.

'Let's go and warm up,' I say, taking my phone back from Mum.

The clouds have rolled back over New York today and the temperature's dropped. With the snow falling it looks like the colour contrast of the city has been dialled down, and I'm keen not to send Mum back home with frostbite.

'It's got to be time for food now, surely. What classic New York morsels do you want to try?' I say, leading Mum back across the bridge. 'Let's see . . . frozen hot chocolate at Serendipity 3, or oysters from Grand Central Oyster Bar?'

Mum answers, 'Or how about both?'

The remainder of the day goes too quickly, time slipping by in a haze of festive feels and family fun.

That night I drift to sleep in our shared hotel room for the last time, and what feels like only moments later I'm being woken up by Mum sitting on my bed, the room still dark.

I switch my bedside light on. 'Mum? You're not leaving already?'

'It's time, honey,' she says, stroking my mad hair away from my face. 'The hotel car is picking me up in ten minutes to take me to the airport.'

'But you just got here,' I whine.

'I had such an amazing time.'

'So did I. Thank you for coming out.' I mean it with all my heart.

'Of course. And thank you for hosting me. Thank you for showing me your New York; I can see why it means so much to you, and meant so much to *my* mum. Now, am I taking your robe home with me?'

'No way.' My dressing gown is under the duvet with me because it's snuggly, and I want to be able to wear it around the apartment in Greenwich Village.

'You'll have room in your suitcase for it come the end of January?'

I nod. 'But maybe you could take my jumper home with you, and give it a spray with some stain remover? Pleeeeease?' I find the crumpled jumper that I lobbed barbecue sauce down in a heap on the floor by the bed, and hand it to her.

'You don't have stain remover here in the USA?' Mum teases.

'I'm just trying to make sure I have a little extra room in my bag.' I give her my best-daughter-ever grin.

Mum pulls me into the biggest hug and I melt into her for a moment. It's been a tonic, having her here. 'I've loved every minute of this,' I tell her.

'Me too. Now off you get, I need to get going.'

I jump up and pull on my robe and slippers, pocket a room key, and help her wheel her suitcase down to the lobby, where the concierge directs her to her car.

'Make sure you get a seat on the right-hand side of the plane,' I tell her. 'You'll get the best views over London.'

'Already booked,' Mum says. I smile. I must have given her that tip before.

We wish each other a final merry Christmas, and with lots of love and kisses, wave goodbye.

I head back up to the room where I plan to have a nice, steamy, spacious shower and hang out in bed for a little longer, before I too check out and make my way back to whatever, or whoever, awaits me in Greenwich Village.

# Chapter 34

I'm not really expecting River to have come back from upstate already. Considering he didn't get home for Thanksgiving, and he'd been looking forward to Christmas, I'm guessing he'll be there much of the following week. Though he did make a mention of watching the Ball drop in Times Square on New Year's Eve ... he must be planning to be back by then.

When I open the door to a silent Greenwich Village apartment, though, my shoulders sag, and I drop my keys on the floor, along with my bag. Sigh.

Nope! I shake off the feeling of disappointment. Literally, I stand in the living room having a good wriggle about. I then set about unpacking my stuff, finding a nice hook on the back of the door to keep my new dressing gown, and having a bit of a general tidy-up around the place, since following the madness of our last day before River went home, the flat isn't looking its freshest.

Once all that crap's out the way, I sit down with a cup of

tea and admire my familiar view, from my window, sitting on my sofa bed.

A notification lights up my phone screen for a second. Is it really the twenty-seventh of December? But I fly home on the twenty-sixth of January. Huh. I really am into my final month here, now.

Being with my mum these past few days has washed me with nostalgia for my past and for home. And being here, looking down on Manhattan from my little perch, showers me with possibilities about my future. Could I be open and enjoy the ride, like Mum said? Rather than focusing on the perfect ending?

My first thought when I wake the next morning is that there's someone I should call and thank.

'Hi, Hugh.'

'Hi, Ashling.'

'I just wanted to ring and say . . . thank you for coming out and meeting my mum, and keeping her company.' I take a breath. I also want to say, *What did you and River talk about at the bar the other night?* But that feels more like a question for River than for Hugh.

'Oh, it's no problem,' Hugh says, his voice soft. 'Did you have a good Christmas?'

'We did. Did you?'

'Yeah,' he replies. But I don't feel like I believe him.

'You sure?'

'It was okay. I should have gone home really, to the UK, but it is what it is.'

'Why didn't you?' I ask.

'I said I'd be available to work, if the office needed me.'

Ah, Hugh. 'Do you like your job?'

'I do,' he answers, and he sounds truthful. 'It's a lot but it clicks for me. I think it feels like how you used to describe piloting.'

'That's good, then.'

I'm about to ring off when Hugh says, 'Hey, what are you doing for New Year's?'

'Uh . . . I'm planning to go to Times Square. I hear it's the place to be.'

Hugh laughs. 'Me too.'

'Oh.' I hesitate. I should invite him to join me. It would be the nice thing to do. But he's not the person I want to be with at midnight. My gut twists at the thought of him being lonely.

But then he ends with, 'Maybe I'll see you there.'

A small sigh of relief escapes. I don't think he heard. 'Yes. Maybe see you there.'

With thoughts of my mum's visit, and the past, present and future swirling about in my mind like a gentle snow blizzard, I head out for a walk, aimlessly meandering up Seventh Avenue until I reach Midtown, and I find myself in Times Square, albeit three days too early for the New Year's festivities.

But as luck would have it . . .

'Would you like to say "Good Riddance" to something from the past year?' a woman asks. I've paused beside a small assault course that's been erected in the plaza below the neon lights that swim across the buildings. She hands me a piece of paper and a marker pen.

'Good Riddance Day?' I read from the top of the paper.

'It's a tradition – inspired by a tradition from Latin America where, at New Year's, people burn dolls in which they put things that represent bad memories from the past year.' She taps the paper. 'On here you write down what you want to say good riddance to. Then you can rip it up inside our mini assault course, which represents what you've overcome.'

She sounds very chirpy and I like her immediately. 'I can write anything?'

'Sure.' She shrugs. 'Anything. Maybe it's something you didn't like about last year, something tough you dealt with, regrets, embarrassing moments, exes, diet culture . . .'

'God, the list could be endless, couldn't it?' I laugh.

'The more things the merrier,' she says, and wanders off to hand a sheet to another passer-by.

Hmm. Should I put Hugh's name down? Close that chapter once and for all? But then I might run into him on New Year's anyway, so that feels a bit redundant.

The obvious thing to say good riddance to is my career. My dreams. My goals. But that's a bit much, isn't it? A bit rash?

Now that's a cute assault course. Inside the railings, people are throwing their ripped papers into a bin, with gusto, I should add, giving a punching bag a good wallop, and then following a runway of cones until they pass under a big inflatable archway. This is all so unexpected and isn't exactly the zen way I would have chosen to let go of troubles, but . . . Mum told me off for trying to create 'perfect' so I think I should just go with it.

*I want to say Good Riddance To:*
*Expectations.*

There. I click the pen lid back on, and make my way to the course before I change my mind. I rip my paper in half and throw it with ritualistic zest into the big Good Riddance Day bin and then whoop for myself as I punch the punching bag with my weight behind my good shoulder, then run in a circle and then out the other side and back into the plaza.

I'm beaming. Part of what's been clawing at my heels and tangling up my thoughts has been my unwillingness to shake away and make peace with things I can't control anymore. I'm not quite convinced I've suddenly let go of harbouring expectations altogether, but I do feel like I've made a small step forward by making the *decision* to let them go. It's a start!

The woman approaches me again with a congratulations, and says, 'Now, if there's something you're hopeful for for the year ahead, and you have a minute, you could also go and write something on the NYE Wishing Wall.' She points down the street to where a cart is set up beside a screen covered in little colourful squares of paper. 'That's confetti, and you write down your wish or a goal and it gets added to the confetti that gets released when the Ball drops.'

'That sprinkles down over Times Square?' I clarify, picturing myself standing below a thousand wishes at midnight.

The woman nods. 'You have any dreams you're hoping to manifest?'

She has no idea how non-black-and-white that question is. But she also probably has better things to do than listen to my life story, so I tell her that yes, of course I do, and I trot off down to the Wishing Wall.

Accepting a tissuey square of lime-green confetti and a pen, I think of what to write. 'How specific should I be?' I ask the man in charge, as if I'm penning a letter to Santa.

'That's up to you, I guess,' he replies. 'For me, I always feel like the more specific the goal the better?'

'Hmm,' I reply, and tap the pen against my forehead. Should I write, 'Find new dreams'? That's kinda vague. And kinda what I've been tiptoeing around for the past two months anyway. How about 'Stop focusing on trying to create the perfect future and live in the moment'? Seems a little wordy for a small bit of confetti. The stars and the universe don't want to read a bloody essay when the clock strikes twelve.

'Figure out who I am now'. Yes. Not who I was in the past, not who I need to aim to be in the future, but who is Ashling as of right now? That seems to encompass what I know I need – want – to do, and also there are now three people waiting to use my pen.

Tacking it onto the wall, I kiss my fingertips and then place them against my bit of confetti. When midnight strikes, I hope I'm kissing a certain someone instead.

*Good luck, little wish ...*


I spend the next couple of days catching up on social media, having video calls with friends about their Christmases, and pottering about the apartment by myself, bringing snow in on my boots every time I go out. I check in with

Rebecca, who's away for Christmas flying to and from Dubai and soaking up a little winter sun during her hours off. I'm envious, for a second, but I don't let it consume me.

'I thought he was coming back today, but there's no sign of him,' I say into the microphone of my headphones, chatting to Flo as I leave the apartment the morning of New Year's Eve.

'Can't you text him? "*Where the hell are you, handsome man, and where's my snog while you're at it?*"'

I lock the door and make my way down the stairwell. 'No, I don't want to be that person that's chasing him around.'

'You aren't – he said he'd go to Times Square with you and he's disappeared.'

'He might still show up. Anyway, I'm heading to the shops to get a few provisions to keep me going this afternoon and evening. What are you doing tonight?' Let's take the subject off me for a moment.

'I'm staying in and watching TV. It's cold here and I can't be bothered to scamper about with icy legs paying eighty quid for a cocktail.'

'That's a very sensible idea, Flo, well done,' I say, reaching the bottom of the stairs and heading for the apartment building door. 'Speaking of watery cocktails, there's nowhere to go to the loo once you're inside the barriers at Times Square tonight. What do you reckon about stacking a few sanitary towels on top of each other—Ohmygod, hi!'

I've flung open the door mid-sentence just as River's done the same from the other side, and we've bashed into each other.

'Hi,' he says. He's bundled up in his coat, scarf, gloves

and hat but he looks well and rested. He has nearly a week's worth of stubble so I'm guessing he forgot his razor, but it suits him, plus probably adds a little warmth to his face, which must be nice right now. I know my legs appreciate their fuzz in the winter months.

'Hi,' I say again. In the fluster I've forgotten to be annoyed at him for shutting down on me, and reach over for a quick hug.

'What's happening?' Flo's voice says into my ears.

'Uh, sorry, Flo, just ran into River as I was coming out of the building, one second.'

'Is he back for you?' I hear her ask and I pull one of the earphones out.

'Are you still coming to Times Square?' I ask him.

'Um, sure, yeah, I just need to . . .' He gestures to his bag, on the ground by his feet. 'Are you going now?'

'No, no, just getting some things from the shops. Snacks. Granola bars. You want anything?'

'Some granola bars sound good, thanks.'

'Sure.'

'No drinks, though.'

'No, HAHAHA!' Oh, please, please, please don't have heard my sanitary towel comment. Pretty sure he did.

'Okay, I'll see you when you get back.'

'All right, bye, River!'

I wave him into the building and put my earphone back in my ear. Immediately, Flo says, 'Way to tell him off.'

'Shut up,' I reply. 'I was all surprised to see him and whatnot.'

'And how was it seeing him?'

On my provisions list is not just food, but also extra thick socks, some paracetamol, maybe a few other bits and bobs, so I head towards a bigger cluster of shops in Greenwich Village rather than just the corner store. I could do with a bit of time to get my head in the right place now River's burst through the door and back into my life, anyhow. 'It was ... nice. And I'm annoyed that we're pretending the near-kiss didn't happen rather than that I'm annoyed at him doing anything wrong. I'm glad he's back, to be honest.'

'So you can go to Times Square?'

'I would have gone without him.'

'But then you wouldn't have had anyone to kiss,' she points out.

I laugh, the sound bouncing against the buildings in the quiet street. 'Oh my god, I nearly forgot! He has to kiss me at midnight!' I pump my fist in the air, then quickly add, 'He doesn't *have* to kiss me, of course, I just mean it's an opportunity we could both consensually take part in, if he wants to.'

'I think he'll want to.'

'I hope so.' I really hope so, and then I stop and sit down on a stoop. 'Wait, do I? If this all really is because he's still hung up on Delilah, I don't want to be some consolation prize just because I'm the only one here.'

'Just enjoy each other if it feels right *because* you're the ones that are there.'

'Hmm. I'm not sure if that's genius logic or you just want me to have my snog,' I say.

'Probably both,' says Flo. 'Oh, honey, I've got to dash, my next client is here. Today is jam-packed with everyone wanting to start the New Year with bangs. Or curls, or balayage.' She titters at her own joke. 'Text me at midnight, good luck with the peeing situation, enjoy watching the balls drop, and happy kissing.'

'Thanks – and it's a ball, singular. Good luck with work today and think of me while you're all warm in your PJs in front of the TV.'

'Will do!' She hangs up and I stand, shaking the cold from my legs. I'll need to be careful standing in one spot for hours and hours today in this temperature. Maybe I'll do squats in the middle of the crowds to keep warm and look like a pro at this.

An hour later, I'm returning to the apartment with far too many snacks, two pairs of men's ski socks in case River wants some as well, some water bottles, some earmuffs that look like the Brooklyn Bridge that I fully believe are cool, and a lip-balm stick since all I have are pots and I don't want to have to remove my gloves to be able to pucker up for midnight.

You know, just in case.

When I get in, I hear River in the shower. That's a good idea – I could do with toastying myself all over before we go too.

'Hey,' he says, emerging.

'Hi, welcome home.' I smile, definitely not looking at his chest because he's only wrapped in a towel. He still hasn't shaved and it makes him look more rugged, less inner city.

And even from here in the living area the orange shower gel on his skin emits a sweet citrus scent.

'I went to the deli and got us a couple of really huge subs. If you want one. Maybe you've already eaten, but I just thought they might keep us going. They're on the side in the kitchen.'

'Thank you, that's really thoughtful. I got you some socks.'

'Oh. Thanks.'

'Just so our feet have extra squidge. And warmth. If you want them.'

'That's great.' He takes a step towards me and stretches his arm out to take the socks, meeting my eyes. 'Thank you. Very thoughtful.'

We are both being as awkward as if it were my first day in New York, but that'll pass, I'm sure. Nothing like standing in the cold and needing to pee for ten hours with someone to bring about a bonding experience.

'What time should we get there?' I ask, just before he heads into his room to take off his towel, I mean get changed.

'Pretty early if we want to see anything. Some people might be there already.'

'Already? But the Ball doesn't drop for, like, twelve hours.'

He smiles, and instantly I smile back, like it's infectious. 'It's quite an experience. I would say maybe let's aim to get there by three?'

'I have time to shower, too?'

'And have something to eat.'

I nod. 'And put on thick socks. I'm excited! I think we should walk there.'

'Makes sense, stretch our legs a bit.'

'Exactly, and the exercise will get us all pumped up and warm.'

We dither for a second, him in his doorway, me looking anywhere but below his neck, and then he retreats inside his room and I head for the shower.

# Chapter 35

We're power-walking through New York City and I feel like I'm the at climax in a dramatic rom-com and I only have twenty minutes to catch my love interest and explain how I never meant for him to find out I was an undercover restaurant critic! Not like this!

With the showering and eating and packing bags and then me repacking into a smaller pouch when River clocked that rucksacks might not be allowed, we haven't really had much of a chance to chat, and conversation has remained very surface level. Now, we're dodging other pedestrians and zigzagging via quieter blocks on our way to Times Square.

The sky above is heavy with thick, white clouds, the kind of ones you know are considering dropping a shit-ton of snow at any moment. But the forecast thinks it'll hold off. Nevertheless, I'm in my bulkiest jacket, zipped all the way and with the hood up, though with the speed we're walking

I'm beginning to feel a tiny trickle of sweat on the back of my neck.

And suddenly, we're there, slowing to join the back of a crowd that's being carefully siphoned through security measures into railed-off sections. We shuffle into our pen and it's all right. It's not too cold. We have a little space. We can see the stage and the big screens and . . .

'There's the Ball!' I shout, as if River won't hear me over this crowd unless I do so.

'There it is,' he replies at a normal volume, his face upturned towards the glittering bauble, twelve feet wide, covered in Waterford Crystal triangles, and sitting level with the skyscrapers atop a giant flagpole. It actually stays up all year round now, but there's still something special about seeing it on its big night.

River glances down and sees me looking at him, and he smiles, and for the first time since we reunited, as it were, he says, in his warm and genuine voice, 'Happy New York City New Year's Eve.'

'Happy NYC NYE to you, too,' I reply. 'So . . . I guess we just stand here for the next, what, nine hours?'

'Yep. We've got about two hours before all the main music and performances on the stage start, but they might start handing stuff out before then, like special Times Square New Year's hats and things.'

'I like freebies.' I sparkle. 'Now, tell me, how was your Christmas?'

'It was really nice,' River says. 'Very relaxing. Lots of, you know, nature and food and sleeping in and seeing old friends.'

'Matching pyjamas, singing Christmas songs around a piano, chopping down your own tree,' I say, adding to his list. 'That's what American families who live outside cities are always doing in holiday movies.'

'No matching pyjamas, unfortunately.'

'Mum gave me and her matching robes, so I guess I win.'

'I guess so. How was your Christmas with your mom?'

I inhale a big breath of happy air. 'It was brilliant. And she had a really nice time, I think.'

'Do you do a lot of mother-daughter trips?'

'This is actually the first one abroad, unless you count a couple of times she's come with me in the early piloting days when I've had a long layover somewhere in Europe. But this worked so well, and we had such fun. We did a lot, but had a very chilled Christmas Day. I'm glad you had some downtime, too.'

'Yeah, I needed it. After all that pushing at work, and then you and I had a pretty full-on day together, you know, just before I went home . . .' Somebody bumps lightly into River and he stumbles into me. 'Sorry,' he says to me, placing a protective hand on my arm before saying, 'No problem,' to the bumper behind him who's apologising.

With his hand still there, I say, 'I'm sorry I didn't end up taking your offer to come with you for Christmas.'

'No, don't apologise. I'm really glad you had such a good one.'

Alrighty, time to address the elephant in the railing enclosure. I start off gently. 'I guess it might have seemed a bit much for your folks for you to be suddenly bringing home your new flatmate for Christmas. Instead of a girlfriend or whatever. And strange for you.'

Nice one.

River hesitates, like he's collecting some words from his mind and wondering the best way to string them together. Or like he's trying not to hurt my feelings. 'I mean, I'm really glad your mom came to town. I think she's great for doing that. But I wouldn't have asked you if I didn't want you there.'

'No?'

'No.'

Well, that explains pretty much nothing then. I need to be more direct, otherwise I'm going to spend the next nine hours wondering whether or not this guy wants to kiss me at midnight. Or ever.

'Excuse me,' somebody says beside me. 'Do you know if there are any toilets?'

'I don't think there are any,' I answer. 'And I heard that if you leave you probably can't come back in.'

'Bollocks,' says the girl, and smacks the water bottle away from her friend's lips. 'I told you. Stop drinking.'

The other girl giggles. 'Oops.' They're young, British-sounding, and maybe late teens, perhaps the same age I was when I first came to New York.

'Are you on holiday?' I ask.

We chat to the girls for a little bit, by which point a few others around us have started a group trivia game to keep our pen entertained, and as much as I'd like to get to the bottom of things with River, I guess I'm not going anywhere for a while so there's no rush.

But as the natural light fades and the sky-high neon of Times Square seems to become even more pronounced, that's when the cold really kicks in, and I find myself trying to concertina my neck down into my coat like a turtle going into its shell.

'Are you getting cold?' River asks.

'Huh?' I say, extracting my ear from its Brooklyn Bridge ear muff.

He leans into me and my lips are right by his neck. 'Are you cold?'

'Yes.'

River opens his arms out, indicating I can warm up against him, but he waits for my reaction before moving towards me. I squint at him, and then step inside his coat, and press my nose against the soft maroon of his sweater. Mmm, I think it might be cashmere, very nice.

Then I feel him sigh against me.

I step back, not letting go completely, but creating a space between us that the cold air tries to seep into. 'What are you doing?'

'What?'

'Don't say "what". Don't act like I'm imagining what happened. What *nearly* happened.'

River bites his bottom lip as I press mine together, defiant.

I carry on. I have to do this. 'You nearly kissed me, and I nearly kissed you, in that lift. And then in the morning, when it was just me and you alone again, something had changed. Was it all just adrenaline? Was it that my mum had shown up? Did Hugh say something to you at the bar?'

The smallest frown appears on River's forehead, like he's wincing from a pain. His eyes study me and for a moment I think he might just grip me, dip me and plant a smooch on my lips right there and then. But then he angles away, moving to speak in my ear, and I brace myself, my breath caught, for the truth.

'*Welcome to Times Square!*' shouts a voice over a loud-speaker, which drowns out anything River says, if he even managed to utter a syllable.

The crowd roars into a deafening cheer and I instinctively turn from River to see what's happening, as we're directed to watch the Ball ascend at the top of the One Times Square flagpole, above a big screen saying that we have six hours to go. The Ball shines a vibrant array of colours and rises into the dark sky, and after, the bass of a song starts beating and I swear it's to the same beat as my heart.

I can't hear a thing River might have to say now, but he hasn't taken his hands from my arms. I know there's about fifty feet of padding between his fingertips and my skin, but I feel him like there's nothing. Like it's just him, with me, and it doesn't matter if a million people and thousands of lightbulbs are surrounding us, or that it's so loud I can't hear myself think, or that it's dropped below freezing. If I look down all I can see, all I can feel, is his hand on my arm.

River's arm moves around me from behind, crossing me from shoulder to shoulder, pulling me in close so the warmth of his chest is against my back. And then his lips are beside my right ear, so close he doesn't even need to shout, and his voice makes me close my eyes for a moment.

'I just can't,' he says.

I turn slightly and look up at him, beckoning him to lean down. 'If you can't then why are you doing this to me?' His arm flinches but it's like he can't let go, and I don't make a move away either. 'Is it her? Just tell me.'

He moves his head, his eyes on mine, the small movement of shaking it from side to side.

'It's not because of Delilah?'

'It's you.'

I must have sunk or deflated a little or something, because his arm tightens a touch and he adds, 'I don't mean like that. You know I don't. It's that you're going home soon. And your home and my home are thousands of miles apart.'

'So it's a long-distance thing?' I'm confused. He isn't willing to try – if it even comes to that?

River leans his forehead against the side of my head and his eyes close as he speaks. 'I'm afraid. I'm afraid to let myself fall any further for you, and then for you to leave and not want anything to do with me any more.'

That's it – my answer. He's protecting his heart, not wanting a repeat of what happened with Delilah.

I can't make him any promises for the future, or iron-clad guarantees, all I know is the thought of not wanting anything to do with him, even if we were a million miles away from each other, seems an impossibility.

And right now we're not a million miles apart, only millimetres.

I shake my head, my hair brushing against his face. 'What about now?'

River doesn't hear me and leans in closer, and I put my fingers on his neck to hold him steady. As I do so he blinks, and looks sideways at me in a way that nearly sends me weak.

'Someone told me recently not to only try to plan for a perfect future, but to just see what happens. So what do we do now?'

River turns me around so we're facing each other now, his hands on my shoulder blades so he can speak into my ear. I need to put my arms around his torso, under his coat, to stay steady. He moves one hand to cup my neck, holding me upright, holding me close.

His lips brush against my temple. It's not a kiss, it's a sigh, a battle inside his own mind, but it's still sweet.

On the stages, the performances and announcements are beginning, and though River tries to answer me, his voice is lost in the crowd and it's becoming impossible to hear each other.

What can I do, but stay close to him while I let myself go to the music, the atmosphere, the lights and the last hours of this maddening, and maybe slightly magical, year?

It's late. The new year is near.

I take my phone out to snap a photo and spot a message from Hugh. I hold it up for River to see. 'Hugh's here. He says he's in a pen alongside . . .' I trail off and look around me. 'I think he must be nearby?' I scan the crowd and type out a quick response, wishing him a 'Happy New Year'.

River studies me, biting his lip.

'What?' I ask. It's still hard to hear each other, but there's a small lull during a performance changeover.

'You two have such a history. Do you know he still has a thing for you?'

I shake my head. 'That's not true.'

A message comes back instantly: Come find me – I think I'm in the next pen over to you. Can we talk?

Not now, Hugh … I check the time and it's a quarter to midnight. Another time?

'Do you still have feelings for him?' He doesn't ask it with anger, or hurt. He asks it with a gentleness, an openness that comes so naturally to him.

'No. I split up with *him*. Why would you think I like him?' *When I so clearly like you?*

'There's an ease between the two of you. And you call him a lot. Which is obviously fine, and none of my business; I just don't want to get in the way.'

Where did he get that idea from? I guess Hugh must have implied it? 'I'd hardly call a couple of times in the past two months "a lot".' River looks like he wants to believe me but doesn't know whether to or not. I continue. 'He's part of my past, part of my home, and I had a lot wrapped up in him for a long time. But being here,' I meet his eyes, 'has made me want to not live in the past any more.'

As if reading my mind, Hugh sends another message. Really quick, while it's quietish. One last time this year. Come on, Ashy?

'Ugh.' I break away from River. 'Listen, he's bugging me to talk about something. I'm sorry, I'll be back in just a minute.'

'You can't leave the pen, you won't get back in,' River

302

reminds me, and I detect sadness in his eyes though he's covering it as best he can, like he's taking care not to influence me or my decisions.

'I'm not leaving,' I press. 'I promise. Back in a mo.'

I push my way through the crowd, a stream of apologies pouring from my lips as I duck under waving arms and get bopped by no less than five tube balloons. I reach the barricades and scan the faces of the neighbouring crowd until I spot Hugh's, looking for me, further down the fence. I wave to try to get his attention, but he doesn't see me, so I wriggle through the hordes, my belly against the railing, until he's near.

'Hugh!' I call, and he turns, his face breaking into a lop-sided grin.

'Hey, you came to me,' he says.

'I came to see what you wanted to talk about,' I reply. I'm pointed with my words, but I think the nuances have floated into the air with the music.

He beckons me closer, and cups my cheek to hold his lips close to my ear. 'I just wanted to say ... it's been good seeing you again. I didn't think I'd see you this year.'

'It's been good seeing you, too,' I say, keeping my voice level. 'It's nice that we're friends now ... right?'

Hugh nods, holding my gaze, then reaches over the railings and pulls me into a squeeze, swaying me to the music.

I squeeze him back, one last time, right? Then I detangle myself. 'It's nearly midnight – I have to get back,' I tell him.

'No, wait,' Hugh says, grinning at me. 'Stay here. See in the new year with me.'

I shake my head. 'I can't. You head back to your friends.'

'Ashling . . .'

'Hugh.'

'Wait, I just wanted to say . . .' He pauses, and somebody bumps me from behind. I glance up at the huge digital clock. On the stage, Chelsea Cutler is singing a soulful performance of the John Lennon song 'Imagine'.

'What?'

'Stay. With me.' His familiar eyes are pleading, lonely. I hate that he's lonely.

The sixty-second countdown begins.

Sixty seconds. That's all that's left of this year, the year I felt like I lost so much. Then I took myself to New York City.

Below the Ball is a big screen counting down the seconds, one by one, moment by moment. And the crowd, who were singing and dancing only minutes ago, are now all focused on calling out the descending numbers.

Just like that, the hours of waiting feel like nothing, the ache in my feet has disappeared, the numbness from the frosty air thaws, and I'm caught up in the moment. This is it.

And I'm in the wrong place.

'I have to go,' I shout over the noise to Hugh. 'Happy New Year.'

He reaches for my hand but I turn away, my stomach dropping like that glistening big ball is about to at the thought of not reaching River before the countdown ends.

Leaving Hugh in my wake, I squeeze under arms and through packed torsos. My vision is blurred by gold-and-purple Planet Fitness top hats dancing before me. The crowd is pulsing, whooping, a sea of smiles and laughter, and I have to jostle to push through them since none of them can hear my polite requests to pleeeeeease move.

As I duck under a couple who haven't been able to save their kissing for the stroke of midnight, I'm struck by an almost heart-stopping awe that I'm *here*. Despite everything I made it to New York, I'm living, I'm breathing, I'm in the moment.

New York City. They say you never sleep, but I wholly believe I'm about to make some new dreams here with you.

Starting at midnight.

I have thirty seconds.

I stand on tiptoes to try to spot how far River is from me, and I can't see him. I can't see anyone I was standing near. I don't get it – I haven't left the pen. Did he?

'River?' I shout into the air, my voice a little fish swimming among the tide of numbers being hollered up into the night.

Come on, come on, come on, where are you?

Twenty seconds.

I whirl around, searching, calling, my heart choking my words as it rises to my throat.

A hand encloses mine, firm, familiar, and I'm pulled in between two friends singing arm in arm, and all of a sudden there River is. He found me.

He holds my hands tight in his, not letting go.

'You came back,' he says, bringing himself close to my ear, the smile unable to hide itself in his voice.

'Of course.' I'm croaky from dehydration, but I don't care.

All around us, people are cheering and waving and snapping photos, but it's just confetti in the background when River takes a step closer to me, bringing his hands to the nape of my neck.

'TEN!'

Ten seconds.

'I don't know how to start the year with you, if . . . if that's all it can be.'

I shrug. 'I don't know either. What are you going to do about it?'

I hold his gaze, take in his dark eyebrows, his green eyes, the kind crinkles around the outer corners, and my lips curve into a half smile. My hands are shaking. My heart is booming in sync with the countdown.

I may have my head in the clouds, but that's where I'm usually at my most calm and in control. Maybe I don't need to be up in the air to feel that feeling. Maybe I can be just as brave right here, on solid ground.

Time to shoot my shot, live what I'm feeling right in this moment. 'We could just . . . see what happens?'

He looks to my lips and a smile forms that matches mine.

I pull my gaze from him and watch the countdown. 'Six! Five! Four!' I shout along with the crowd.

I've had a little turbulence, but right now I'm up on cloud nine, and for a while there, I didn't think I'd be able to soar that high again.

I face River again and reach up from my good arm to touch his hair.

That grin, the one that comes and goes and feels sometimes like it's only for me, spreads across his face, and as I'm saying the words 'Two' and, finally . . .

'One.'

River pulls me to him, lifting me to my tiptoes, and his lips meet mine.

Finally.

His kiss is like a sweet maple whisky on a cold evening and I savour it. *About time*, I find myself thinking, as I kiss him back.

Confetti laced with a thousand wishes and dreams, including my own, sprinkle down on us like snowflakes. Fireworks explode into the night air overhead. All around us, people are celebrating the start of a brand-new year, and I pull back from River just in time to see the Ball finish its descent.

'Happy New Year,' River says into my ear. That big grin of his is still there, like he can't wipe it away. I have a feeling I might look the same.

'Happy New Year.'

I don't know how long this moment will last. For now, I'm going to stay in this dream and keep my River close.

'Auld Lang Syne' spreads its melody across the city, and I kiss my guy on this wintery midnight.

## Chapter 36

I'm slow to wake up on New Year's Day, and by the time I open my eyes I can tell it's late morning. The light outside my big, arched window is brighter than usual. But not just due to the sun being higher in the sky – something's different outside.

I sit up on my sofa bed and shuffle forward towards the glass. In the distance, the top of the Empire State Building is misted in soft cloud, and the building roofs, tree branches and roads of New York are under a white duvet of snow.

Not your tiny little wispy sprinkles from Christmas. Thick, plush, still-falling snow.

I must have made some kind of 'ooh' noise, because behind me, in bed, River stirs.

Nothing *happened*. We didn't do anything last night, but after the Ball drop and the singing and the kissing, we joined the hordes filtering away from Times Square. Attempting the subway rush wasn't worth it, so despite the ache in our feet and our jelly-like legs, we walked home. Hand in hand. Ahhhh.

We were shattered by the time we arrived back, sometime after one in the morning. Because no alcohol is allowed in Times Square, after chugging giant glasses of water and having a freshen-up in the bathroom, we changed into PJs and finally had a cold glass of bubbly on the sofa. Since I already turned it into the bed before setting out (thank you, Ashling of last year!) we ended up sinking lower and lower, leaning into each other, sweet, prosecco kisses shared, and that's where we both ended up falling asleep.

I turn from the window just as River's eyelashes flutter open. He looks momentarily confused about his surroundings, then he focuses on me, and he smiles.

'Happy New Year,' he croaks out.

'Happy New Year.' I hadn't known what to expect this morning. Would he wake up worrying about where the two of us could possibly go considering I was leaving later *this month*? But his face is soft and open, and he sits up to join me by the window, his hand finding my back.

'Did it snow?' he says as he shuffles his way over.

'So much. I've never seen New York like this.'

'I think it's going to be this way for a few days now. Do you want a coffee?'

'Oh my god, I'd *love* a coffee.' Now he's mentioned it, a coffee feels like the only thing missing from this scene.

River stands up and stretches. 'I'll run down the street and get us some interesting ones. What do you want?'

'Something creamy, maybe hazelnut flavour? And big.'

'Got it.' He disappears into his room and comes out moments later in jeans and a hoodie, over which he slings his coat, and grabs his keys. 'Back soon. Stay warm.'

While he's gone, I lean against the window frame and watch the snow fall. Wow. Last night . . .

River and I kissed, finally. Part of my brain is trying to get through the tangles and make me think about the future and what this could or couldn't mean, but I focus on the snowflakes falling in front of me, drinking in the perfect peace that is right now.

I'm deep in a daydream of River cupping my neck just as the clock was hitting midnight when he returns, coffee cups in hand, snowflakes dusting his dark hair.

'What's it like out?' I ask as he hands me my cup, plus a lovely-looking pastry dotted with pecans.

'Tropical,' he quips, then chuckles at his own joke, which makes me chuckle in return. River joins me back on the sofa, slotting in beside me, and we settle into a position of us both facing the window, with me leaning back against his chest. 'It's actually freezing out there. A good day to stay inside on the couch.'

I turn my face to see him. 'That sounds nice to me.'

We haven't actually kissed yet this morning, but his face looks open, a little shy, and I think we're both waiting for the green light from the other.

Taking a sip of my coffee feels like an elixir and I let out a colossal, happy moan. It's heavenly creamy with a rich, nutty depth. I am the living version of a winter Pinterest board right now, complete with delicious leading man beside me. 'What did you go for?' I ask the delicious leading man.

'Vanilla. You want to try some?'

I mean, if that isn't an opening, I don't know what is, so I take a chance and kiss him softly on his warm lips. 'Yummy,' I conclude.

'Well, now it's only fair I try yours,' River says, and his lips touch mine again. He nods. 'Yep, yummy.'

We might just be the cutest.

We drink our coffees slowly, letting the new day, and new year, settle in, and watching the snow as it drifts down in thick flakes past our window.

'Do you think we would have made it to midnight if this snowfall had started yesterday evening?' I ask, reaching for my pastry.

'It would have taken more than this to make me leave there,' River replies.

'Really? I didn't realise you were so into the whole Times Square New Year's thing.'

'I waited on my feet for nine hours just for the chance to kiss you. You think I'd give that up because of a little snow?'

Of course I've just chomped down on the pastry, so now have to wait until I've chewed and swallowed this giant hulk of buttery goodness. When I can, I say, 'You wanted to kiss me all along? I thought it was a last-second decision, literally?'

'It was, but that doesn't mean I hadn't been thinking about it since, well, for a while actually.'

'Since the lift?'

311

'Since Vermont.'

That warms my heart instantly and I kinda want to punch my fist in the air in victory, but I don't. 'Vermont was a bit of a turning point for me, too,' I admit.

We don't talk about what any of this means beyond these walls and beyond today. Time seems to stand still on New Year's Day, like the whole world is sleeping in or taking time for themselves or being still in the last moments of peace before life starts up again. So, we do the same.

River and I spend it in the apartment. We relive the evening before, we watch two people on the street below trying to dig their car out of snow, we stick the TV onto an old movie, we even play a game of chess, which I win, so maybe I could be a bit of chess shark after all. It's a lovely, lazy, languid day, and, before we know it, the sky has turned back to black, the lights of the city are on again, and the freshly falling snow has coated over the day's footprints on the ground.

'What did your parents think of you quitting your job?' I ask River that evening as he lies beside me, trailing his fingers through my hair. I think we're going to fall asleep on the sofa bed together again, and that is just fine with me.

'I think they were actually pleased,' he replies. 'They just want me to be happy, and they could see I wasn't, there.'

'Since the Italy thing fell through?'

'Even before then, hence the book. It was a good job. Solid. Benefits. Stability. But it wasn't everything and it kind of was becoming everything.'

'It was taking over.'

'It was like it was becoming my whole identity, but it wasn't even something I loved doing.'

I think about this for a moment, about how broken I was – am – about no longer being a pilot. That it is – was – a huge part of me, but I'm lucky to have also loved it, right in my soul.

River continues. 'When I was sent back from Italy, I thought I needed to fix myself within that company. But I needed to start by throwing away what wasn't actually working for me, and starting from fresh.'

I nod. I don't have anything to add – he said it so perfectly. I just hope I can get to the place of peace with my life that he is right now. I think I'm getting there. I know I am.

'How do you feel today? About life? Has coming to New York helped you find some new dreams, do you think?'

'I don't quite know how to answer that yet,' I tell him. 'If I was going back to the UK tomorrow, I wouldn't know what to do with myself. I don't have a new list of goals. I can't close my eyes and see what the next five, ten, fifteen years are going to look like. But ...' I close my eyes, trying to see what I *do* see. 'It doesn't feel as dark out there as it did before, like I don't have a torch. Now it feels like—' I open my eyes and point out the window. 'Like that snow. It's making the street glow even though it's dark out. I feel like I can see where to put my feet, I can see a whole criss-cross of ways to walk, even if I can't see where I'm going yet. Does that make sense?'

'It does.' He nods.

We're silent for a while, like he's giving me space in case I want to elaborate further with my ramblings about snowy sidewalks, but this is enough, for now.

# Chapter 37

On the second of January, the snow is still falling, and today I want to get out there and see Manhattan in all her magical winter wonderfulness.

River's taken himself out for the morning, meeting a career-counsellor friend of his for a coffee. He asked if I wanted to come along, talk through my situation, but I didn't want to get in the way.

I've been thinking about Grooms a lot since Mum went back home, and I feel like I have more questions than ever for her. How did she know coming to New York to dance would pay off? How did she feel when she achieved her dream? I wish I could still ask her.

My plan today is to sling on my most waterproof leather boots and walk from Greenwich Village up to the New York Public Library, through the snow, and I'm going to spend a happy few hours researching through the old newspaper records just in case there's any mention of my gran in them.

It's a long shot, but you never know, and it would be so fun to see her named somewhere.

Also, I'm sure I could totally do all this online, but when in Rome, and by Rome, I mean New York, why *wouldn't* I go get out there and hang out at one of the most famous bookish landmarks?

I'm just deciding whether a skirt, tights and boots is cute or really too cold, when the buzzer rings. Crap. Pulling off the skirt and swapping it for leggings, over my tights, I hop over to the intercom but by the time I've pressed the button and said, 'Hello?' I can already hear the front door clicking back closed. Somebody else has let the visitor in.

A minute later, there's a knock on my door, and I open it to find a person I was never expecting to see in real life.

'H-hi,' I stammer, face to face with Delilah. River's Delilah. THE Delilah.

I don't need to look at the photo on the shelf beside me, the one of her and River at the canyon, to know it's her. She has shorter hair now, but it's still a rich, chestnut brown. She has the same pale blue eyes; she's even wearing a white sweater similar to the one in the picture. Her smile is different; in the photo she's grinning, her teeth on show, but as she looks at me now her smile is polite but a little forced, her lips sewn together. In her hands she's holding a woollen hat, gripping it tightly.

'Hello,' Delilah replies. 'Is River here?'

'He's actually out this morning,' I say. Do I invite her in? I don't know the protocol. 'I'm Ashling, I'm, well, I was subletting the apartment and then River came home, as you know, of course—' Her eyes narrow just a tiny amount. It

316

would have been imperceptible if I wasn't going overboard with the whole making-eye-contact thing. 'Um, and he let me stay. On the sofa bed.'

Well, I couldn't very well tell her he was my boyfriend now or something; he and I haven't even begun discussing that.

'I'm Delilah,' she says, by way of reply. She doesn't offer any further explanation, and I think we both know that we both know who she is. 'Mind if I come in and wait?'

'Urrrrrrm, yep, sure.' I stand aside and she comes in, hanging her hat on the hook at the back of the door, the hook that my dressing gown is on. This is too weird.

'Actually, I was about to head out so it might be better to come back later?'

'Can I just wait here?' she asks. The redness of her eyes, the slump of her shoulders, everything about her gives away that she's clearly tired. Not in a mean way, I'm sure I look tired ninety per cent of the time.

'Okay. Do you want a coffee?' I ask.

'Yes, please.'

Delilah takes a seat on the armchair and looks out the window and it's not lost on me how at home she seems here. I busy myself with the coffee machine and shoot a quick text over to River.

Hey. Delilah's here. She just came over. I let her in – is that okay?

It's read immediately and a reply comes right back. It's definitely Delilah?

It's someone called Delilah who looks a lot like the one in your canyon photo.

I'm on my way.

I'm not going to allow myself to twist into acrobatics about whether his quick response means he's excited to get home and see her. It's none of my business.

Nevertheless, I don't quite know if I should leave her here alone. Not that I think she's about to ransack the place or take off with River's mug collection or something. But I wouldn't want an ex roaming around my space without me there, it just wouldn't feel right to me.

I bring a coffee to Delilah and sit down with one myself.

'I thought you were heading out?' she says. 'I'm okay waiting here by myself.'

'No, I am, but I was just going to have a coffee first.'

Delilah nods, and looks out the window. 'Are you British?'

'I certainly am, guvna.' I tip the hat I'm not wearing and internally call myself an idiot.

'How long are you here for?'

She might be sounding me out, I can't tell, but she says it with a smile. Perhaps my weird 'guvna' thing made her think 'this chick is no threat to me'.

'Just to the end of the month. I'm on the ESTA visa waiver, just a tourist, so I'm living here but not *living* living here. I have ninety days and I got here early November, so ...' *No, please, Ashling, tell her more about your life story.* 'How's Italy? That's where you're based now, isn't it?' Smooth.

'It's okay.' She sips her coffee and looks out of the window again. 'I just got in last night.'

'Oh, New Year's Day. Happy New Year.'

'Yeah. Happy New Year.' Delilah does not sound happy.

318

But what do I know? Maybe this is her sounding happy. The only things I know about her are from River's side of the story and, although I believe all he's told me, it's always going to be biased when you're the one who's been dumped. I'm sure I come off as a total villain to many of Hugh's friends when he talks about me, and I don't think I'm too bad.

We sit in silence for a little while, and I act very invested in blowing on and sipping my coffee to try to hide the fact I'm searching for things to say that don't involve River's kissing techniques or something. Delilah doesn't seem to be having the same internal struggle. She's gazing out at the snow, lost in thought.

'Can I get you anything?' I ask after a while and she pulls her gaze from the window, a sad smile on her face.

'How's he been?'

The question throws me and I open and close my mouth a few times like a fish.

'I don't mean about me,' Delilah clarifies. 'I'm sure you don't talk to him about that. I mean about the job, about the Italy thing falling through and coming back home.'

'Oh. Well. He's . . .' What do I say? Should I even be talking to her about this? I pretend to drink from my mug again to buy myself time but it's empty so I make a faux-slurp noise to make it look realistic. Pretty sure she knows I'm faking. 'Well, he was sad, I think. But he got back into work and did what he could but I guess it just didn't feel like the right fit any more.'

'What do you mean?'

'Him. And the company.'

'Did he quit?'

Ah, shit. I kind of thought someone at work would have told her. 'No,' I say quickly. 'Uh, yes, he did. But it was all his decision.' Dunno why I felt the need to slip that in. 'I'm sure he'll tell you all about it.'

'Does he know I'm here?'

'I let him know. Just because I don't know what his schedule is today and I didn't want you waiting around all day long or something. There are snowmen to be built out there!'

'Right.' She chuckles, then pretends to carry on drinking her coffee too.

Four years later, River finally walks in the door and though he spots me first, his eyes immediately flick to Delilah.

'Hey,' he says.

'Hey.' And then she starts crying, and the first thing I notice is that she's quite a pretty crier and I wonder if I should tell her because nobody's ever said it to me and I think it would be a nice thing to hear.

'Delilah.' River says her name like it's the most familiar sound in his mouth. He walks towards her and I step out of the way, heading to put my mug in the kitchenette. As we pass each other, he brushes his hand against mine, and I know it was on purpose.

'I'm going to go out now and leave you to it,' I say.

I try to face away as I'm putting on my coat, but out of the corner of my eye I see him reach her and hesitate before he sits down and puts his arm over her shoulder. She leans into him and he looks over, meeting my eye. 'Okay,' he says, and then he mouths, 'Sorry.'

I shake my head and mouth back, 'It's okay.' But he doesn't see. He's already wrapped back around Delilah, speaking to her softly. I slip out of the door.

Once I reach the stairwell, I have to stop and take a breath.

Here are the facts: River and I have kissed. River and I have not discussed any kind of relationship, beyond him telling me his fears about giving his heart to someone who would be leaving the country. Again.

His ex, Delilah, is back from Italy. I knew this was happening sometime in January. She is crying. He is comforting her.

Here are the things I don't know and will *not* let myself ruminate on because I am a grown-up with more important things to think about. Such as what the hell to do with myself now I am only three weeks away from turning thirty. I don't know if River and I will ever be more than a holiday romance. I don't know why Delilah came to see River after only getting back yesterday. I don't know why she's crying. I don't know how long she'll be there for. I don't know if the two of them will kiss. I don't know if I'll come back to find her in a post-coital glow and wearing my dressing gown.

So I guess I'd better stick to my plan and go to the library.

# Chapter 38

I'm not gonna lie, that walk was a slog. The snow is thick, and it's not having time to turn to slush as more snow keeps falling. It was like walking on soft sand for forty minutes, and it was beautiful, but my calf muscles are feeling it.

I reach the library and climb up the steps and in through the massive arches, removing my scarf and gloves as I do so, and stamping the snow off my boots before I go inside the revolving doors. Wow, this place. Before I start my research, I take a good look around, quietly walking through great halls with warm chandeliers dangling above them, admiring the bookshelves and the murals, smelling the paper and listening to the silence. It's a sanctuary in here, and it quietens my mind so I'm definitely not thinking about River and Delilah.

After speaking to a nice lady at a nice desk, I'm set up with an account and directed to a computer where I can search masses of digitised newspapers for keywords.

I can't ask Grooms my questions any more. But there's

just a chance that her dreams were documented somewhere here in the city, to inspire the world like she inspired me.

I type in my gran's name, making sure to use the right spelling, and several hundred results come up. Hmm. Clicking on the first one, I see it's an article from the seventies about how a woman with my grandma's name was angry at the local politician for digging up her favourite tree. I'm going to need to be more specific here. I type in Grooms' name again, along with 'dancer'.

Finally, something! A small write-up about a cabaret act, and a little photograph. Just a couple of lines about the dancers being in time and making the audience laugh, and then naming four women. One of which had the same name as my gran. I zoom in, and there she is, it's her, in her cabaret get-up, standing with her dancer colleagues, outside the NightNight Lounge Cabaret Club, New York City.

I want to take a victory lap. I love that I found this! My Grooms, immortalised here in New York.

But it doesn't tell me a lot that I didn't already know.

I click onto a small advert, the next entry down. It's old, sparse, a call-out for information about a missing person, the same surname as Grooms. And it lists her as the contact.

I sit back in my seat. What in the . . .? Who was Grooms looking for? I pull out my phone and drop a quick message to my mum.

Hi Mum. Just at the library doing some research, trying to fill in some of the blanks in Grooms' life. Do you know if Grooms had an older relative out here? A man? And if so, why she was looking for him in New York?

A friend? A boyfriend? Unlikely to have the same surname as Grooms though . . .

While I'm waiting, I search the newspaper archives for my own name, because why not, and find an article about a namesake of mine who committed a double homicide.

A message comes back from Mum, but rather than any details it just says, Honey, can you give me call?

A trickle of worry seeps in, and I log off the computer and pack up my things, after taking a quick print-out of the cabaret article and accompanying photo. Exiting the library, I walk around the quiet side, away from the ice rink and Winter Village, taking a seat on a bench, brushing the layer of snow off, first.

The phone rings only once, and then Mum picks up.

'Hi, honey,' she says.

'Mum, are you okay?' I ask without hesitation.

'Yes, yes, fine,' she says. Her voice is sunny but there's something in her tone that isn't quite right.

'Did you get my message about Grooms?' I ask.

*Now* she hesitates. 'I did, and, look, I need to tell you something.'

'What?' I feel cold, and not because I'm surrounded by snow.

Mum takes a big breath; I hear it down the line. 'There's something about your gran's time in New York that she wasn't completely honest with you about. It's not a big deal, really, but you know Grooms, she was always so into this idea of you and her being these big dreamers.'

Huh? 'What are you saying?'

'I'm saying that my mum did go to New York, that all happened exactly as she told you, but it was for another reason.' Mum takes another breath. 'She always fed this idea to you that she had big dreams of becoming a dancer in New York City and made it happen, but that wasn't quite how it panned out. Her dad, my grandad, left my grandma when Grooms was a teenager. He moved to America, and they didn't hear from him again. Grooms, a few years later, decided to follow him out there, to talk to him, bring him home, but then she ran out of money trying to find him. In fact, she never found him. The dream failed. She used her talents as a dancer to earn more money, and it became a life she loved. Then, she discovered she no longer needed his support or his approval. And that's where she found her family – in her new friends.'

My brain scrambles to keep up, to hold on to the details Mum's telling me. She came out here to find her dad? She just fell into dancing? But ... my gran prided herself, instilled the pride into my mum and me, that she never let a man – anyone, actually – stand between her and her dreams.

I said goodbye to Hugh after he stopped supporting mine.

Wasn't Grooms' life, and all she achieved, her *own* making, thanks to hard work and following her heart? 'You're saying, she wasn't the big success story who followed her dreams ... after all?'

'Honey,' Mum says soothingly. 'I'm saying her path altered, and she found her true dream in an unexpected place.'

'But why wouldn't she tell me all this?'

'She always wanted you to believe following your heart

was worth it. She wanted you to think she'd achieved her wildest dreams. She was happy,' Mum adds. 'She never lied about how New York made her feel. I know she loved her life there and her experiences, all of them.'

'Okay,' I say, inhaling an icy breath, hearing the crunch of snow under city feet walking by. 'Okay, well, I suppose it's no big deal. I'm just being silly. All right, Mum, it's really snowy and cold here and I'm outside at the moment, so can I call you back another time?'

'Yes, of course, honey. Thanks for ringing.'

'Thanks for letting me know. Chat soon!' I ring off and the smile I've pasted on falls like snow off a rooftop.

I sit for a while on the chair, the cold seeping into my leggings, and feel a numbing pooling from my inside out. Which is really silly. I'm happy for Grooms, that she found her happiness, I don't care what road she took to get her there. I didn't believe in having dreams just because Grooms fulfilled hers. That was a source of inspiration for me, sure, but I didn't base my life around it.

What's causing me to shut down as I sit alone in the snow, though, is the realisation that I never really knew her at all. She hid herself from me, and now it's too late to ever get to know the true her.

# Chapter 39

My bottom is very cold now.

A while has gone by and before I get stuck to the chair or something, I lift myself up and walk a lap of the park, wondering what to do with myself. I don't want to go home – I don't want to interrupt River and Delilah, if she's still there. I don't want to wander around the shops having to keep putting on a smiley face to the lovely sales assistants. I don't want to go and sit in a coffeehouse as I feel sick at the thought of eating or drinking anything.

I want to talk to someone, but not Mum, she'll just worry. I try Flo but it goes to voicemail, which usually happens if she's with a client. I just want to speak to someone who knew Grooms and can help make some sense of this with me.

'Hi,' I say, standing outside Hugh's door.

'Come in.' When I called, Hugh said he was working from home, but said that I could come over and see him for an hour or so and he'd mark himself as being in a meeting.

'I'm really sorry to show up like this.' I mean it. A big part of me knows I shouldn't be here, shouldn't be anywhere near poor Hugh when I'm aware how he feels about me, and how I don't feel about him. But he knew my gran, spending countless hours with her over the years and they got on so well. He seemed like the right person to call.

'It's not a problem.' His voice is a little frosty, but it thaws when he takes me in. 'Have you been crying?'

'A little.'

He gestures for me to take a seat on the sofa and brings a fresh cup of tea out of the kitchen for me. Proper tea, made how I like it. That makes me smile. He sits beside me. 'What happened?'

'It's nothing really, it's so silly,' I say. His face is full of concern and it makes me want to reach out and rub the frown line out, like I used to do, but I keep my hands around my mug. 'It's just something about Grooms that I just found out.'

I offload through a long sigh, telling him about my call with Mum, and when I'm done, I just sit still with it for a little while and let him put his arm around me.

'I feel stupid crying at you. Crying at all because it's not even a problem.' I sniffle. 'She was happy and she had a great life out here. My gran didn't wallow at not reaching her dreams; she just turned them into new ones. I'm just really facing the truth that it's too late to talk to her about anything now.'

'I know . . .' Hugh soothes. He always was soothing, and

I was grateful for that. I hope I was a good girlfriend to him, at least most of the time. He lets out a small laugh. 'Remember that time your gran tried to give me a tap-dancing lesson?'

I giggle at the memory, a bit of snot bubbling out of my right nostril. 'She said your toes weren't "Ginger Rogers standard". And then you tried to teach her the guitar.'

'Tried? Thanks to me she could play the opening bars of "Smells Like Teen Spirit" on her own.'

I forgot all about that. It took Hugh and Grooms all day but she nailed it by the time the slow cooker at Mum's had dinged for dinner that Sunday. I pictured her tucking into the stew, then sprinkling garlic powder onto hers when Mum wasn't looking. (Mum always pretended she wasn't looking). 'Remember the garlic powder she carried with her wherever she went?'

'Of course. And the surgical gloves.'

'"Just in case she needed them."'

This was nice, talking about my gran, talking about things I knew to be true.

I wish, *I wish*, I could turn back time and take that trip with her. I wish I hadn't said we should wait while I saved up money to take us on the Orient Express. I'd give anything to go back in time and just take her for a week in a caravan in Cornwall or something, anything, anywhere I could just talk to her and hear all of her stories, her real stories, and ask her all the questions I have right now. I wish I could have gotten to know the person she was, not the person she wanted me to think she was.

My heart feels heavy. Exhausted. Confused.

I wish I could go back and change so much. I wish the me of ten years ago picked different dreams and goals up at the top of the Empire State Building. Then I might not have lost them all.

'What's going through your brain right now?' Hugh asks, bringing me back from my wish land.

I sigh and look at him, and another wish materialises. I wish I hadn't hurt him. 'Just thinking about how I should have done things differently.'

Hugh reaches his hand up and mops at my tears with his sleeve.

'I don't want to think about these things. I don't want to think about all the things I've lost.' I squeeze my eyes shut, trying to close the door on these feelings. And now I've probably lost River, too.

Was I ever going to find happy again?

'You've not lost me,' Hugh says, his voice low.

I open my eyes. 'No, Hugh.'

'What if I said you could go back in time?'

I do want to go back in time. Right now, it's exactly what I want. Hugh leans over, cupping my cheek with one hand, and kisses my other cheek, softly.

His hand is warm, his touch familiar, his heart good. Even after everything I put him through, he'd still take me back. He keeps his lips close and says, 'What do you think?' He kisses my cheek again, a little closer to my lips.

I know what he's offering me. If I say yes to this, I have the chance to claw back one of my dreams, to be with him again, and, maybe, down the road, get married to him, like the plan always was. I wouldn't be so lost.

After all, I'm still the same me I was ten years ago, I still want the same things. Losing them just made me realise how empty I feel, all the time.

There's a tug at my heart, a nagging in my consciousness. A little voice trying to poke holes in my current mindset. *Sure, Ashling, some things we lost before we were ready, but others, like marrying Hugh ... if the dream doesn't fit any more, it's okay to wake up, right?*

And what about River?

*But what about Delilah*, my mind counterargues.

I meet Hugh's eyes. They are still home. Aren't they? Maybe just one kiss is all it'll take for us to be righted again, knocked back on course?

He kisses me again, a centimetre from my mouth, and whispers, 'Come on. I'm going to help you get your life together. I know you're sad to have missed the chance to really know your gran, but you can get to know me again.'

Urm, what? I jerk away, just as his phone rings on the coffee table. Was that a really crappy thing to say? Or is he telling the truth? And, wait – is that my face on his screen? And my name?

Am I having an out-of-body experience, or something? How am I phoning him right now? Am I butt-dialling?

Hugh pulls back and glances towards the screen, then leaps away from me like a cat jumping at a loud noise, grabbing his phone and cancelling the call. No ... my phone is in my coat pocket. The coat that's draped over a chair, on the other side of the room.

'Who was that?' I ask, coming back to reality. 'Why did it look like I was calling you then?'

'I don't know, I must have accidentally put your photo against someone's contact details.'

That little liar. I know that face. 'You accidentally put my name on there too, Hugh?'

He sits back on the sofa, leaning his head against the backrest, and puts his hands over his face, groaning into them. 'Look, it's nothing.'

'*What's* nothing?' I demand, and a memory of River saying to me, 'You call him all the time,' pops into my consciousness. 'Tell me what's going on.'

He rubs at his forehead, and after a couple of minutes, and a couple of sighs, he looks at me. 'I did it because I wanted to put River off, okay? I didn't want you dating my colleague. So I wanted him to think we still had something going on. I know, I know, I'm a bell-end.'

'I don't understand what you're talking about.'

'I changed someone's contact info so they have your name and your photo come up when they call me.'

'Who is it? Who just called you?'

'My mum.'

'YOUR MUM? Your mum calls you four times a day, and all this time River, and anyone else, has been thinking it's me?' No wonder River thought I was still secretly into Hugh. Hugh has probably been telling everyone I came to New York to be with him again, knowing his track record.

'It's not *four* times a day,' he replies gloomily.

Oh, River. What was I thinking, coming here, risking

what's brewing with him for this. Sure, I might get back to the flat and have lost him already. But your heart is worth taking a risk for, right?

I stand up. I have to get out of here. I have to get out of Hugh's life.

'Don't go. I'm sorry,' says Hugh, but I shake my head.

'No, I am. This isn't what I want, and it's not because I'm a bad person, it's because I've changed. Not completely, but in so many ways. And now I'm not good enough for you.' Hugh opens his gob to protest, but I shrug and continue. 'I'm not. Because I would only be with you because I was trying to go back to something I knew and I loved. And you deserve someone who knows you and loves you now. And so do I. So I'm going to go. And I'm going to keep my distance now. I'm sorry I didn't before.'

I half expect him to resist, but he doesn't. Instead, he walks me to the door of his home, and I say goodbye, to Hugh, and to the dream I once had for us.

And that's okay.

# Chapter 40

I'm going home now. My temporary home. My lovely flat in Greenwich Village, to my window with a view of the Empire State Building and hopefully, to River.

It's late afternoon by the time I get back, twilight in the city, and car headlamps are creating puddles of amber light on the snowy sidewalks.

I reach the apartment and listen at the door as I take off my gloves and hat. Silence.

Inside, all is quiet too. I go to hang my coat up and see that Delilah's hat is gone, my dressing gown on its own on the hook again. I stand for a minute, looking around. River's door is closed. The mug I made Delilah's coffee in is washed and on the draining board. I put my hand to my chest. The photo of the two of them is gone from the bookshelf.

At that moment, River's bedroom door opens and out he steps, in a sweater with too-long arms, dark blue jeans and his hair a mess. He looks tired. He looks great.

'Hey,' he says, and then seeming to once-over me too, adds, 'You okay?'

'Yeah,' I reply with an exhausted vagueness. 'How are you?'

He runs a hand through his hair and leans against his door frame. 'All right. Thrown. I wasn't expecting Delilah to be back in the city for another couple of weeks.'

I want to butt in with questions but my befuddled brain won't form them, so instead I start making two cups of coffee. I'll wait for him to talk it out.

'Turns out,' he continues. 'The whole team got sent home from Italy. There's been a one-eighty on the idea of the European branch and now the remaining five have, you know, met the same fate as the rest of us did back in November.'

Whoa, this I was not expecting. Delilah must feel like a prize dick for letting River go because of long distance. Ah, hang on, she probably *does* feel like that, and that's probably what this visit was all about. 'So, she's back in New York?' I clarify, attempting to keep my voice really neutral.

River nods, slowly. 'Yeah, I guess so. She was pretty cut up about it all. I mean, you remember the mood I was in when it just happened to me.' I smile. That first night. Was it really just two months ago, or a million years? 'We talked for a while, she apologised . . .'

He trails off, and I don't push him. To me, the silence is filled with the sound of my heart thumping, my shallow breath. I'm trying to play it cool, but I'd be fooling myself to think this might not affect whatever was beginning to brew between him and me. He has history with Delilah, a shared

335

life before he even met me. And who's going to be here after I've gone back to the UK? Her.

'Complicated things, exes,' I say with a small sigh, and hand him his coffee.

Our fingers touch as the mug passes between us and we both leave them where they are for a moment, before I move away and sit on the couch.

River sits beside me, and we both slump down onto the sofa, staring forwards, our mugs resting on our chests. Really, it's quite the image of domestic bliss.

'Tell me about your day,' River says. 'You look how I feel.'

'Thanks,' I reply, and take a beat before looking over at him. 'I went to see Hugh.'

'Oh?' He raises his eyebrows.

'Something – not Delilah, just so you know – something to do with home, with my gran, had upset me and I went over there to talk it out with him. It was kinda nice but I shouldn't have gone because he then made it very clear he wanted to get back together. Which I knew beforehand so it really was a mean decision to go over there.' I pause. 'We nearly kissed. But we didn't. And we won't. I just wanted you to know.'

River nods. 'All right. Thanks for telling me.'

A laugh pops out of me. 'Oh and by the way, turns out he switched his mum's caller ID to my name and photo. That's why you and half of New York have been thinking I've been calling him non-stop. She calls him *constantly*.'

River chuckles at this too, thankfully.

My laughter dies down. 'I'm not telling you any of this

to try to influence anything between you and Delilah, I'm just . . . telling you.'

'I appreciate it. And just so you know, I'm not back with Delilah. That's not what I want.'

I let that sink in. Okay. That's good, for now. But . . . 'I don't expect you to make any choices or decisions or anything without letting the fact she's come back settle, in your mind. Maybe you should just sit with it for a bit and then see how you feel about, you know, everything.'

We sip our coffees in unison.

'What upset you about home?' River asks after a while. 'If you want to tell me.'

'Well, you know I told you about my gran, who followed her dreams to New York to be a dancer?'

'Sure . . .'

I tell him what I found out, and then let out a tired chuckle. 'She just rewrote the beginning of her truth, all to inspire me to go after my dreams.'

'Even though hers changed?'

'Exactly, they just altered course, but that made her happy.' I shake my head, as best I can in this slumped position. 'But the thing that makes me sad is the fact that I feel like I never got to take her on the big trip I planned, where I think I could have finally got to know the real her. It's too late now.'

When I look over, I'm expecting River to have that frown on his face still, but he's smiling, his eyes twinkling at me.

'What are you smiling at?' I ask.

'I'm so happy for you.'

'Um, thanks?'

He sits up, rolling up his sleeves. 'Ashling, you're on a trip, in one of her favourite places in the world, and here you are, you're getting to know the real her.'

I blink at him, his words seeping into my soul. He's right. My heart lifts a little, like the heavy snow on top of it is being brushed away. So my dream to get to know my gran didn't crumble completely . . . it just had to alter course, the best it could. River knew exactly what I needed to hear.

I fall back into silence, thinking, mulling, remembering, and after a while a long, giant yawn comes out of me.

'It's been a day. Wanna order some pizza? Watch TV, and go to sleep?' River asks, sitting up and stretching his back.

'That sounds exactly what we both need.' I nod.

Night has fallen and I open my eyes to the sound of shuffling. It's River, moving quietly through the apartment, switching off the TV, putting the pizza boxes on the side, and pulling my blankets over me. My eyelids are puffy and tired, and they droop again rather than waking up fully.

I'm aware of him heading into his own bedroom. He's planning to sleep alone tonight. For a moment a little sadness drifts into my consciousness, until he turns around at the last minute and comes close. 'Ashling, are you awake?' he whispers.

'Mmm-hmm,' I reply in my dozy state. I feel him stroke the hair from my face and I open my eyes again and look into his.

'I just wanted to say . . . New York can't tell you who you

are, only you can do that. It's not outside, at a place or a landmark, it's in you. So rather than listening to all the external sounds, listen to yourself.'

He's always encouraged me to take control of my own life, ever since our first breakfast together, that November morning. Now, I take his words, in his lovely New York accent, and hold them close as I drift into sleep.

## Chapter 41

Figure out who I am now

I'm going to miss the sunrises. I'll miss a lot of things when I go back home, but the sight of the morning sun as it first hits the Empire State Building, and pools like silk through the streets, waking up the architecture and chasing away the dark, that's one thing I'll miss a lot.

This morning, the sky is a mix of pale blue and wispy clouds, and I take my time dressing, one layer at a time, bundling up warm. I leave the apartment with a quiet *click* and begin the long walk up to Central Park. I'm painfully aware of how little time River and I have left together, but I need to focus on me before I can think about us.

I've brought a bag with me, in which is a cushion and my Brooklyn Bridge earmuffs, and I duck into a store to buy a new, clean sketchbook and a set of pencils.

On the walk, I don't allow my mind to wander off to revisit the past, or imagine scenarios in the future. The morning traffic and strum of city life getting back to business after the holidays fills the air around me. Warm aromas spiral up from pretzel carts. The cool wind tickles my cheek and I absorb the sight of the city, with her window ledges and curbs and tree branches topped with snowy ledges.

When I reach the edge of the park, I keep walking, through tunnels of wintery leaf-bare trees and past icy lakes until I reach a string of benches with few other people around.

It's so quiet, the buzz of the city no more than white noise, dulled by the thick snow. I place my cushion on the bench, take a seat, and take a breath.

And then, I let in my mum's advice, the same advice I passed on to River only the day before, but had never really taken on myself. I stop. I stop thinking, planning, doing, panicking, I just let myself sit, settle, and allow the feelings in.

For the first time since I had the news three months ago that I wouldn't be able to pilot a plane again, I allow myself to feel sad. Proper, actual, mournful sad for the life I loved that was no longer mine, and for the way that knocked me irreparably off course and made my heart feel like it was being squeezed to nothingness in my chest.

The tears come thick and silent, and I'm a touch nervous that they'll freeze on my cheeks and I'll end up with mascara icicles, but I still let them come.

At one point, a passing guy kneels down to where I'm hunched over, crying into my hands. 'Ma'am, are you okay?'

I tell him I am, wiping at my snot.

'Can I get you anything?'

'No. Thank you, though. Just ... taking a much-needed moment.'

'All right.' He smiles and walks away, and ten minutes later, somebody else sits beside me on the bench.

I lift my face from my hands to see a woman, about my age, in running clothes, including a long-sleeved top and a beanie hat. She's panting.

'Hey,' she says.

'Hi.'

'You letting it all out?' I nod, and she gives me a nod back. 'I've had my share of Central Park ugly-cries. Here.' She hands me a bottle of cola and a chocolate bar. 'I got you these from the kiosk. Keep your sugar levels up.'

'You got these for me?'

The woman nods again, pats me on the back, then sticks her AirPod back in and resumes her run before I can even say thank you.

I eat my chocolate bar and drink some of my soda and draw patterns in the snowflakes under my feet with the toe of my boot, while my mind deals with the feels, like it needs to.

A while goes past, and I'm cold. And hungry. I find a nearby restaurant, where I order a big bowl of French onion soup with sourdough bread and let the warmth bring me back to life a little.

From the window, one of the ponds lies still and calm. Is that ... kinda ... me right now?

My birthday is in two weeks – my thirtieth birthday – the deadline I've given myself to have rebuilt my life and know exactly what I want my future to look like. I don't even know what I want my birthday to look like.

But I'm actually not worried, as I sit here. I'm not stressing. I don't quite know why – maybe it's the release of all those tears, maybe I'm in denial, but something has changed. I exhale.

Re-warmed, I make my way towards the Wollman Rink, and take out my sketch pad to draw the scene in front of me. Drawing for fun, like I used to do, before nobody but me told me to stop.

The skaters blur on my page as they swoop in circles, snow on the banks and tree branches that look over them.

One skater, a woman around my age, spins in the centre of the rink, lifting up into the air as she does so and lands with a confident *swoosh* as her blade hits the ice and she becomes grounded again.

Like I have. Thanks to New York.

I smile to myself, as winter sunlight breaks through the clouds and glitters the snow in the park.

At times I've worried that I wasted my time here in New York, frittering away the days following directions from anyone other than me, because thinking about what *I* really wanted seemed so hard. But bit by bit, as autumn leaves blew away to reveal holiday sparkles, which have now been blanketed by New Year's snow, I think I've managed to let some things go. Or, perhaps, let them be.

I study my drawing. I may have missed out on the Young Artists' Residency, but, for the first time in years, here I am, actually drawing again for *me*.

Hugh didn't get my happily ever after, in the end. And a tiny flat in Greenwich Village (with perhaps a dash of Vermont cabin) have opened me up to new places for my heart to explore.

I would have loved to have had extra time with Grooms. Even one more minute to know just that little bit more of what made her the woman she was. But River was right. In a way, New York gave me that.

And no, I didn't look up at the skies above the Empire State Building and find an immediate replacement for my failed dream of being a pilot. Of course I didn't. Because I never failed. What a disservice to my years of training, to those sunrises from my cockpit seat, to the people whose fears I've helped fade, to the friends I've made and the places I've seen and the feelings of ascending up into the atmosphere, to pretend it was all for nothing. I was a pilot. I fulfilled that dream, even if I can't live it forevermore.

I owe it to me from ten years ago to not pretend the last decade didn't happen. I owe it to me now to not let the last decade define the next.

I'm a dreamer, I dream big and I make things happen; I don't know why I ever limited myself to five. My life isn't over. I can have a thousand dreams and goals and some may glow and some may fade, some may be small and some may be as big as a city.

It's kind of exciting, now I think of it that way.

# Chapter 42

It takes approximately one hour to walk between the ice rink in Central Park to my apartment in Greenwich Village. And that's not accounting for thick snow, and pretty damp boots.

If I take the subway, I'd be there in twenty minutes. But I know what I want now, and I don't want to miss a single footstep here on Manhattan while I move towards it.

With pink cheeks and numb toes, I race through the streets. Down Fifth Avenue, its giant shop façades towering above the snowdrifts. While I'm walking, a new dream is forming, something that clicks, and sticks. I call my mum, hoping she's still up.

The phone rings a couple of times before she picks up. 'Hello, honey,' she says down the line. 'I was just sitting here with Madeline telling her all about our ice skating over a glass of wine. She doesn't believe how good I am so we're going to go to an ice rink together next Saturday where I can show off my skills.'

345

I laugh. 'Good for you, Mum.'

My heart warms at the thought of her and Madeline holding mittened paws around an ice rink.

'How are you doing?'

'I'm good. It's all good. Listen, Mum? I was thinking . . .'

'Yep?'

'I had the best time in New York with you. Shall we take more trips together? We could start with Iceland, and the Blue Lagoon.' I mean it. She came all the way out here, my mum, the big worrier. An inspiration.

'That sounds brilliant!' Mum enthuses.

It's time for our relationship to shine, for *us* to take more trips together, for me to ask questions and have her share anecdotes about her own life and goals. It's like my dream for me and Grooms, but altered, and just as amazing.

I speed-walk past the dogs playing on the white-blanketed slopes of Madison Square Park, and type out a quick email on my phone. It's in reply to Living In The Air's HQ, and I tell them that yes, please, I would like to have a call and discuss alternative jobs with them. It's going to be hard to adjust, but I love this company too much to force my heart into something it doesn't really want to be a part of. At least, that's how I feel in this moment, and that's all I can go off, right?

I dodge to avoid a sidewalk snowman and zigzag my way past brownstones and apartment blocks until I'm in front of my own.

I catch my breath and wipe the snot away that's dribbling out because it's cold and sometimes that just happens.

The elevator allows me a few moments to collect my thoughts, and I press my back against the inside of the lift. A little snort of laughter escapes my lips at the happy memory. River and I almost kissed in here.

Yes, I know what I want now. And I know who I want.

My phone rings in my pocket just as I reach the door, and on the screen I see River's name.

'Hey,' I answer, pulling out my keys. I hold the phone to my ear and open the door. There he is, standing by our big arched window, looking out. The panes of glass have snow settled in the bottom of each of them, and tiny flakes have started to fall from the sky, against the near-clear twilight sky. He looks framed with confetti, like he did as the count-down hit midnight on New Year's Eve.

'Hey,' I repeat, and he turns.

'Hi.'

What's he thinking? I can't read him right now. Hanging in the air between us is the possibility that he's decided to rekindle his romance with Delilah. His face is thoughtful, dreamy, and then that whisper of a smile appears on his parted lips, and it's like a gentle breeze has lifted any stale air. I move towards the window, and him.

'I just needed to speak to you,' he says, his coffee-drip voice low and smooth, and he steps closer to me, running warm fingers through my icy hair and sending sunbeams through me.

'You did?'

'I don't need time to think, not about this,' he says. 'Not

when the only one soaring through my mind is you.' His other hand moves to my hair too, and I lean into his touch. 'If you need time, that's okay, but I'm not afraid of a little distance any more. Not when everything else feels like this.'

From the corner of my eye, I see the Empire State Building looking down at me, glowing her signature white, the top sparkling in the way it does to mark the top of every hour. I like to think she's winking at me, telling me she had my back all along.

'I don't need any more time,' I say to him. 'I want to make this work. I don't know how to predict a perfect future any more, but you . . . you and I are in this together. Now. Right?'

He smiles as he leans down to kiss me, and I fold my arms behind his neck. This funny, sweet, shy guy who seems to like my head-in-the-clouds self.

River is a dream I found in the most unexpected place. I'm falling in love, and I'm going to live every New York minute of it.

## Chapter 43

It's my birthday, and it's bittersweet. Bitter as it means I'm leaving New York soon, sweet as life is, finally, sweet again. And so is this cocktail.

I'm having a birthday party at the NightNight Lounge, and by birthday party, I mean a small gathering of everyone I know here in the USA, which is Septum-Ally, the two girls from my hostel dorm, returned from their travels around the US, River's parents, Meg and Ricky, Danny the Pizza Guy, a few neighbours from Greenwich Village and River, though he's running late, travelling back to the city following a job interview.

Well, not quite everyone. I didn't invite Hugh. That whole situation just needs to be left alone now, I think. Besides, it looks from Instagram like maybe he's started dating again, somebody from his work who's just come back into town . . . and I'm happy for him.

Ally is chatting with Danny and I'm sat in between Meg

and Ricky, telling them all about my phone call with Living In The Air.

'They told me they wanted to find a place for me in the company that I really loved, so we talked for aaaaages about what it was about being a pilot that I hated, that I enjoyed, that I couldn't live without. And it really helped, you know?'

'Do you know what they'll offer you?' questions Ricky.

Shaking my head, I say, 'Not yet. But they're going to come back to me as soon as they can. They seemed to like the idea I proposed, and so do I, and if I hadn't come out to New York this winter, I don't think it would have ever occurred to me.' I have a new, altered dream making itself at home in my mind right now. I really hope it works out with my beloved airline. But if it doesn't, I know there are plenty of paths I can follow.

Right, I need to pop outside and do something before I forget. I excuse myself and step out, treading with care between the slush so as not to skid on the icy pavement and tensing my bad shoulder against the freezing air.

Nowadays, the NightNight Lounge is a chic cocktail bar with a vintage feel. I step back between the parked cars that line the dark street and take out the photo of my gran with her dancer friends, and hold it aloft. Yep, the awnings may have changed, the signage is slightly altered and rebranded, there are fairy-light-covered planters now where huge potted palm trees stood framing the door in the photo, but it's still the same place. The shape of the windows, the arch above the doorway, and the street sign just to the left, are all as they were back then. Back when my gran stood right here.

I know, I've visited several places in New York and stood in the footprints of my gran, but, this time, I'm not standing in them to try to find inspiration for use in my own life, but to really get a feeling for hers.

'Hi, Grooms,' I whisper to the space where she once stood, and I can almost hear her laughing, whooping, cackling with her gals. I bet she had a blast, I bet she didn't let it ruin a thing, having to alter her goals.

*Thank you for bringing me to New York a decade ago, Grooms, when I was just nineteen. And now, I've turned thirty. A new decade for me . . . I wonder what my thirties will bring?*

I kiss the photo, tuck it into my pocket, hug my coat around myself, and feel the warmth within me, as I send up a silent *cheers* to my old haunt (Grooms) from her old haunt (her cabaret club).

I'm looking up, between the skyscrapers, searching for the stars, when someone skids into me.

'Whoa!' he cries. The stars align; River's here. I start to slip again and he catches me, pushing my back against the black-painted wall for balance, and coming to a stop in front of me.

Well, this is reminiscent of our time in the elevator.

The past two weeks have been a dream. The two of us have been a super-cute couple of love bunnies, and we're growing closer every day. We've even done some of the date ideas from *New YOLO*, much to River's mild dismay, (haha). I can't believe I have to be moving the other direction from him in a week – the thought makes me bloody well want to cry but I don't want to spend my present here only thinking about what's to come.

Now he's here, in front of me, his eyes as glittering as the snow.

'Happy birthday,' he whispers.

'About time,' I reply. 'How did it go?'

'It went really well,' he says, his voice a murmur. 'I like your hair.'

Earlier today, I finally made it to the salon Flo recommended, and they refreshed my cut, and this time I asked them to melt some copper into the blonde. It's no longer the peach of when I arrived in New York, but it's warm and wintery like a fireplace, and I love it.

River keeps one hand on the wall, his feet planted firmly, pressing his body forwards into mine to keep the two of us steady on the ice, as he moves his other hand down to my face. His thumb strokes over my lips, which curve into a smile under his touch. His fingers, warm from racing through the streets, reach around behind my neck, tilting my chin towards him.

I kiss him in the dark, I kiss him in the cold, I could kiss him right through my dreams and into the morning. And maybe I will.

'Ready for your birthday present?' River says, his hands over my eyes the next morning. He insisted we get to the pop-up art gallery for opening today, and he's led me right through to a spot near the back and promptly covered my vision.

'I really hope you don't have your peen out because this is a public place,' I tell him.

'No peen, I promise. Just this.'

He lets me see again. What am I supposed to be looking at? This weird little picture – a line drawing in a wooden frame of Central Park in the snow? Huh. Where have I seen that before? And why is my name on a plaque beside it?

'What the?!' I look up to River, who's grinning.

'It's only temporary, and we need to be quick. I have a friend who works here and he let me come in last night just before closing time to put it up. It's the first place I went once I got back to the city after my interview. I reckon we've got an hour or so before someone notices and takes it down.'

I return my eyes to the picture – it's *my* picture – the one I drew in the park only a week or so ago. 'How did you ...?'

'It must have come loose in your sketchbook and fallen out; it was on the floor of the kitchen the other day. I rescued it, framed it, and, well, you once told me you always wanted a picture of yours to be on display in an art gallery.'

'So you got me into one in New York City?' I screech with excitement, then clamp my hand over my noisy mouth.

'Do you mind?'

'I love it, I ... I can't believe you remembered me saying that. And did you make this plaque and everything?'

River nods, and I bend down to read it.

Ashling Avalyn

British, born 1993

**Let It Snow**

Beautiful drawing of Central Park in the snow,
sketched using cold fingers.

353

'River, thank you,' I say, and touch my little drawing.

'Don't touch the artwork, please,' he hisses.

We snap a billion pics next to my picture and then, with thanks to River's friend, we make our way out of the gallery before we're thrown out. Outside, New York is glowing in sunlight today, which glitters off the remaining snow, thawing in patches. In one hand I clutch my picture, proud of it for having been in such a prestigious gallery, and in my other hand, our fingers entwined, is River's.

'I have some news,' he says, breaking into my thoughts just as they're about to descend to thinking about how little time we have left. 'I woke up to an email this morning. I got the job.'

'You did?' I stop in the street and face him. 'River, that's brilliant! I think you're going to love it.'

'It's a bit of a change from what I did, though.'

I've seen that look on him before – lips pressed together, eyes glinting, a tinge of pink brushing his cheeks. Excited, happy, nervous.

When his old marching-band director, Max, got in touch after New Year's to say he was retiring soon, he asked if River would be interested in taking the reins.

'But it's perfect for you. I think you'll be so happy.'

'I think so too,' he agrees. 'And I wouldn't have gone for it, if it wasn't for you.'

'Well.' I wave him away. 'Sometimes it's good to have your head in the clouds rather than your feet planted on the solid, sensible ground. So you're leaving New York, too?'

He nods. 'My college is up in Massachusetts, so I'll be

moving back there. It's okay though, I'm ready to leave the city.'

I understand. Though this all feels really strange, us both planning such very separate lives. 'I'm happy for you. When will you start?'

'Well, that's something I wanted to talk to you about . . . Do you know anyone in the UK who might have a sofa to stay on, just for a couple of months? Someone I could win over?'

# Chapter 44

I sit back in my window seat as the plane climbs in the air, the sparkling night lights of New York City, never sleeping, retreating out of sight. Soon, it'll be under the clouds, which the captain will slice through until we're high above them, and we'll be floating in the air like dreams in the dark.

Spending just a winter in New York might not have been what nineteen-year-old me had in mind when she thought I'd 'move to New York'. But my thirty-year-old self is certain that this is exactly what needed to happen to know who I am, now, what I really value, now, and what passions were just waiting to be unlocked.

I'm used to travelling, but I'm not used to staying any-where for more than the length of a layover. I loved that; I could have done that for ever. Then, my life changed. But at my core, I know that it means a lot to me to see the world with my own eyes.

*That* doesn't have to change. And now, I want to

experience living in as many places as I can. A hundred places, maybe! Why not! Feeling a part of a neighbourhood. Making connections. Seeing cities, or countryside, or coasts in close-up.

A new career is fizzing around me, taking hold, settling into my soul. One where I can combine some of what I loved about being a pilot, and some of what I've learnt that I love about life.

Living In The Air are going to help me do that. After talking with them on my birthday, they came back to confirm they can make my idea work. Now, I'll be spending my time between their worldwide offices, helping run their fear-of-flying courses for the public. Not only that, but I'm also going to be involved in the training of new pilots. Immersing myself in new places, challenging myself in new ways, and getting to do it all in the field I love, love, love. Spreading the happiness has never felt so good.

Lost in thought, I grin to myself, my heart bubbling. In the plane seat beside me, River is calm. He's read the safety card a few times, and he looked into my eyes for the whole of take-off, but he's doing well. He glances over at me and smiles.

I forgot to tell him that, actually, we're staying with my mum for a few weeks since I gave up my flat prior to New York. But he's going to be here in the UK with me for three months. We'll find somewhere to live for that time, it'll be fine, and I know we'll make the most of every second. And then? We'll figure out who we are when that time arrives.

My new dreams and goals didn't come to me in a flash of

inspiration in the space of a weekend, this time. This time, New York made me work a little harder, think a little wider. But they came, and they suit the me I am now. And my new biggest goal? To keep dreaming.

I can't believe it's over. But oh my god, the things that are about to begin.

# Acknowledgements

As we begin our descent, I'd like to whoosh out a few thank yous . . .

Firstly, a huge thank you to my editors, Bec, Ruth and Molly, for endless patience, sky-high improvement ideas and helping this novel to grow wings. And a whopper of a thank you to Hannah and the team at my literary agency, Hardman & Swainson, for first-class championing and cheerleading.

Big, huge thanks to the whole team behind the book, at both Sphere and beyond – Zoe, Sophie, Suzanne, Natasha, Laura, Robyn, Bekki and Sarah. Thank you for being dreamy and helping shape *A New York Winter*.

Thank you, Sarah, for sharing so much detailed knowledge with me on all things to do with life as a pilot. You're an inspiration.

Thank you, Ellie, for not only working magic on my mane, but helping me with the finer points of Ashling's peach Rachel cut. And thanks and credit to Chris McMillan, original creator of The Rachel, and Jennifer Aniston for being a total hair goddess.

Thank you, Phil, for always being patient as I'm making up conversations in my head, and for being you. And thank you, Kodi, for topping my writing snacks with dog fur.

Thank you to my family and my friends, the writers who inspire me and the readers who curl up with me.

Finally, New York has a whole lotta my heart, so a thank you to the City is in order. Thanks for being big and brilliant and a great place to build great dreams. I love NY.

Wishing you all a pleasant onward journey xx

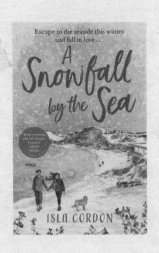

Escape to the seaside this winter
and fall in love . . .

## A Snowfall by the Sea

ISLA GORDON

*A heart-warming, feel-good festive romance
to settle down with this Christmas*

Cleo loves winter in Wavebreak Bay. The tourists
leave as the temperatures drop, the fairy lights go
up and it really starts to feel like home again. It
also happens to be the time of year that her best
friend Eliot comes back from San Francisco.

Though the seasons change, not much else in Cleo's life
does. She's in a people-pleasing rut, taking the worst
shifts at the family restaurant, pet-sitting for her parents
and making little time for herself. Cleo has spent so
long thinking about everyone around her that she's lost
sight of what *she* wants. And she wants Eliot. And she's
decided that, this year, she's finally going to tell him.

But as the snow settles on Wavebreak Bay, Cleo's
Christmas-for-two is disrupted by the arrival of her entire
family – and more guests keep arriving. As Cleo works
hard to make sure everyone else is having the most
wonderful time of the year, will she finally pluck up the
courage to stand up for herself . . . and to follow her heart?

*Will the magic of Lapland help
Myla fall in love with that festive feeling?*

# A Winter in Wonderland

ISLA GORDON

***Will a magical winter in Lapland help
Myla fall in love with festive?***

Myla is the UK's least-festive woman. Starting the year she found out the truth about Santa Claus, everything bad that's ever happened to her occurs around Christmas. Nowadays, she wants nothing to do with this time of year, so of course she would lose the bet with her sister and be forced to put herself forward for a seasonal job in Lapland, welcoming tourists to Santa's winter wonderland for the holidays.

Ten weeks, temperatures well below freezing, days that are mostly dark, and the need to stay brimming with Christmas spirit doesn't fill Myla with joy as she heads off to the arctic circle for winter in Finland. But as she discovers that Lapland is more than Santa Claus's Village, the very last person she ever thought she'd fall for turns out to be a man who plays an Elf, and who is bound to stay in character at all times.

Will a little love under the Northern Lights convince Myla that her bad luck might finally have come to an end?

**'A heart warmer'** *Heat*